TRUST
ONLY ME

An unputdownable psychological thriller
with a breathtaking twist

MCGARVEY BLACK

JOFFE
BOOKS

Joffe Books, London
www.joffebooks.com

First published in Great Britain in 2023

Cover art by Nick Castle

ISBN: 978-1-80405-709-4

Chapter 1

I remember the moment it started as if it were yesterday. When everything spiraled out of control the only recourse was — let it play out, for better or for worse.

It was a Tuesday morning and I was on the phone in my second-floor home office. Despite finishing my third cup of coffee, I was still feeling the effects of the two bottles of red wine my husband Teddy and I had consumed the night before. We had celebrated my thirty-fifth birthday. He cooked — crab cakes with mango-cilantro salsa and quinoa, finishing with a peach prosecco sorbet. His presentation was, as usual, spectacular — one of the many perks of being married to a chef who the *New York Echo* called one of the "Top 100 Rising Culinary Stars".

Still on hold, I tapped my pen on the desk as if it would make time go faster. I was waiting for a "yes" from my client, which would mean a big commission check for me. As an executive recruiter, you learn pretty fast every scalp is worth something — some more than others. The one I was waiting for was worth a bundle.

During the week, I placed people in jobs. But on nights and weekends, I wrote dark thrillers about psychos and serial killers. They often included dead bodies, severed limbs, explosions and the occasional torso without a head. The number of casualties in my stories depended on my mood. I once slaughtered an entire fictional town after I got a letter from the IRS saying I owed back taxes. I didn't have the extra eight hundred dollars the US government said I owed. When I received the notice, everyone in my work in progress died. It was strangely therapeutic.

As I waited patiently for my client to give me a green light on the job offer, I played around on Instagram, watched stupid pet videos, and checked email. A familiar alert sounded from my phone. That's when I got that bombshell text from my BFF Natalie. I didn't know it then, but her message marked the beginning of the nightmare about to unfold. I didn't see any of it coming.

Chapter 2

My best friend, Natalie Bloom, the quintessential Type A personality almost always got what she wanted. Right after college, she had landed her dream job at a boutique PR firm in Manhattan. The company was fast-paced and demanding, so she rarely communicated with me during the workday. That's why I was so surprised when I received her text that Tuesday.

—Where ru? I called ten times!!!!!!!

Jeez, maybe I was in the shower. There was always drama with Natalie, but I texted her back.

What's up?

—Something weird on Twitter.

What?!

—Twitter trolls posting crazy conspiracy crap about your first book. You don't want that kind of publicity. Trust me. Get it down. Here's the link.

I clicked. Somebody named @Aussiegirl9876 had been tweeting about my first novel, *A Burning Desire*. Aussie Girl had even tagged me in the tweet.

Anyone notice drone explosion and fire in SW Connecticut eerily similar to @JillianSamuelsAuthorbook #ABurningDesire? #copycat #explosion #lifeisstrangert- hanfiction #realcrimecomestrue #WTF?

WTF is right. I spotted three more Twitter notifications from total strangers all talking about me while commenting on the local explosions and comparing them to my book. I was about to do a Google search for "fires in Connecticut" when my client came back on the line and told me to extend the job offer. For a second, I completely forgot about Twitter as I calculated how much commission I'd make — twelve thousand dollars. Nice. Teddy and I needed the money and I hadn't made a commission in months. I only got paid if I placed someone, which didn't happen every day . . . or every month for that matter.

Until that day, my only aspiration was for one of my novels to become a bestseller and translated into twenty-seven languages. Over the years, friends and family had encouraged me to write, but I think I became an author because of my mom. Suddenly a single mother after my father decided he didn't want to be one anymore, she held what was left of our family together. I was ten and my sister, twelve. Camille was older and should have been looking out for me, instead she made my life a living hell.

After getting the thumbs up on the new job offer, I called my candidate to share the good news. He was thrilled and truthfully, so was I — twelve grand was a lot of money. Teddy was trying to save up to start his own restaurant and the commission would get us that much closer.

With my job placement secured, I Googled "explo- sions in SW Connecticut". Within seconds, pages of listings splashed across my screen. I clicked on a link from a local newspaper, the *Connecticut Advocate*.

EXPLOSION IN BARRINGTON CT, POLICE INVESTIGATING.
By Tommy Devlin.

Late Thursday afternoon, an empty warehouse in Barrington went up in flames. The Medford Police and Barrington Fire Department were called to the scene and soon brought the blaze under control. Shortly before the explosion, two residents from Barrington saw "something" fly overhead in the direction of the warehouse. Both witnesses reported the flying object looked like a mini-Superman.

"I was taking my dog Riley for a long walk when I heard this faint humming over my head. I looked up and thought my eyes were playing tricks on me," said Michael Clinton, 68, a long-time Barrington resident. "I thought, what the hell is that? Must be one of those drones. Probably just some kids playing around, I figured. I watched it for a bit and saw it fly in the direction of that building that blew up. I could only see the roof above the trees but it looked like that flying thing was going to crash right into it. Then, there was a big boom."

Liz Gill, 52, lives a quarter-mile from the warehouse on Franklin Street. She was gardening when she saw something that looked like Superman fly over her yard. "I was down on my knees pulling out weeds and saw a funny shadow on the ground. That's what made me look up and I saw a blue and red man with a cape soaring over my head. At the time, I thought it was kind of amusing. Then it disappeared and a few minutes later I heard a loud bang in the distance."

5

*While the cause of the empty warehouse fire is incon-
clusive at this time, police are investigating drone activity
in the area. If anyone has any information, please contact
the Medford CT police department and ask for Detectives
Boris Brodsky or Nick Marino 203-536-7500*

I had to admit, there were clearly many similarities
between that news story in the *CT Advocate* and the plot of my
first thriller, *A Burning Desire*. You could say my journey to
crazy town started *before* the text from Natalie. Technically, it
began years before — the night I finished my first manuscript.

Teddy and I had recently celebrated our first wedding
anniversary and I had just completed my first novel, a thriller.
It was about a demented male teen arsonist who was also a
very popular high school honor student and track star. One
caveat, he had a peculiar incendiary obsession. He enjoyed
reconfiguring drones to make them look like superheroes
among other things. He'd painstakingly craft them into
colorful hot air balloons, Superman, Spiderman, the Titanic,
Wonder Woman, and even Santa on his sleigh. Once his
artistic flying masterpieces were ready to go, he'd load up his
camouflaged drones with explosives and by remote control
send them silently into random buildings. Ka-Boom. Every
boy needs a hobby.

Over time, my pyro-teen sets off a series of massive
explosions and fires all over Connecticut. The first five buildings were empty warehouses or large vacant utility sheds that
no one cared about. But the sixth one — a caretaker had been
napping inside and didn't make it out alive. That's when
things got real for the adolescent pyromaniac. Turns out, he
also liked to blow up reptiles and had wet his bed well into
his early teens. Add in the fires and you've got the trifecta
for a serial killer.

Still focused on the Twitter storm unfolding, I scrolled
through numerous posts and articles about the real local
fire until I heard the sound of tires on gravel. From my second-floor window, I saw a Medford police car pull up in

front of my house. A uniformed female officer with a short brown ponytail got out of the car and walked slowly up my front walk. Her car radio loudly crackled instructions from the distance as I opened my door.

"Are you Jillian Samuels?"

"Last time I checked," I said, attempting humor she clearly didn't appreciate. The cop wanted to know if I had any information about the drone fire in Barrington. Someone at the Medford PD had looked at social media and seen the postings referencing me. According to her, the cops had checked out my books, and thought there might be some connection. I told her I knew absolutely nothing about it and she scribbled something in a notebook retrieved from her breast pocket.

"Anyone ever show any unusual interest in your books, Ms Samuels?"

"Why? Do you think someone is getting ideas from my thrillers?"

"Don't know," she said, as she handed me her card. "Could be a copycat or simply a coincidence. Too soon to tell. If you have nothing else to add, I'm going to turn this information over to the law enforcement team that deals with arson. Someone will contact you if they need anything further."

She turned toward her car, took a step but then quickly spun around. "Anything else unusual happen recently?" she said, one eyebrow raised.

I debated whether I should mention the green SUV I was sure had been following me the last few months. I tried to tell Teddy about it, but before I got all the words out, he rolled his eyes and said I was being paranoid. I told Natalie, and she thought it sounded very strange and insisted I copy down the license plate the next time I saw the car.

"Actually," I said to the cop while leaning on my open front door, "this may be nothing and purely a figment of my imagination, but I think a green SUV has been following me around town."

The officer looked at me with, thankfully, an appropriate amount of gravitas. She fired back a series of staccato questions. How often had I seen the car? Did I know if the driver was a man or a woman? Did I get the license plate? When and where was the last time I saw the vehicle?

I answered succinctly to match her rhythm so she'd take me seriously. "I think I've seen the car a total of five times. It looked like a man driving but I couldn't be sure. I didn't get the license and the last time was about three weeks ago."

The officer nodded and made a few more notes. "If you see that green vehicle again, try to get the plate number, but stay away from the car."

That night, Teddy got home from his dinner shift at the restaurant around 12.30 a.m. I had waited up specifically to tell him about the drone explosion and subsequent Twitter frenzy. Since I was agitated and knew he'd be late, earlier in the evening, I had taken a hot grapefruit-scented bubble bath. I had even lit the matching grapefruit candle to give myself a full immersive citrus experience. Baths normally have a calming effect on me, but not that day, I was too wired. After Natalie's texts, the explosion, the Twitter storm about my book, and the visit from the cop, my simple country life was turning into a plot from one of my thrillers.

When Teddy walked into our bedroom, he looked tired and mumbled something about "brushing his teeth and going right to sleep". It was obvious he was exhausted but I really needed to talk to him, so I plunged forward.

"Long night?" I said, easing into a conversation only I wanted to have.

"Unbelievable. The main dining room was beyond crowded. We were completely overbooked," he said irritably as he pulled off his clothes leaving them in a pile on the floor. I nodded sympathetically and tried to ignore the heap of dirty clothes he had just created.

"Management needs to get some front-of-house people who know how to schedule reservations. I'm shot. All I want to do is close my eyes," he said climbing into bed and giving me a kiss on the cheek before rolling over with his back to me. "Turn out the light, Jills."

"I need to talk to you about something?" I said to the back of his head. He groaned. "Please Teddy, it's important."

Slowly, he turned over and looked at me, his eyes half open. "This isn't about your sister again, is it? Camille is gone. You've got to let her go." He pulled the blanket over his head, signaling our chat was over.

Nice try, but it wasn't about my sister. But, what if it was? Aren't husbands supposed to be there for their wives when shit happens? Well, shit was happening and I needed to talk. I had a lot of stuff to unpack that night. I didn't bother him at work, even though I wanted to. I had waited hours for him to come home so we could have this conversation without any distractions. He was acting like he was doing me a big fat favor by staying conscious for five more minutes.

Don't get me wrong, Teddy was usually very supportive. In fact, the first time he read *A Burning Desire*, he was brimming over with praise.

"The story is clever but also poignant and quite sad," he had said. "A real commentary on family and growing up in society today. It's really good, Jills."

Natalie had loved it, too. "I don't know how you wrote an entire book," she said, shaking her spectacular head of thick, dark-brown hair while flashing a big supportive red-lipped smile. "I can barely put together a one-page press release and you write a three-hundred-and-seventy-six-page novel? You're amazing, Jills. Someone will definitely publish it. You'll see."

When I met my husband, he was already head chef at a mid-sized New York City bistro. There was chemistry between us pretty quickly and it wasn't long before I moved into his apartment in lower Manhattan. Six months after our wedding, my mother started to struggle with memory issues and we had to shift gears. Our move to Connecticut had been Teddy's idea. To be closer to Mom, we bought an old fixer-upper in Medford, CT, about an hour and twenty minutes northeast of the city and only minutes from the assisted living community we eventually moved my mother into. That's when I essentially said goodbye to the Big Apple and set up my office at home.

Every morning, I played the country wife as he dashed for the crowded commuter train to New York. Though my dream was to write a bestseller, my husband had his own entrepreneurial aspirations. Over the years, Teddy had made a number of investments — some good and some bad. Most of his "sure things" that were supposed to "make us millionaires" never materialized. If you looked at the math, the net proceeds of my husband's investments actually put us underwater. I never said anything to him about it. He worked so hard and I knew he was doing the best he could. I always wanted to be supportive.

"Something really weird happened today," I said, speaking directly to his blanket-covered head. "There was a post on Twitter about a warehouse explosion in Barrington. The person said what happened was identical to the plot in Jillian Samuels' *A Burning Desire* and—"

He groaned and removed the blanket from his face. "It's 1 a.m. and you want to talk about Twitter? Now? I don't know anything about Twitter. I don't even have an account anymore."

"But there were these fires and—"

"That's why we have fire departments. Fires happen all the time."

"Not fires started by drones," I said looking at him like he had three heads. "According to the article in the *CT Advocate*, witnesses said they saw a drone that looked exactly like Superman fly overhead right before the explosion. Teddy, that's exactly how it happens in my book. Then, random people on Twitter started speculating that there's a copycat using my book for inspiration — like a blueprint."

"You're blowing this up, Jills. You always do this and I'm too tired to play games tonight. Can we go to sleep? We'll talk about it tomorrow."

"A Medford police officer came to the house today and asked me about the connection to my book," I said with a certain amount of satisfaction as a surprised look crossed his face.

"The police? I thought only your friends read your books."

Ouch. It was true I didn't sell many books but he didn't have to say it that way. "Not *everyone* who bought my book is someone I know. A few copies were bought by random strangers. The police came to see me, so clearly they think there's something there."

"The cops have to cover their asses and check out everything. That's their job. They asked you a few questions, it doesn't mean they think there's a connection. You know how your imagination goes on overdrive," he said, his eyes closing again. I was losing him.

"But, don't you think it's strange?"

"Of course, but there's probably a rational explanation. Now, turn out the light," he said as he rolled over again signaling our conversation had concluded. Within a minute he was snoring, a soft rhythmic growling that I found oddly comforting.

Lying in bed feeling the warmth of his body, I snuggled up next to him. Even though our conversation hadn't gone the way I'd hoped, I loved him. Teddy was someone who knew what he wanted and always went for it, no matter what. I loved that about him and strived to be more like that. He was making things happen for himself. He was a rock star on his way up in the food world. My writing career on the other hand was practically on life support. I wanted to keep up with him. I laid in bed for an hour plotting and planning my next move. My first three books were self-published and that night, I decided I was going to find a literary agent and take my career to the next level.

I eventually did find an agent, but soon after signing with him, all hell broke loose.

Chapter 3

Ask anyone who has tried, looking for an agent is an emotional rollercoaster. To keep myself sane during the process, I focused on all the positives in my life. For starters, I had the most amazing husband who let "me be me" — alone worth its weight in gold. So while my professional life was in flux, my personal one remained calm and steady. I liked to think of Teddy and I as two peas in a pod. People said we bumped when we walked, always in sync. We had a life strategy and often talked about our future including children. But at that time, I wasn't ready to be a mother and he was consumed with his huge professional plans. There was no time for kids then, so we put a pin in the baby conversation and saved it for another day. Truthfully, neither one of us had had a stellar childhood and we wondered if we were equipped to become good parents. In the meantime, we were blissfully happy and talked about getting a dog to fill the void. We never did get the dog. I would have liked that.

Natalie often said, especially after a few glasses of wine, that I had "hit the husband jackpot". It sounds like a cliché, but my husband actually *is* tall, dark and handsome and oozes with charm. Since I can't tell cumin from coriander, having a partner who knew his way around the kitchen was a tremendous bonus. Without him, I would have spent my entire adult life eating takeout, frozen dinners and bowls of cereal.

Teddy and I both had big dreams. He worked twelve-hour shifts, six days a week in a restaurant kitchen, while making plans to roll out his restaurant empire. We didn't see each other much then because of his long hours, but we both knew it was only temporary. One day it would all pay off. So, while he worked the night shifts, I used my evenings home alone in Connecticut to write.

When I finally finished my fourth thriller, *The Soul Collector*, I deliberately pushed thoughts of the explosion, fire and police out of my mind. For the next few months, I meticulously hunted for an agent using a series of metrics and spreadsheets along with a self-devised tracking system. I was positive having an agent would be the turning point in my writing career. I fantasized about book signings, interviews, fans, even a movie deal or a limited TV series. I dreamed about my novel being selected for Oprah's book club. That would have been something. Sure it was unlikely, but dreams don't cost anything so why not go big?

I sent personalized query letters to forty carefully vetted agents and crossed my fingers.

"You know what they say," said Natalie in her usual matter-of-fact tone when I told her about the letters, "bad luck comes in threes and since this is your fourth book, the negative spell will have been broken. This will be your break-out book, Jills. You know I'm witchy like that."

After the agent letters went out, I bit off all my nails, waiting and hoping, refreshing my email a thousand times a day like a gambler sitting in front of a Vegas slot machine. Then one ordinary weekday, I received both a voicemail and an email from a New York agent named Matthew Donovan with the Sanford Weston Literary Agency. He wanted to set up an in-person meeting with me. After listening to his voicemail praising my book, I re-read his equally complimentary email seven times. He wrote, and I quote, "I adore your manuscript" and that my new thriller, *The Soul Collector*, "has the potential to become a massive bestseller". Wow! That all sounded pretty great to me. I was giddy. Who wouldn't like that kind of praise? All I could think was that I was finally on my way.

After doing an embarrassing victory jig in my office and unable to wait until Teddy got home that night to tell him the news, I called him at work.

"What do you think?" I said breathlessly after relaying all the info.

"Sounds like he wants to represent you. Congratulations," said my husband after I read Matthew's email to him a third time. That night Teddy brought home a bottle of Veuve Clicquot from the restaurant and we celebrated.

"I'm so proud of you, Jills. All your hard work paid off," he said as he refreshed my glass of champagne. I shifted gears while savoring the tiny bubbles trickling down the back of my throat.

"I went to see my mom this afternoon so I could tell her the news," I said placing my glass down on the table and looking into my husband's beautiful dark eyes. "I'm not sure what I expected. I tried to tell her my good news but she didn't understand anything. Old Mom would have been thrilled and so proud. New Mom didn't know who I was or what I was talking about."

"Try again next time," said Teddy gently touching my hand. "You might catch her on a better day. Sometimes she understands things."

I shook my head. "You haven't seen her in a while. She doesn't remember much anymore. She called me the C-word today."

Teddy grimaced as he reached over and rubbed my other wrist.

"That's only because you and your sister Camille look so much alike. Your mom has dementia, it's not surprising she confuses the two of you."

"But I want my mother to remember me. I never gave her a single problem. How could I with Camille wreaking havoc on a daily basis?"

Looking back on everything now, one might say that signing with my agent somehow triggered a series of events that led to terrible, hurtful things. Eventually, more strange and scary stuff started to unfold, and social media wasted no time connecting the dots. I'll tell you one thing, when it comes to the internet and social platforms, nothing stays under the radar for long, no matter how much you might want it to. Once that evil genie was out of the lamp, trust me, there was no way back for anyone involved.

I inked the deal with my agent only months after the first explosion. In retrospect, I think he was a little intrigued by the mini-conspiracy Twitter storm because he kept mentioning it.

"I think we can do something with this 'life mirroring fiction' situation," said Matthew in one of our early conversations. "There's got to be a way to monetize this."

He had a point. All three of my self-published novels together only generated a few hundred dollars. If I'm being honest, most copies had been purchased by friends, family, co-workers and a few supportive neighbors in Medford. Only a handful were bought by people I didn't know. When the investigation got underway over the drone explosion, the police asked me if I had any enemies. Me? Having enemies sounded so exotic. If there was a connection to my writing, the cops thought it more likely the person behind the crimes was someone I knew, someone with an ax to grind. I led a very quiet life and couldn't think of a soul.

My agent, Matthew, eventually brokered the book deal I'd always dreamed of. Meanwhile, Teddy was also making progress on his own business plans. Our future looked so bright. It should have been smooth sailing for the two of us. But not long after my book was acquired by a publisher, my life took a hard left turn as more and more crimes from my old thrillers started to happen. To add insult to injury, Mom got worse and was convinced that I was my sister, Camille. That may have been the worst part.

Chapter 4

My sister Camille had always been a troublemaker, rule destroyer and heartbreaker. Given a choice of two paths, one good and one bad, she always took the wrong one. Sometimes it felt like she did it on purpose just to freak out the people who cared about her. My sister was selfish, reckless and determined to do things her way regardless of who she hurt or the consequences.

I was the polar opposite. I never stepped on the lines and always followed the rules. If Camille did something wrong, which was practically every day, I made up for her atrocious behavior by being extra good. When she used drugs or slept around, which was often, I went to church on Sundays with my mother to pray for her and did volunteer work at a local animal shelter. My poor mom had so much on her plate as a single parent and as the mother of Camille, that I never wanted to add to her load. I always tried to be the perfect daughter and for a time, I think I was.

Though only two years apart, my older sister and I were not close. Thick as thieves when we were really young, we were best friends then. No one was more fun than Camille. But when she turned twelve and I ten, without warning, she got mean. By the time we were both teenagers, she was so overtly nasty to me that I stayed out of her way whenever possible. She regularly doled out physical violence, and had a nasty habit of punching me hard whenever she passed me in the upstairs hallway. Sharing a bedroom with her only made things worse. It got so bad that my mother finally let me sleep with her for my own protection. To put it simply, my older sister was a first-class bitch.

Then there was her constant drama. Frankly, it was exhausting. Camille would run away for weeks and not tell anyone where she was. Frantic, my mother would often call the police. Sometimes they found her and other times she'd come home on her own when she was hungry or out of money. In order to cope with the frequent upheaval, my mother and I created a life for ourselves that didn't include my sister. We had to, it was self-preservation, our only way to have and keep a family.

Once, after Camille had been gone for nearly ten days, we received an incoherent letter in the mail from her. She was staying fifteen miles away squatting in an unfinished low-income housing project primarily inhabited by drug addicts. She needed money. At first, Mom wanted to give it to her even though we both knew she'd use it for drugs. I convinced my mother not to, and soon the pleading phone calls started. After each call, my mother was left in a puddle of tears. The pleas eventually turned to threats and we dreaded whenever the phone rang but Mom always answered it. She had to. She explained to me, "I'm her mother".

At sixteen, Camille ran away two weeks before Thanksgiving. Within days, she was calling and asking for money. Mom begged her to come home for the holiday but my sister only laughed, saying she had nothing to be thankful for.

Despite all the constant upheaval, we had established one family tradition of going into New York City on Thanksgiving Day to watch the big Macy's parade with all the giant floats. It was something we had done as a family even when my "waste of space" father was still in the picture. For some unknown reason, my father was nice on Thanksgiving and Christmas, even jolly. The other three-hundred-and-sixty-three days a year he couldn't have cared less about us. But, he loved the holidays and for those two days each year, he kept his nasty side in check. Let me be clear, two days of nice don't make up for all the rest. He died when I was seventeen and I hadn't seen him in years. I didn't shed a single tear.

My father had been long out of the picture on that particular Thanksgiving when my sister took off. To put the absent Camille out of our minds, Mom and I decided to keep with tradition and go into New York City for the parade.

That night, we were supposed to have Thanksgiving dinner at a neighbor's house and stopped at home after the parade to pick up the three pies my mother had made. When we pulled into our driveway the garage door was wide open.

"Did I forget to close the garage before we left?" said my mother shaking her head, annoyed at herself for being so careless. As soon as we walked inside it was evident the place had been ransacked. Among other things, all of our jewelry and some loose cash had been stolen. Neither of us said it but we both knew it was Camille. She had taken things only a family member would know existed, she knew where they were hidden. That Thanksgiving Day, Camille broke into our house and took anything of value she could get her hands on.

We didn't call the police. Mom didn't want my sister to be arrested, so we just carried on as if nothing had happened. We straightened up the house, grabbed the pies and went to the neighbor's for dinner pretending everything was normal. Camille came crawling back a few days later looking like shit. Mom told her if she was going to stay in our house she had to stop using drugs. My sister stayed clean for a while but like everything else with her, nothing ever lasted for long.

When Camille died a few years later, Mom took it hard, but honestly, I was relieved. My sister's destructive presence was finally gone from my life and I had my wonderful mother all to myself. Given my sister's shitty lifestyle choices, I had always expected something bad was going to happen to her. I just didn't know when. Waiting for the inevitable was the worst part.

With my sister gone, it was just Mom and me and eventually Teddy, who thankfully was nothing like my father.

"Sometimes, when I visit my mother she has these occasional moments of clarity," I said to my husband, a tear trickling down my cheek as I looked across the kitchen table into his eyes. "I get so excited when she seems to understand me. I try to keep the conversation going. But it's like sand slipping through my fingers. Then it's over, and I wonder if I'll ever get another chance."

Teddy squeezed my arm gently.

"When I was leaving her place today, I waved to her and you know what she said?" Teddy shook his head. "She said, 'I love you so much, Camille.' It was like a knife going through my heart. I'm the one who's taken care of my mother. My sister's been dead for seventeen years but she's the only one Mom remembers. It's not fair."

"Your mother doesn't mean it. Her brain doesn't work right anymore," said my husband gently. "You know she loves you."

"Last week, she asked me if I knew where her daughter was? I said, 'Mom, I *am* your daughter, Jillian.' She started to cry and chanted Camille's name over and over like I didn't exist. It broke my heart."

"You're spiraling again, Jills. Don't let it get to you. This is your day for celebration. You got your first agent, be happy. Go upstairs and take one of your spa baths. Fill up your champagne glass. Light some candles and put on some music. That always gets you to your happy place. Tonight we toast to your achievement," said Teddy as he topped up my wine. "You wait and see, one day *The Soul Collector* will be on bookstore shelves from coast to coast. You're on your way."

People say "be careful of what you wish for", and "if it sounds too good to be true, it probably is". I didn't think of either of those harbingers at the time. All I knew was, some-body liked my manuscript and that was good enough for me. I was a hundred-and-fifty percent on board. To be honest, I was so desperate to have my book traditionally published that I would have signed my life away. Turns out, I nearly did.

Chapter 5

The first time I met Matthew Donovan, I pushed open the double glass doors of the Sanford Weston Literary Agency on East 45th Street in midtown Manhattan, and took a deep breath. The waiting room was gray and sleek, all metal and glass and had a cool vibe. For days leading up to the meeting, I had gone through my wardrobe fifty times looking for the perfect "literary agent signing outfit". I settled on a pair of black designer pants I had been told made me look two sizes thinner and a pair of four-inch black heels. I selected a champagne-colored Armani jacket that I'd bought for a steal at a high-end consignment shop. Armani delivered the right amount of gravitas while providing a little touch of glam.

My fine, straight, strawberry blonde hair (the same color as my mom's) was pulled up into a loose but professional looking knot. I added my best pair of gold hoop earrings, dabbed on some lip gloss and looked in the mirror for a realistic assessment. I have been told I am pretty in that girl-next-door sort of way and looked better with less makeup. My best features were my almond-shaped blue-green eyes and my peaches-and- cream complexion (another gift from my mother). Could I stand to lose ten pounds? Probably — okay yes, who couldn't? But I tried to mitigate the slight extra padding with numerous forms of exercise and flattering wardrobe choices. The yoga, Pilates, running and swimming didn't burn off enough calories to put me at my ideal weight but they kept my body in reasonable shape. It is what it is.

The night before my first agent meeting, I test drove my full ensemble by twirling around for my husband in our living room.

"You get a 'like' from me," said Teddy sticking out an upturned thumb. "You look fantastic, Jills." I appreciated my husband's admiration but he *was* a guy and I wasn't convinced his fashion sense was on point. To be sure, I wanted the approval of the chief fashionista, Natalie, and sent her a few screenshots of me in my outfit. She'd give it to me straight, she always did. I waited for her response fully expecting her to tell me to scrap the whole thing. To my amazement, she approved . . . of everything.

"But, wear red lipstick. Red leaves an indelible impression," was the only thing she added.

I was ready for my big day.

When I entered the agency's lobby, an older female receptionist looked up.

"I'm here to see Matthew Donovan," I said as I tucked a loose strand of hair behind my ear.

The woman looked down at her computer and smiled. "You must be Jillian Samuels." I nodded. "You're going to love Matthew. He's a doll. I'll let him know you're here."

Crossing and re-crossing my legs while I waited, my feet fidgeted nervously on the floor in front of me. The fingers on my left hand tapped uncontrollably on the metal arm of my chair. After a minute or two and a couple of sideways looks from the receptionist, I became aware of my movements and tried to calm myself down. *Stop fidgeting, she'll think you're having a seizure.* Using whatever self-control I had in me, I commanded my body to be still and took several deep breaths. Soon after, a young, good-looking male hipster with sandy-brown, slightly spikey hair, which I presumed had product in it, opened the glass door to the reception area.

"Jillian?" he said smiling as he shook my hand with a firm self-assured grip. "I'm Matthew and let me say once again, I — love — your — manuscript."

He made me blush but it was music to my ears. One can never hear that kind of effusive praise too often. I was so elated I couldn't feel my feet as I followed him through a second glass doorway and down a long hall. We sat in his small office with a single window overlooking First Avenue. I could hear the city traffic below as he gushed over the different sections and characters in my book. I wasn't accustomed to such robust praise from a publishing professional, and I'm not going to lie, I loved every second. I could have listened to that all day.

"I've gotta tell ya, Jillian, *The Soul Collector* had my pulse racing from the first page," said Matthew. "I couldn't put it down. It was so riveting. Really hooks you and doesn't let go. I don't want to bore you but, you've got an amazing writing style."

You're not boring me, Matthew, keep going. Tell me more.

"Love the title, too," he continued. "Brilliant on all fronts."

"Thank you," I said overwhelmed but so freakin' happy.

"I think your book can go all the way to the top," he said as he rattled a litany of things off in rapid fire. "I mean it. You're the real deal. If we play our cards right, I'll bet I can get a bidding war going for your book with some of the big houses. How does that sound?"

"Really?" I said, my eyes as big and round as dinner plates. "I'm sorry, but what exactly does that mean?"

"It means a whole bunch of big publishers fight to acquire the rights to your book and you and I make a lot more money."

"You can do that? A bidding war? That would be amazing."

"Your novel would make an incredible movie, too. We've got a kick-ass film rights department here that can handle all of that," he said as he proceeded to pitch me on his representation skills and achievements, not to mention his agency's clout on both coasts. "Don't even get me started on foreign rights. We blow the doors off foreign editions. You're going to make a bundle."

A huge smile spread across my face, so wide that soon it started to hurt. I had to consciously relax my mouth. Everything was finally happening, the way I always knew it would. My elusive dream was coming true.

"Jillian," said Matthew looking directly into my eyes, "I'd be so honored if you'd let me represent you and take *The Soul Collector* out to the marketplace."

The rest of our conversation was a little fuzzy because I was walking on a cloud somewhere in the stratosphere. I remember nodding enthusiastically and saying something like, "I'd be honored to have you represent me". Next thing you know, he pulls out a contract already filled out and hands it to me saying it was "all very standard".

"Look it over and send it back and we can get started. In the meantime, I'll reach out to some of my better contacts and start seeding the soil. Together, we're going to make your book the next blockbuster bestseller," he said brimming with confidence.

That should have been the best day of my life but what I didn't know at the time was, Matthew Donovan had been put on a very short leash at his agency. Technically, he *was* a junior agent, but was still expected to fulfill clerical administrative duties for several of the senior agents, which took up a lot of his time. And apparently, signing me didn't come with the full support of the agency's founder and managing partner, Charlie Weston.

It's a long story and the fact that Matthew didn't share the sordid details of his intercompany woes with me until several years later comes as no surprise. The truth was, my prospective agent had been having an affair with Charlie Weston's wife (also a partner), although her husband could never prove it. Let's just say, being Matthew's client at Sanford Weston Literary made me a bit of an author non grata.

When I got home that night, Teddy called one of his friends who was a lawyer and asked if he'd look over my contract. After everything checked out, I happily put my signature on the bottom of the document, scanned it and sent it back to the agency. I officially had literary representation.

Signing with Matthew Donovan should have been the beginning of an incredible new chapter. Instead, it was the beginning of the end of my life as I knew it.

Chapter 6

After eagerly accepting representation with Matthew and Sanford Weston Literary, I was reborn. I was about to embark on a brand new and more exciting phase of my otherwise ordinary life. A few days after I sent the signed contract back, Matthew invited me to his office so we could "properly kick things off".

I looked forward to learning the publishing business from him. He was the pro and I knew so little about the inner workings of the industry. He repeated that he was going to make me a bestselling author and that my manuscript was "genius". Who wouldn't follow that Pied Piper to the edge of the pier and into the water? I can swim for miles.

I took the train into the city the following Monday for a 10 a.m. working session with *my* new agent. Though Matthew was five years younger than me, I was his devoted student. Once in his office, I placed my notebook dutifully on the table between us ready to consume his pearls of literary wisdom. I expected he'd explain the process of shopping my book to different publishers, what our strategy would be, how it would be marketed and how I might augment his efforts using my own social media channels.

"Must feel good to be on your way?" said Matthew, smiling as he sat at the table peeling back the plastic lid of his paper coffee cup.

"You've made my dream come true," I said, my eyes flashing. "I'm still floating."

"Better get your feet on the ground," he said, "the hard part starts now."

"I thought writing the book was the hard part." I said accompanied by a little laugh.

Matthew laughed too. "Don't misunderstand me," he said. "I have the utmost respect for what authors like you do. I couldn't write a book if my life depended on it. You've got a talent I wish I had. Now, we are moving over into the business side of writing. This is where I'm going to try and sell your book for as much money as possible. Remember, when you make money, Sanford Weston Lit makes money, the publisher makes money and everybody wins."

"Sounds good to me."

"Which brings me to your role in the selling process," said Matthew taking a sip of his coffee and looking me straight in the eye. "We're on this freshman journey together. This is your first traditionally published novel. I've had a lot of experience working with one of our senior partners, Ellen Sanford. While I've put plenty of deals together with her, this is my first time flying solo."

"Oh," I said, learning that fact for the first time. Had he mentioned that detail before? I knew he was a junior agent but I hadn't realized it was his first time at the rodeo. My poker face must have left something to be desired because he suddenly shifted gears and tried to reassure me.

"Don't worry about anything," he said leaning forward. "I've got your back. Remember, a truly good book will always find its audience. You trust me, right?"

"Of course," I said trying to cover up my disappointment. "We're in this together."

"Exactly. Now, the first thing we need to do is get some serious and consistent buzz going on you. We need people talking about Jillian Samuels and your book. "

"How do we do that? My book isn't out yet."

"Right now, you need to start building the Jillian Samuels brand. With so many agents vying for a piece of the pie, publishers have thousands of manuscripts to choose from and limited time and budgets. For every book that's pitched, only a handful get bought."

"But when we spoke last week, you talked about bidding wars."

"Did I?" said Matthew as he polished off the last of his coffee. "That could still happen, but we have to be realistically optimistic. Editors are looking for authors and books that will make a splash when they're released. We need to do something that will get people talking on social media. Maybe you can create a TikTok video that goes viral."

"Tell me what to do and I'll do it."

"I like that positive attitude, Jillian. You'll need to use all of your contacts. Post on social media every day. Use all the channels — Facebook, Twitter, Snapchat, TikTok, LinkedIn, Instagram, YouTube and Pinterest. Post positive reviews of other books on Goodreads and Amazon. Write a weekly blog related to *The Soul Collector* and the thriller genre. See if you can get yourself profiled by local newspapers, magazines and websites. Contact your college alumni office and get them to do a "small-town girl makes good" story. Do any kind of outreach you can think of."

"I can definitely do some postings and sign up for all those accounts. I'm not very good with video though. To be fully transparent, I should tell you about this weird thing that happened with one of my older books." I told him about the drone explosion and fire, and to my surprise, he was delighted.

"What a coincidence," he said with a grin. "I love drones. I've got a dozen of them in all shapes and sizes at home. But I assure you, I don't load them up with bombs. I'm an amateur photographer and use them to take aerial pictures. Do the cops have any idea who's doing it?"

"The police think it might be a copycat who read my book, but they're not sure. They said it could be someone who sets fires for fun and might have been inspired by the drone story in my novel. Thankfully, no one's been hurt."

"You know what they say, better they talk smack about you than not at all," said Matthew with a laugh. "I say we exploit these explosions and get people talking about you and your books."

I nodded and made a note.

"Also, isn't your husband a name in the New York food scene? He's the chef at the American Bistro, right? When we take on an author here at Sanford Weston, we look at their whole package. I'll be honest, your husband's high profile was a factor in our decision to sign you. Maybe he or his restaurant can post some mentions of your book on their social channels. They could post how their chef's wife is an up-and-coming author. I've seen a few articles mentioning your husband. You can surely get some rub off from him. I'll bet his restaurant would let you do a book signing there. The American Bistro gets a ton of high-profile customers."

I nodded and made another note.

"We'll take publicity any way we can get it," said Matthew. "You having that chef husband and restaurant connection will be a great selling point when I'm talking to publishers."

I did a quick mental inventory of my social media experience and savvy. I had Twitter, Instagram, Facebook and LinkedIn accounts, but hardly ever used them. Instagram photos of food or smiling people visiting places I had never been only annoyed me. And, I absolutely hated Twitter. People were always screaming about something and used really awful language. Don't get me wrong, I occasionally use the F-bomb when necessary and appropriate, but Twitter was a cesspool. Half the stuff was made up and the rest so twisted it made me cringe. So many of the tweets were bitter and angry. Honestly, I found the Twitter world a little scary.

When TikTok first came out I tried doing a video to see how it worked. It was a disaster. A bunch of haters posted things under my video like "Nooooo", or "Wrong on so many levels". After that, I opted out of TikTok. It wasn't the medium for me. I should have been honest then and told Matthew that I had stopped socializing online a long time ago. I rarely ever posted, but I said nothing. I didn't want to jinx anything. Some things are best kept to oneself.

During that first working meeting with Matthew, it was clear I had to change if I wanted my book to be a success. If my agent wanted a social media butterfly, then that's what he'd get. I could carve out a few hours each morning to grow and work my social contact lists. I could certainly post pithy or humorous anecdotes and pictures of my dinner several times a week. If Matthew Donovan needed that kind of author support to make my book a bestseller, I was ready, willing and able. I wanted him to know that Jillian Samuels was a team player.

Reading something on his phone, Matthew pulled his chair closer to the table.

"So," he said looking up at me, "let's talk about next steps on your manuscript."

I sensed a little apprehension in his voice but thought it was my own insecurity coloring my perception.

"I've passed your manuscript around the agency and everyone loved it," said Matthew with too big a smile making his statement seem insincere. "I spoke at length about your book with our senior partners, Ellen Sanford and Charlie Weston. I used to be Ellen's right-hand man, we're very close. They've been doing this a long time and had some very specific thoughts on the best way to take your book out to market."

"Great. I'm so excited," I said with too much enthusiasm. "Two heads are better than one. What's our first move?"

Matthew paused for what felt like a really long time. "We want you to tweak the first few chapters."

Tweak? What happened to "genius" and "brilliant" I wondered as alarm bells went off in my head.

"Okay," I said trying to remain calm while making sense of this turn of events. "What kind of 'tweaks' did you have in mind?"

"We think the world of your book. Ellen totally loves it. It's more Charlie. He thinks your manuscript is terrific, but needs a little more polishing before we take it to our contacts at the publishing houses."

"What exactly needs to be polished?"

"You have a three-hundred-and-eighty-seven page manuscript and Charlie feels the story starts on page one ninety-two," said Matthew. "He thinks you should begin the book there."

The rest of the meeting was a blur of rewrite instructions. I took copious notes and agreed to revisit the manuscript and pull the story further forward. I think it's safe to say, the day had not gone as I had envisioned. Matthew walked me to the elevator and gave me an encouraging smile.

"Please don't feel bad about the revisions. We do this with all of our clients," he said observing the change in my mood. "We want you to put your best foot forward. Trust me and we'll have a hit. I promise."

"I do trust you," I said mustering up as much phony cheer as possible, though completely deflated inside. "I'll work on all the changes we discussed. I know I can do this."

Matthew gave me a thumbs up as the elevator doors closed. I started to panic as the elevator went down. Devastated, I stepped out of the building onto the Manhattan sidewalk and it started to drizzle. Tears filled my eyes as dreams of bestsellers, book tours, awards, glowing reviews and movie deals crumbled around me.

Chapter 7

As I raced through the rain down Second Avenue toward Grand Central Station, I tried to make sense of what had just happened. The first time Matthew and I spoke he had been so upbeat and positive. He convinced me *The Soul Collector* was going to be a blockbuster. When he told me to rewrite my entire novel and kill the first half of the book, I was surprised and so disappointed — in him, in me, in the world. Oblivious to the tears streaming down my face, I picked up my pace in an effort to outrun the rain and the nausea in my stomach. After several concerned looks from people passing me, I realized I was full-on crying. Wiping the tears from my face with my sleeve, I commanded myself to "get it together".

It was only after my book was finally published that Matthew told me the true story of how everything went down. Behind the scenes he *had* fought hard for me but had been constantly overruled by his boss. For five years Matthew had been Ellen Sanford's personal assistant, gatekeeper and occasional paramour. All manuscripts that landed on her desk went through him first. He had a great eye and had picked a bunch of bestsellers over the years. If Matthew didn't like a manuscript, Ellen Sanford never saw it.

Ellen and Matthew had worked closely together for years. Her husband never had any proof that anything had gone on between his stunning forty-something wife and her younger male assistant, but he had suspicions. Bottom line — Charlie wanted Matthew out of the agency and far away from his wife.

I eventually found out that Ellen and Matthew *had* been romantically involved. Though Matthew enjoyed every minute, he also expected that one day she would help him move into an agent role. That payday finally came when a junior agent spot opened up and Ellen insisted the job go to Matthew. Her husband didn't think the young man had the experience, good sense, or right contacts.

For weeks, Ellen hammered on Matthew's ability to spot a good manuscript and his numerous contributions to the agency. Barely speaking at home and exhausted from his wife's incessant badgering, Charlie eventually capitulated and promoted Matthew to the coveted junior agent position. His one condition — Matthew's desk would now be located on an entirely different floor from his wife. Matthew would use a different elevator bank making future interactions with Ellen highly unlikely. Also, Charlie told his wife, he intended to keep Matthew on an extremely short leash. If the young, self-important hipster made even a single mistake, Charlie would cut him loose.

Matthew's promotion on paper satisfied different agendas for all concerned. Matthew got the dream job he always wanted. Ellen was still able to slip in an occasional romantic encounter and Charlie had moved a perceived threat to his marriage far away, or so he thought. If there's such a thing as a left-handed promotion, Matthew Donovan's elevation to junior agent was surely that. Charlie made it crystal clear that not everyone thought he was ready. If he had "one little screw up" or "took on loser authors that didn't result in revenue", he'd be out.

Worried he was on borrowed time, Matthew got to work. Focusing his energies on building his own list of authors, he hoped to discover that "one in a million" bestseller somewhere in his slush pile. They say timing is everything. While Matthew was on the hunt, my query letter for *The Soul Collector* was one of hundreds of emails waiting in his inbox. He later told me he started reading my manuscript at 8 p.m. on a Thursday night and stayed up past 3 a.m. to finish it. I take that as quite a compliment. Nothing makes an author happier than a reader losing sleep.

The next morning, bleary-eyed, he took my manuscript directly to Ellen and Charlie. They listened to his pitch and asked for a copy to read over the weekend at their beach house in Sag Harbor.

On Monday morning, Charlie summoned my future agent to his office. Charlie wasn't sold. He didn't love my manuscript the same way Matthew did. The agency wanted large up front advances for their authors. Those typically came from the bigger publishers. Charlie thought only a small indie publisher would be interested in acquiring my book. He also thought my novel needed a significant rewrite. After much back and forth with Ellen intervening midway through, Charlie gave in. The agency would take me on under one condition. If Matthew didn't sell my book for a decent advance, he'd be out of a job.

My manuscript had been dangerously close to being dropped back into the abyss. My entire future rested on Matthew Donovan's shoulders and he didn't have the full support of his company behind him. If I had known the full cloak-and-dagger backstory before I signed, I'm not sure I would have.

In the end, Matthew's agency took a chance on me. I tried to stay focused on the positive. I had my agent and was on my way up the literary ladder. With my head swimming in the endless possibilities of fame and fortune, I continuously reminded myself it was a long road until publication. Having an agent was no guarantee anyone would publish my book. I had been told that a thousand times. Still, I remained hopeful.

I'm a very resilient person. Even that awful first official working meeting, when Matthew suggested (ahem, insisted) a massive manuscript revision was required, only dampened my enthusiasm for a few days.

"You've got to be thick-skinned in this business," said my new agent. "I'm only giving you constructive criticism. Trust me, it will make the book better."

Call it what you will. From my vantage point at the time, he was tearing my novel apart chapter by chapter. At first, I was a bit defensive until a little voice in my head said, *Calm down, he's trying to help you.* After a day or two of licking my wounds, I took a deep breath and accepted Matthew's advice.

In the weeks that followed, I drafted and redrafted every chapter of the novel Matthew had originally called "brilliant". It didn't feel so "brilliant" by my seventh new draft. But I wanted my book to be a success, so I persevered.

After resubmitting all the revised chapters only to be told they didn't quite hit the nail on the head, I started to go to a dark place. Matthew appeared to be a smart and savvy thirty-year-old, but who anointed him the god of all things literary? He never used the word "genius" again like he had at our first meeting. There were moments when I wondered if I should get out of my contract.

"Give your agent a chance to show you what he can do," Teddy had said when I shared my concerns on one of the rare evenings my husband was home for dinner. "It's a process. You always want everything to happen yesterday. Relax. Give it time."

As usual, Teddy was right. It wasn't like anyone else was beating down my door to sign me. I had nowhere else to go, so I sucked it up and got busy and did what Matthew told me to do. Eight weeks later, I was glad I had stayed the course. Matthew announced that my revised manuscript was ready for prime time and he was going to start the submission process.

"You did a great job with all the rewrites," he said. "I know it was painful but the final result was worth it."

"I agree," I said, and I meant it. Matthew had been right about everything. All the revisions he suggested did make the manuscript tighter and better.

"So," said my husband early one morning in the kitchen when I told him my novel was going out on submission, "what kind of an advance do you think you'll get?"

"Matthew told me it depended on what other books were circulating and competing with mine."

"Are we talking ten thousand or fifty?" said Teddy as he sliced an apple on the cutting board.

"I'm hoping it's fifty grand. Wouldn't that be something?" I said. "We could invest it in the new restaurant."

"I'll be counting on that."

Chapter 8

A few weeks later, there was another explosion and fire set off by a drone. After the first drone explosion, a uniformed officer had stopped by my house. This time, a utility shed had blown up in the neighboring town of Barrington causing a raging fire. According to news reports, it took fire departments from three small towns to put it out. Not long after that, I received a second visit from law enforcement. Suddenly, my quiet sanctuary in the woods had become exceedingly busy.

Medford is a small and usually quiet place where most houses have two acre zoning. We share police services with a few surrounding communities like Harwich, Barrington and Hastings CT. That joint police force is headquartered in Medford, not because we're special, but because we're geographically in the center.

I was in my home office one afternoon trying to convince a reluctant client to hire my candidate when my doorbell rang. Since my work call was going nowhere, I ended it and headed downstairs to answer the bell.

Through the glass panes on the side of my front door, I saw a tall attractive man around forty leaning against the white pillar. I was about to open the door when I caught a glimpse of my own disastrous reflection in the glass. I quickly ran my fingers through my unkempt hair and smoothed it into place. Then, as I'd seen Natalie do a thousand times, I wiped my front teeth with my index finger and opened the door.

"Ms Samuels?" said the handsome man with a broad engaging smile and gleaming set of neon white teeth. It struck me his teeth were too perfect and I immediately suspected they were veneers. He handed me his card and said, "Tommy Devlin, reporter with the *Connecticut Advocate*. Got a minute?"

It was a warm, sunny day so I stepped outside closing the door behind me. I wasn't about to let a strange man into my house, not even a good-looking one with a business card. You can never be too careful when you live in the woods with no visible neighbors. I could scream my head off and no one would hear me through all the trees. Anyone can have fake cards made up. I've heard about deranged killers who even have fake police badges. You can't trust anyone these days.

I looked into the man's light blue eyes and had a flicker of recognition. "I know who you are," I said as I squinted at him. "You wrote the article about the drone explosion here in Medford and the one in Barrington."

He smiled, enjoying the recognition. "Then, you know why I'm here."

"Not exactly," I said. Okay, I did know why, but I wasn't going to serve it all up for him on a silver platter. And truthfully, I didn't trust him — gut instinct. Always follow your gut.

"Some people are saying there appear to be significant similarities between the explosions and the events depicted in your book, *A Burning Desire*," said Devlin gazing into my eyes as if to hypnotize me. He almost did. "Do *you* have any theories, Ms Samuels? Know anything about those incidents?"

"I wish I did," I said. "When the first one happened, I was as surprised as anyone. I only heard about it when my best friend texted me after she saw some chatter on social media. She's in PR and practically lives on Twitter."

"According to my sources in the Medford PD, they're conducting a criminal investigation. You don't think there's any connection to your book?"

"Look, I know you're after a story, but I don't have one for you. The truth is *A Burning Desire* originally only sold a few dozen copies in total, mostly to friends. I hate to admit it but hardly anyone even knows my book exists."

"I figured as much, but had to ask," he said. "For the record though, don't you think the explosions are almost identical to your book?"

I smiled. "You've read my book?"

He smiled back. "As a matter of fact, I have."

"Did you enjoy it?"

"I wasn't reading it for pleasure, I was reading it for research," he said. "But, yes, I did. In my opinion, the similarities between your book and the explosions here are too close to dismiss. Drones that look like superheroes? Even I know that's on page one hundred and seventeen of your book."

"You did your homework."

"I used to be a reporter for CNN. I'm well trained," said Devlin feigning humble but not succeeding. I wondered, if he had worked at CNN, why the hell was he now working for a small regional paper in Connecticut? The writer in me was very curious about that. Obviously, he was looking for some admiration from me, so I played along. Feeling generous, I gave him a few crumbs.

"CNN, really? It must have been so cool to work there. Were you on TV?"

"Of course. I worked on a lot of important cases and then did a year of fieldwork in Alaska."

"Wow. You're a big deal." I said, a little impressed. "As far as the explosions go, to be honest, I probably know less about these local crimes than you do. I only know what I've read on Twitter or on news sites."

"Let me ask you, have you had any trouble with anyone or is there someone who might want to sabotage your writing career? Another author maybe?"

I shook my head and looked at my watch. "I can't think of anyone who dislikes me that much or would do such destructive things. I'm sorry, but I have a conference call starting in a few minutes."

Devlin nodded. "You have my card. Call or text me if you think of anything else. You do admit the explosions and drones are quite similar to your book."

"Yes. I suppose it's possible someone read my book and that's what gave them the idea. But I still know nothing about it."

I watched Devlin get into his car as I closed the front door. Surely, it must have been a slow news week if a former CNN reporter was making house calls on something as minor as a couple of small fires. When I got to my desk, I checked Twitter. There were more posts about the fires tying them to me. On the plus side, four people had posted they had just bought my book. I checked my Amazon account. Over the last few days, thirty-four copies of *A Burning Desire* had been purchased. That was more than I'd sold in total before all the Twitter craziness started. I had to admit, the uncanny similarities between reality and my novel were definitely selling books. Woohoo!

I immediately called Matthew.

"A local reporter just came to my house. He was covering the fires and made the connection to my first book. Are you ready for this? Because of this weird coincidence, my old books are starting to sell."

"I didn't see that coming," said Matthew smiling through the phone. "I'm going to milk these conspiracy theories for all they're worth when I'm pitching your new book. Publishers eat up this kind of thing. Free publicity is free publicity."

I ended the call feeling excited. It looked like real life arson was actually helping my books catch fire.

Chapter 9

The first time I met my husband was at the American Bistro on West 47th Street in New York City. Natalie and I had gone there with a few friends for dinner. Since my BFF did PR for high-end hotels and restaurants, she had insisted we go to that particular restaurant. We found out why after we arrived.

As with everything in Natalie's life, our girls' outing had a dual purpose. She had hoped to make a connection with the manager or the owners of the place while we were there having dinner. The American Bistro had been growing in popularity and she wanted to pitch her public relations services. Right after we ordered however, Natalie found out from our waiter that the owners were off the premises for the evening.

"Shit. Nobody who counts is here tonight," she said gritting her teeth, her bright red lips turning slightly downward. That's when I realized why we were all there.

Halfway through our dessert, the young handsome chef of the Bistro, Teddy Samuels, made his dinner rounds in the main dining room. As he got closer, Natalie turned her charm meter up to high and went for it. Another dual purpose — the chef might have sway with the owners and help her get her foot in the door. Also, she found him very attractive.

I had already had two glasses of wine, okay, four, when Teddy approached our table asking if we had enjoyed the food. His chef whites enhanced his dark complexion. From the far side of the table, I admired the shine of his thick, wavy, almost black hair. He had that close-cropped beard thing going on which made him look sexy in a southern European sort of way. He could have been Italian or even Middle Eastern. Natalie, who always gets to the bottom of everything, later told me that Teddy was Greek-American. He caught my eye the minute he entered the main dining room and I watched him move from table to table charming each person. I remember thinking it must be nice to be able to do that so effortlessly — charm people. I didn't have that skill set, I had to rely on my smarts.

When he finally made it over to our table, his charisma was on full display. He was warm, self-effacing and up close even more handsome. His dark-brown eyes with their killer lashes made me practically melt. With a downward glance followed by a bashful grin, he deflected every compliment lobbed at him by our enthusiastic group of eight. When he blushed, everyone at our table, including me, swooned. How could anyone resist that? My crush on Teddy Samuels started at that moment.

Usually the center of attention, because she was both beautiful and bitingly funny, Natalie monopolized most of the conversation with the handsome chef. A femme fatale of the first order, Natalie was gorgeous and used it to her every advantage. Like a samurai with a sword, she wielded her cascades of chestnut brown hair, enormous hazel eyes, perfect upturned nose and lips as full as they were pouty with absolute precision.

Naturally thin with plenty of curves, Natalie was smart, ruthless and hated more than anything to lose. But, if you were ever in trouble, she was definitely the person you wanted in your corner. She was also fierce and when she attacked, she didn't mess around. She went right for the jugular. Some people found her a little intimidating but not me because I knew she had my back. She was a party in a box and always up for anything. I treasured our friendship. As for men? They found her electric energy irresistible. That first night at the restaurant when my BFF laid it on as thick as honey, Teddy Samuels took the bait.

While fishing for information about the restaurant's publicity plans, Natalie inched close enough to Teddy so that he could feel her body heat and smell her expensive Jo Malone London fragrance. Only the best for Natalie.

"I don't get involved on the business side of things," he said to her. "My job is to keep the kitchen from burning down and to make sure your food is perfect."

Licking her lips, Natalie was about to ask another business question when I uncharacteristically butted in. I couldn't help myself.

"How did you make that amazing molten lava chocolate cake?" I said a little breathlessly. "We all shared one. It was incredible." Teddy blushed again and looked directly into my eyes. I felt my body temperature shoot up and gripped the edge of the table to steady myself.

"Share?" he said winking at me. "That's so wrong. Each one of you ladies should have had your own. A delicious dessert is one of the greatest pleasures in life. Since you liked it so much, I'll give you my secret recipe. Then, you can make it at home. But, if you give it to anyone else, I will have to find you and kill you."

Everyone at the table giggled and it was my turn to blush. I tried to tell him I didn't know how to cook, but he only smiled. I could have sworn he was flirting with me and was about to respond in kind. Then Natalie jumped in peppering Teddy with questions and kept him engaged until he was called back to the kitchen.

"Oh, my God," said a blonde woman in our group who worked at Natalie's PR firm when Teddy was out of earshot. "That man is so hot. I'm dying."

"He's like one of those Michelangelo statues," said Natalie letting out a breath and fanning herself with her hand.

"And his eyes," said another woman at the table. "I could look into them all day. My pulse is racing."

"He's very attractive," I said. "And, he seems nice, sweet and kind of vulnerable."

"Attention," said Natalie taking the floor, "I'd like to make an official announcement. Just so we're all clear, I'm going to go out with him." Typical Natalie wasting not a minute. Before any of us had a chance, she had already staked her claim. Honestly, it broke my heart a little.

Twenty minutes later when we got up to leave, I took one last look around the dining room hoping to catch a glimpse of the handsome chef. He was walking across the main floor directly toward us, a piece of paper in his hand.

"If you have any trouble while you're making this cake," he said as he handed me the recipe, "call me and I'll walk you through each step. My private phone number is on the back."

"Given that I don't know the difference between rosemary and thyme," I said trying to be funny and feeling loose because I was a little drunk — okay, a lot drunk. "I may just have to call you."

He smiled and I flushed pink again as Natalie shot me a warning look. "Nice to meet all of you," he said to our group. As he walked back through the crowded restaurant, Natalie swiped her finger across her front teeth, presumably to make sure the new thick coat of red lipstick she had just applied hadn't settled in the wrong places, and went after him.

We all watched as she caught him before he got to the kitchen door. They were on the other side of the room so we couldn't hear what they were saying. But I got a good sense of the conversation from their body language. She was playing with her long hair, and touched his arm not once but three times until she finally left it there. I'd seen her in action plenty of times and knew how she operated. She was going in for the kill. Whatever she said made Teddy laugh and then I saw her press her business card into his palm. He looked at it and grinned. She turned and sashayed back to our group with a big, satisfied, red smile on her face. The whole time, I watched him watch her.

"I gave him my number," said Natalie, her hazel eyes orb-like as she poked me in the arm and giggled. "He'll call."

It sounds crazy now but for me, it was love at first sight. I *wanted* Teddy Samuels, but unfortunately, so did my best friend.

I've never been good at girly games or feminine trickery. I certainly wasn't going to compete with my BFF over a man. That's so 1950s. As much as I was drawn to Teddy, for the sake of my friendship with Natalie, I decided to step aside. I remember feeling rather noble when I made that grown-up decision. Besides, Natalie was much more glam than I was. Teddy was clearly a player and I convinced myself she was the better match. But she had a history of going through men fast. I wondered if in two weeks Teddy would be in her rearview and my sacrifice all for nothing.

I was certain he'd have chosen her anyway. If that makes me sound insecure, I'm not. Natalie was always the star of the show when it came to men. I didn't mind. I'm more of an introvert anyway. Natalie was smart, funny, entertaining, always eager to take center stage. No one on the planet made me laugh harder than she did. I'm more comfortable on the sidelines. Our respective roles worked for us and enabled me to stay in my social comfort zone. Despite my disappointment over Teddy, girls gotta stick together, right? I wasn't about to have a fight over some guy we had just met. Still, I couldn't get over the feeling that Teddy and I were meant to be together, but I never told her.

Chapter 10

The day after I met Teddy at the restaurant, I woke up thinking about him but knew there was only one choice. I had to
put my feelings for him away to preserve my friendship with
Natalie. But it was hard getting him out of my head, he had
hit me like a semi-truck. In the week that followed, I thought
back to that first meeting at the restaurant a thousand times.
I replayed the moment he looked at me with those big brown
soulful eyes. When he spoke to me, I was the only other person in the universe — at least that's how he made me feel.
His laugh was so contagious that I giggled even when I didn't
understand his joke. He made me feel good, really good.

Not long after their first meeting, Natalie and Teddy went
out on two dates both initiated by her. I wanted to warn him
that her boyfriends didn't last long. I predicted she would keep
Teddy around for a few weeks, maybe even a month, because
he was so cute. Then, she'd redirect her focus to someone new.
That was her pattern. I'd seen it happen a million times.

Natalie's beauty and passion were both a blessing and a
curse. Relationships started out great, but she was like a hum-
mingbird flitting from one blossom to another. She'd drain the
man emotionally and almost instantaneously fly away in search
of a fresh untouched flower. My BFF was the poster child for

high-maintenance and despite her good looks, men eventually grew weary of all her demands. When she sensed a change of heart, often before the man knew it himself, she'd dump him first to save face. Nine times out of ten, those same men would come crawling back, begging her to reconsider. By then, she'd already have moved onto someone new. There were a few brave souls who didn't come crawling back. To say rejection irked her is putting it mildly. On the rare occasion *she* got dumped, she'd lose her freakin' mind. Sometimes, things got messy.

One man started seeing someone else right after Natalie ghosted him. Within six weeks he was engaged to the other woman. When Natalie found out, things got ugly. The man and his fiancée eventually had to get a restraining order against her. It wasn't my BFF's finest moment and unfortunately, not the only time something like that had happened.

Let me be clear, she didn't boil bunnies or anything like that. Although, once she deliberately let a boyfriend's cat out of his house because it got its white fur all over her black designer sweater. True, she had slashed a few tires over the years and once poured a bottle of maple syrup into someone's gas tank completely ruining his new Jaguar. I met that maple-syrup guy once and he was kind of an arrogant jerk. Even I agreed he probably deserved the syrup.

After each of these erratic incidents, I was always there for her. They weren't entirely her fault. She acted out because everything came so easy to her and she grew accustomed to always having things her way. She thought nothing about dropping a man the second he displeased her. But, hell hath no fury like Natalie when she was the one who was blown off.

The next time I saw Teddy was during Natalie's second date with him. She had brought him to one of our friend's birthday party. That night, she and I couldn't have looked more different. Two hours before the party, I had undergone a complicated root canal that left my right cheek and eye puffy and swollen — not a pretty picture. I didn't feel or look good and had planned to only make a brief appearance, say happy birthday to the host and leave.

As usual, Natalie made a grand entrance in a skintight, black knit dress that she must have just bought because I'd never seen it before. Her six inch red heels were also new. She made decent money but spent almost all of it on designer clothing and her expensive personal maintenance. Routinely coming up short at the end of each month, she typically used one credit card to pay off the other. "Looking good doesn't come cheap," she had often said after complaining about all her bills. With not a hair out of place that night, she looked like a movie star — a real A-lister.

Natalie walked into the party first with Teddy following behind. They were both so beautiful that they should been on the cover of a magazine. One was almost better looking than the other, although both were gorgeous. To be clear, Teddy wasn't a big deal chef back then. He was still building his career and reputation but was fairly well-known in some eclectic foodie circles. When he walked into that party, a few people recognized him and went over to introduce themselves. While Teddy greeted his handful of admirers, Natalie, teetering on her heels, walked over to me. As she air kissed both of my cheeks with her big, glossy, red lips, I caught a whiff of her signature fragrance lingering in the air around my swollen face.

"You remember Teddy, don't you, Jillian?" she said loudly pointing to him as Teddy moved toward us. I attempted a smile but it felt wildly crooked from my afternoon surgery and anesthesia.

"I went to the dentist this afternoon," I mumbled, trying to cover my mouth with my hand. "I'm still a little numb. Root canal."

"Aww. Poor you," said Natalie making a fake sad look with her mouth as Teddy came up behind her. He flashed his thousand-watt smile at me and I felt my body go limp.

"Did you say root canal? Been there," he said. "I completely understand how you feel."

Behind them, there was some movement in the crowd as a distinguished looking man in his fifties reached over and gently but firmly took Natalie by the arm.

"Sorry to interrupt. We've got a little problem, Natalie," said the older man. He was one of her biggest clients and said he had an urgent business crisis that desperately required her expertise.

"Of course, Ty. You know I'm available to you twenty-four-seven," she said all breathy as she followed the older man into another room. Teddy and I looked at each other not knowing what to do.

"Would you like to sit down?" he said pointing to an empty table in the corner of the room.

I attempted another crooked smile as we sat at a small table for two. The irony that it was me sitting with Teddy that night and not Natalie didn't escape me. For the next hour, while Natalie was occupied with her client, Teddy and I got to know each other. I tried to think of things that would interest him.

"I remember the dessert menu at your restaurant had baklava? That's one of my faves, all the gooey honey and nuts," I said trying to make relevant small talk. "Is it hard to make?"

"Not if you use a lot of butter with the filo dough and work fast," he said smiling again, making my heart beat faster. "Some dishes need time to marinate, others require speed. People are the same, don't you think?"

I laughed out loud because it was kind of true.

"I can show you how to make it sometime," he said, "if you'd like."

A little later, I shared my dream of becoming a successful author and he talked about his own big plans. He loved being a chef, but also had much grander aspirations. Teddy Samuels didn't just want a single restaurant, he wanted to build an empire. Our conversation flowed effortlessly.

"I'm going to start small with just one restaurant and grow the business from there," said Teddy. "I want to have locations all over the world. Being a chef is only the beginning."

I'm not going to lie. I was impressed by his lofty goals. Why not shoot for the top? If you aim for the middle, you'll end up near the bottom. I ate up his big ideas and the way his eyes flashed when he spoke. I also had big dreams, so I understood him. We talked and laughed with never a dull moment in the conversation. Before I knew it, an hour had passed and it was like I'd known Teddy Samuels for my entire life.

He had just said something funny and we were both laughing when Natalie finally returned with her client in tow.

"Teddy," said Natalie all syrupy, "forgive me for leaving you alone for so long. You know how work can be."

"But, I wasn't alone," said Teddy giving me a wink. "I've had an amazing conversation with your friend here." I blushed as I felt Natalie's death stare boring into the side my skull.

"Jillian, you're an angel staying so long and keeping Teddy company. I know you weren't feeling well and really wanted to go home." She cleared her throat which I knew was her signal for me to get up and let her take my place at the table. I looked over at Teddy and thought I detected disappointment in his eyes. But I told myself it was probably wishful thinking. What could I do? I started to get up when suddenly Natalie's client came rushing up behind her again.

"Sorry to do this," said Ty, "I'm afraid I need to steal Natalie away for the rest of the evening. We've got a situation going on and Natalie being our PR person, well, it can't wait until tomorrow. We're calling a board meeting for tonight."

I took that as my cue to leave. "I'm going to head home. Still not feeling great," I muttered.

Teddy stood and put out his hand. "I really enjoyed our conversation, Jillian," he said as his hand shook mine creating an electric shock that traveled all the way up my arm. His touch nearly made my legs buckle. "Come by the restaurant sometime and try the baklava. I'll fix you something special."

I blushed, nodded, and turned to go.

"Feel better, Jillian," Natalie shouted before shifting her attention back to Teddy and her impatient client. When I got to the front door and looked back, Natalie was making oversized hand gestures. I figured she was apologizing to Teddy a second time for leaving him high and dry. I opened the door and left. I didn't want to get in the middle of that.

Chapter 11

The next morning, Natalie called me first thing to tell me every gory detail of the previous night.

"My client's timing couldn't have been worse. The whole thing was so awkward," she chattered away, her keyboard clicking in the background. "I mean, I've been trying to get Ty Griffin's attention for months. He's the SVP on all the Hillman Preferred Hotels business. He's always been cordial and polite but never showed any personal interest in me beyond PR. Don't you think he's handsome? He's old, but sexy old, right? I don't know if it was the wine, but last night he wanted to take things up a few notches. That's why I had to ditch Teddy. Who knew when I'd get another shot at Ty."

"You dumped Teddy Samuels in the middle of your date for another man? You're unbelievable."

"I know, Teddy's amazing. But it wasn't my fault Ty Griffin finally made his move last night. What could I do? Ty's very well connected and super influential in the travel and hospitality business. He could make or break my career."

With a snap of her perfectly manicured fingers, chef Teddy Samuels was history. A few weeks later, Natalie turned the page on Ty Griffin after he took a new position running marketing for a large appliance company. The man had assumed his relationship with Natalie was on solid ground and would continue after he switched jobs. Unaware that a large part of his appeal was his influential position in the hotel industry, he was quickly put out to pasture. Like I said, everything my BFF did had a dual purpose. She would never do PR for an appliance company — far too pedestrian. And just like that, Ty Griffin was out.

The week after Griffin started his new job, Natalie spent the night with an airline pilot. According to her, he had "washboard abs and a chiseled chin". She met him on her way back from a business trip to Boston. With Teddy Samuels now buried in her boyfriend graveyard, I decided to take him up on his offer to stop by his restaurant. I waited for a cold, wet Tuesday night. I figured it would be slow because of the weather and Teddy might have time to chat for a few minutes.

Taking a seat at the bar, I ordered a glass of Sauvignon Blanc and nonchalantly asked the bartender if Teddy Samuels was around. He told me he'd let Teddy know I was there. Nervously, I waited for a response.

When a smiling Teddy emerged from the kitchen, I scrutinized his grin and decided it looked genuine. He told me he could only stay for ten minutes but ten turned into twenty. It might have been magical thinking on my part but I thought there was clicking going on between us. That night was when I learned his name wasn't always Samuels.

"My family on both sides is Greek. When my great-grandfather got to America, he changed his name from Samaras to Samuels to sound more American," said Teddy. "I've often thought of changing it back."

"You should to honor your ancestors," I said, finding him more interesting with each passing second. "That's why you know how to make baklava."

"Shhh. It's my grandmother's recipe. She's little and old but she's still strong and she'd kill me if she knew I was using her recipe at the restaurant. I can teach you how to make it."

With Natalie now legitimately out of the picture by her own hand, I allowed my fantasies of Teddy and me to flourish.

A week later and about a month after Natalie had dumped Teddy, I happened to be at the American Bistro for a business lunch. Truthfully, I had suggested the Bistro hoping to 'accidentally' bump into Teddy. Sure enough, while my clients and I were eating, Teddy sauntered through the main dining room greeting customers. When he spotted me, he smiled and waved from across the room and walked directly over. He wasn't as well-known back then, but he was just as handsome. My clients were thrilled. The charming chef stayed and chatted with us for nearly fifteen minutes, longer than with any other table. Before he went back into the kitchen, he handed me his card.

"I believe I promised to teach you how to make baklava," he said. "If you'd still like a private cooking lesson, text me."

As he walked away, the conversation at our table reached a fever pitch, my clients nearly frantic that the chef had ostensibly asked me out.

I smiled as I tucked his card into the zippered pocket of my bag and contemplated my next move. At the same time, I wondered how this would be perceived by Natalie. She was currently hot and heavy with the commercial pilot and hadn't mentioned Teddy in weeks. Given that, I figured he was fair game. Clearly, she didn't want him. I called him a few days later and soon learned the secrets of his grandmother's perfect baklava . . . among other things.

When I told Natalie I'd gone out with him, at first she seemed annoyed but quickly got over it. She really didn't have a leg to stand on. She had gone out with seven or eight different men since Teddy and, along with the pilot, she was simultaneously dating a Wall Street banker on the down low as well as a few other assorted men. I marveled at her ability to juggle so many guys at the same time. It was nothing short of extraordinary.

"Teddy wasn't my type anyway," she said dismissively after I told her my intentions. "Besides, he works crazy restaurant hours. I need a man who can work around my schedule. You can have Teddy. He's all yours."

To be clear, I wasn't asking her permission. She had rejected him. In my opinion, she had no claim. Teddy and I did start seeing each other. After our first night of baking Greek pastry, everything just came naturally together. The Natalie thing was a little awkward at first because he had dated her and she was my best friend. Neither of us knew what the acceptable rules were, but we figured it out. In a matter of months, Teddy and I were inseparable and I knew he was my soulmate.

Spoiler alert — after one carefree glorious New York City year, Teddy Samuels aka Samaras asked me to marry him.

I said yes.

Chapter 12

Eight months later, surrounded by friends and family, Teddy and I got married on a farm in Connecticut not far from where I had grown up and near my mother's house. Naturally, Natalie was my maid of honor. Was she bothered by the fact that I married someone she had gone out with first? Not really. By the time Teddy and I became a "thing", Natalie was already involved with another Wall Street banker who she declared could be "the one". He wasn't. By the time my actual wedding day rolled around she brought a jazz drummer as her date.

My mom was still okay on my wedding day looking beautiful dressed in a pale melon-colored chemise. She was so happy that day but in the blink of an eye, everything changed. Less than a year after my wedding, Teddy and I noticed signs of what we would eventually learn was early onset dementia. Once it started, it came on so fast it made my head spin.

A few months after our wedding, Teddy and I observed subtle changes in my mother's behavior. First, it was little things like forgetting that we were coming to pick her up or that she was supposed to meet us for dinner.

Once, Teddy and I stopped over at her house and she offered to make us coffee. While we chatted in her kitchen, my mother pulled out the coffee grounds, dumped them in a strainer, held it over a coffee cup and poured boiling water through it. Her clean French press coffee pot, the one that she had used for years, sat only inches away on the counter.

"Mom, what are you doing?"

"You said you wanted coffee, didn't you?"

"Why are you doing it that way? Why aren't you using the coffee pot?"

When I pointed it out she realized something was wrong but tried to brush it off. "I like to make it this way now. It's much easier. I don't have to clean anything afterwards."

Easier it absolutely wasn't. Teddy and I gave each other a look but let it drop for the moment. Soon, there were more what we called "weird Mom things" until they became too frequent to ignore. We started finding little notes all over her house. Some were written reminders of things she had to do and others were where everyday things were kept.

When we finally got her official Alzheimer's diagnosis, she and I both cried. That's when I circled the wagons determined to take the best care of her as humanly possible. And, I did. I made sure she had everything she needed including lots of outings and visits from Teddy and me. He was great with my mother. That was probably because his own mother had died of cancer when he was in high school. He always said it left a big hole in his heart. I guess my mom was the next best thing to having his own. Before his work got so busy, he used to come with me to visit her all the time.

"I made you a frittata today," he had said to my mother one time as he opened up a glass container with a fresh vegetable, egg and cheese pie inside. "I made it especially for you because you like them so much." It was so sweet that he remembered and made the effort, plus she could eat it with her hands. My mother had started having difficulty using utensils and food she could eat with her hands had become the better way to go.

It was soon evident I needed to be closer to her. That's why we ended up moving out of the city and up to

Connecticut. It was partly to get away from the chaos of Manhattan, but more to be near my mother. She was going to need support and a lot of it.

Since my father and sister had both passed away years before, I was all my mother had left. Not that my father would have been any help to her if he were still alive. He had always been more concerned with his own well-being than my mother's, my sister's or mine. Can't honestly say I miss him. My mother would agree, if she remembered who he was.

Teddy and I scraped together every penny we could get our hands on, borrowed some money at a terrible interest rate and bought an old house with a stone wall in Medford, CT. We created our own little countrified universe. About an hour and twenty minutes north of Manhattan, Medford is a rural hamlet loaded with woods, streams, bridges and lots of quiet. Life there was the antithesis of our previous sensory overloaded New York City existence.

Our charming eighty-five-year-old colonial cottage sits on three acres of wooded property and has a large stone fireplace. Situated off a small country lane, the house is surrounded by a dense thicket of evergreen trees providing us with total privacy. After living in the fishbowl known as Manhattan, the solitude of Medford was a welcome change. Seriously, you could play nude volleyball in my backyard, and no one would see you. Not that we ever did, but you could if you were so inclined. Knowing that made me happy in case I ever had the urge to rip my clothes off and spike a ball over a net.

There's a deer path running through our front yard. Sometimes while working in my home office, I'll look out the window for inspiration. It's not unusual to spot seven or eight deer, some with antlers, munching happily on our lawn and shrubs. I'm talking some serious reindeer, like the ones that pull Santa's sleigh. They are magnificent. People in Connecticut say deer can obliterate a flower garden in minutes. Since I'm not a gardener, that was never an issue. I just like looking at those sweet animals. They center me.

There's also a neighborhood black cat that frequently traipses across my lawn. He's probably looking for mice but he'd do better if he went hunting in my basement. I'm pretty sure our cellar is the international mouse headquarters based on the number of droppings I've found and the racket they make. Black cats are supposed to be bad luck. Whenever I see that cat, I throw some salt over my shoulder as a little insurance policy. You can never be too careful.

During the first year of our marriage, Teddy's culinary star was on the rise. The demands of the restaurant required him to work long hours. We didn't see much of each other, but it couldn't be helped. We both understood it would only be temporary until both of our careers were firmly established. I tried to turn that negative into a positive and used that time to work on my first novel. Teddy encouraged my writing every step of the way and his support got me over my first literary finish line.

"Everyone needs to pursue their passion," Teddy had said to me shortly before we got married. "I create things with food that make people happy. Cooking brings me joy. Do the same with your writing, Jills. Don't give up." Teddy's enthusiasm was what kept me going. Every time I got another rejection, he'd build me back up.

"That's one person's opinion," he'd say as he wiped away a tear in my eye with his thumb. "Try someone else. You know what they say, 'all it takes is one'." My husband was all in on me and my writing and his faith gave me the strength to keep going. At the same time, I couldn't have been prouder of all that he had achieved in the restaurant business. It sounds corny, but our life then was like a little slice of heaven.

Over the next few years, Teddy's reputation as a chef grew. He did a few guest stints at some hot food events in the city and even appeared once as a guest chef on a cable TV food reality show. He wasn't a household name or anything like that, but things were starting to percolate.

Meanwhile, I had finished writing my first thriller, *A Burning Desire*, and was nearly through with my second. To be honest, while Teddy's career was soaring, my writing career was tanking. I tried repeatedly to find an agent to represent my finished manuscript but had no luck. No matter how hard I tried, I was still only an executive recruiter who liked to write. I was not an author. Despite my disappointments, my husband remained steadfast in his support of my writing and eventually encouraged me to self-publish my book.

"What have you got to lose?" he said one night over a bottle of red wine. "Your books are great. Get them out into the world so people can read them. Maybe you'll get an agent that way."

Years of work were sitting in a documents folder on my laptop doing nothing. He was right. What did I have to lose? It was Teddy's prodding and a few nudges from Natalie that got me off the couch and into the self-publishing business.

"I loved your drone, explosion, fire book," said Natalie. "You write with such passion. I can visualize everything. You've got a real gift, Jills. You owe it to the world to put your stuff out there."

I took the advice from my two favorite people and set out to learn the process of self-publishing. At that point I had completed three novels, all thrillers. After several missteps, I figured it out but said nothing to Teddy or Natalie. When my books were finally loaded, visible and ready for sale, I invited Natalie up to spend the weekend with us in Connecticut. That Friday night I surprised them both and showed them all three of my book listings on Amazon.

"Now, you're an official author," said Teddy giving me a kiss. "I'm so proud of you."

"I want a signed copy of each one," said Natalie as she gave me a hug and whipped out her phone. "I'm buying ten books right now and giving them to my clients."

"Don't spend so much money," I protested, secretly pleased that she would do that.

"I'll charge it to the company, client gifts," she said as she tapped into her phone.

That night had been so full of joy, hope and support. Even now, after everything that's happened, it's hard to believe how everything eventually changed and not for the better.

Chapter 13

While I plugged away writing, Teddy did the same in the food world. His creativity in the kitchen combined with his earthy good looks and quick wit occasionally landed him in New York newspaper and website gossip pages. He wasn't a celebrity exactly, but he was fairly well-known in culinary circles, his reputation solid and growing.

"One of the top high-end restaurant groups approached me about opening a new place downtown," Teddy had said over dinner as he unpacked his big news. "They want to use the Teddy Samuels' brand to build a following for a whole new type of epicurean venue. They want to call it 'T. Samuels'. Cool, right? I'd have a restaurant in New York City with my name on it. What do you think?"

It was huge news. I had picked up a little knowledge about the restaurant biz while married to him. Launching a four-star restaurant in Manhattan was an expensive proposition requiring a lot of sweat equity and even more money. According to my husband, this group of investors had a stellar track record and a big wallet.

At first Teddy was flattered, but there were stumbling blocks. His biggest concern was that he'd be doing all the heavy lifting as the chef and face of the restaurant, while the investors made all the money. They had offered him a 0.85% interest in the business in addition to his salary. Teddy mulled it over but wasn't convinced the numbers worked for him and declined. Less than a one percent interest for all the extra hours as the public face of T. Samuels seemed not enough.

Eventually, the investors came back and sweetened the pot. They crafted a plan where Teddy would get a one percent interest for lending his name and running the place along with his salary. This time they offered him the opportunity to invest his own money in the business. They structured it so he could purchase two shares for the price of one for up to ten percent of the company.

"It's a really good offer," said an excited Teddy the night he laid the new deal out for me. "These are seasoned successful restaurant investors. This is the same group behind Arrandales's, The Loft, St Eve's and a bunch of others. They know what they're doing. They've never failed."

"Do it," I said. "It sounds amazing. How many times have you said you wanted a career like Wolfgang Puck, Thomas Keller or Gordon Ramsay?"

Chewing the inside of his cheek, something he did whenever he was anxious or unsure about something, he waited a moment before he replied. "It's not that simple, Jills. For me to purchase ten percent of the company, their accountant said I'd have to come up with nearly half a million dollars."

"Wow, that much?" I said trying to wrap my brain around the humongous number. I did a quick inventory of our financials in my head. We had less than five thousand in our savings account and barely squeaked out our bills and mortgage payment each month. Our money was tight but not because we didn't earn a decent wage. Over the years, my ambitious husband had speculated on a few real estate deals. We had taken every penny we could out of the house and borrowed more from several banks. One of his deals simply died and another turned out to be a scam. We lost everything and owed a lot of money to a lot of people. I had been down this investment road with my husband before and was a little skittish about going into more debt. Now, he wanted to find half a million dollars and put it into a restaurant. Half a million we didn't have.

"An opportunity like this doesn't come along twice," he said shaking his head. "If I say no, I may never get another shot."

"Could we take more money out of our house?"

He shook his head. "We're tapped out on the house."

"Your family?"

"We can't ask my father, he practically lives on Social Security. He doesn't have it, nor does anyone else in my family."

I sighed. One of the things I loved most about Teddy was his ambition. I understood it because I had a ton of my own. Still, you can't squeeze blood from a stone. If this restaurant went the same way as some of Teddy's other investments, we'd be financially screwed forever. On the other hand, I didn't want to crush his dream. "Do you have to let the investors know right now?"

"I don't think so. They're serious about moving forward, but they're still in the planning stage. Nothing concrete would get going for a while. That gives me some time to come up with the money for the shares. But, there's a catch. I'd have to sign on to T. Samuels now with the smaller percentage. I'll have to commit without knowing for sure if I'll be able to raise the money in time. That means if I don't come up with the cash, I'm locked in with only a tiny stake. They want my answer now, or they'll look for another chef."

I looked into my husband's anguished brown eyes. "Do it, Teddy. Commit. Worst case scenario, you'll see your name up in lights on a hot New York City restaurant. You'll still get your salary and 0.85% of a successful food business isn't nothing. Plus, you'll get your picture in the paper on a regular basis while you continue to build your brand."

"But they'll own my name." Teddy said as he hung his head. He was torn but didn't want his big break to slip through his fingers. This opportunity was exactly what he had been working toward his whole career. If we could somehow come up with the money to make the bigger investment and the restaurant was a success, Teddy would be able to open more restaurants and fulfill his big dream.

I reached across the table and touched his arm. "We've still got time. We'll figure out a way to get the money over the next few months. I promise. If my book does well and becomes a bestseller and I got a movie deal like Matthew said, who knows how much I could make?"

We both burst out laughing because at the time that was such a pie in the sky fantasy. The next morning Teddy called the investors and told them he was on board. He would be the face of T. Samuels, a quintessential American eatery with a little touch of Greece. In the meantime, we had a little breathing room to find that money.

To celebrate his new venture, I wanted to get him something extra special. I shouldn't have spent the money because we were supposed to be saving, but I couldn't help myself. For as long as I'd known him, my husband had coveted a set of Yaxell knives. According to Teddy, these Japanese blades were among the best in the world.

"You can do things with those knives that you wouldn't believe," he said when we passed a Yaxell display in a store window. "They're so precise. You can cut beef paper thin."

I wasn't sure why anyone would want "paper thin" beef. Personally, I liked my steak thick and juicy. Regardless, he thought they were amazing. So, I bought him a set of four knives for an ungodly sum. I even paid cash so he wouldn't see the bill and ruin the surprise. I also bought him a carrying case with his initials embossed on it — TAS — so he could take his knives with him wherever he went. When I gave him the gift, he was so over the moon that he never questioned the cost.

While his career was catapulting forward, mine was not. I continued executive recruiting making a few thousand here and there which we immediately put into the bank. My agent had been shopping my book to publishers, but there hadn't been a single nibble and I was getting worried. What if Matthew couldn't sell it? Communication between us had become less frequent and I worried he was losing interest in my book and me. Then one day I received a text from him:

> *Three different acquisition groups looking at your manuscript. Now's the time to pump up your social media. We need buzz to tip the scales right now. Do whatever you can.*

Pump up my social media? I'd already been tweeting, posting pictures, liking and retweeting like a drunken sailor. What more could I do? I blogged, re-posted and tweeted articles on crime and commented frequently on other authors I admired. If someone posted a picture of their half-finished ice cream, Jillian Samuels "liked" it. I hadn't the faintest idea how to create more "buzz". But from the tone of Matthew's text, it sounded like unless I created some extra publicity, my book wasn't going to be sold.

Whenever I had a crisis, my go-to person was Natalie. A professional buzz maker who always had an opinion, more than anything Natalie loved solving problems. She'd know what to do.

"Hate to tell you, I only have two minutes," said Natalie when she picked up my call. "Going to a big pitch meeting in an hour." She was always going into a meeting, so her brevity didn't surprise or bother me. It was part of Natalie's New York girl charm and I was used to it.

'Keep 'em wanting more,' she'd say defensively whenever I'd joked that her abrupt behavior might appear rude to some.

"I am not rude. I'm busy," she said on more than one occasion. "People who have nothing going on in their lives have time to shoot the shit. I don't."

In every other respect Natalie was a great friend. I'd made peace with her occasional "ahem" brevity.

"I have a serious emergency," I said. "I really need to talk to you."

"Okay," she said clicking her tongue, "Dr Bloom is in. What's the problem?"

"My agent says I need to create buzz around my book. I don't know what to do or how to do it."

"That's a big question and not one I can answer in your remaining minute and a half. Off the top of my head, I'm thinking you need to get Teddy involved. He's already got buzz around him. Get a little of his star power to rub off on you."

"That's a great idea. What if I—"

"Time's up. Sorry, gotta go. Love you," said Natalie as my phone went dead. She may not have given me much of her time, but she did give me some critical food for thought.

The following night, after arriving home from her client's new hotel opening in SoHo, Natalie called me.

"Our event tonight was unreal. The hotel critic from Travel Vacay was there. She was super impressed with the decor in the bar and lobby. We're definitely going to get a good write-up from her. And, get this, remember Greg Hayden from the 90s boy band No Connection? He made an appearance at our event tonight. Can you believe it? When he showed up, everyone at the party went insane, especially the middle-aged women. My client apparently had a crush on Hayden when she was growing up. She was absolutely out of her mind when I introduced them." Natalie chattered on, no "gotta go" when the topic was about her. Whenever I brought that up, she changed the subject or rationalized her behavior. But I accepted her for who she was. I loved her, warts and all.

"I talk when I have something interesting and poignant to say. Many people think I'm an expert listener," she had said when I once complained she wasn't paying attention to me. It was hard to believe anyone would have categorized Natalie as an "expert listener". If you wanted to get her full attention, there usually had to be something in it for her.

"Have you given any more thought to how I can elevate my book?" I said leaving no time to change the subject back to her.

"In PR, you have to use what you have. You're probably looking at yourself thinking you have nothing to offer, that you're not newsworthy."

"Actually, I wasn't really—"

"Use what you've got, Jills. You have three self-published thrillers, that's huge. Add in your secret weapon, a very handsome, sexy, fairly well-known chef husband. Tap into both of those things. Promote your older books to lay seeds for the new one. Use Teddy to get some exposure with all the glitterati who dine at the American Bistro. A lot of influential people go to his restaurant and know who he is. Teddy could give away signed copies of your first three books to the people in New York that count and have influence. Maybe he could take pictures or videos of certain customers holding your books. Then, you could post those pics on social media."

Say what you will about my BFF, but she knows her stuff. None of what she recommended had occurred to me. Teddy did have a following and people were always taking pictures with him because he was both handsome and his name often showed up in food columns. Of course, he could only give out so many books but even if I got just a couple of pictures to post, that might satisfy my agent and impress a potential publisher.

Natalie was absolutely right. Until my new book found a publishing home, I had to leverage my first three books to help sell it. Teddy was the glue that would make everything work. At least I thought so at the time.

Chapter 14

According to my agent, several publishers were supposedly evaluating my manuscript. I waited on pins and needles wondering how it was all going to end. With my nails down to the nubs, I continuously ruminated on every worst case scenario. Though I tried to shift my attention and focus on my recruiting assignments, I found it impossible to concentrate.

Despite Matthew's original proclamation that there would be a "bidding war" for my manuscript, nothing close to that ever materialized. As weeks of silence passed, I learned there was only one publisher remotely interested — Linton Books. They were a small independent publisher with a good reputation. If they acquired my book, I'd be in good hands. If they passed, I was toast. I had nothing.

I wondered if Matthew knew what he was doing. What if he didn't have the right connections or any connections at all? I should have thought about that before I signed with him. I was so eager and anxious to see my book in print; an orangutan could have put a contract in front of me and I would have pulled out my pen.

I tried not to bother Matthew too often, didn't want to become annoying and clingy. Nobody likes that. One rainy day however my own anxiety got the better of me. I texted him even though I knew if he had anything to report he would have been in touch. What can I say? I'm only human.

Any news yet?

—*You'll be the first to know.*

You haven't heard anything? Nothing? No feedback?

—*Not yet.*

Isn't it taking too long? It feels like it's taking too long. Should I be worried???

—*These things take time. I'm on it. Trust me. Relax.*

Relax? I hadn't relaxed since I was five. At first, I accepted Matthew's response, but then I wondered, how the hell he'd know if it was taking too long? I was, after all, his first freakin' client. After that lukewarm text exchange, I became convinced no publisher was ever going to acquire my book. That sent me down a rabbit hole.

What I didn't know then was that Matthew *did* have a legitimate connection at Linton Books. Turns out, Linton was his one and only real connection — a young editor named Eric Shaw.

Matthew Donovan and Eric Shaw had gone to college together and had been acquaintances but not real friends. Flash forward years later, they were both ambitious young men in book publishing. When Matthew read a blurb in the trades about Eric being promoted into the acquisitions group at Linton Books, he made a point of attending an industry event Linton was sponsoring. Matthew "accidentally" bumped into the new editor there. Their fortuitous meeting reestablished their college relationship, though their motivations going forward were vastly different.

Matthew needed his first book, which happened to be mine, to be a hit. If it wasn't, he risked getting tossed out of Sanford Weston — something I only found out about much later. Desperate to keep his job, Matthew remembered that Eric, who was gay, had the hots for him in college. Matthew was straight so nothing ever happened, but it didn't stop Eric from forever hoping.

When Matthew read about Eric's promotion, he wondered if Eric could possibly still have feelings for him. If so, Matthew wondered if he could stir them up to his advantage. Apparently, my scheming agent had intended to exploit Eric's feelings to help my book find a publishing home.

The afternoon they ran into each other at the business event, Eric was both delighted and astonished to see his college crush looking better than ever. Their reunion ended with my agent inviting the acquiring editor out for lunch.

A week later seated in a bustling Italian trattoria, the two young men caught up on mutual college friends and associated gossip. After an acceptable amount of time on memory lane, Matthew got down to his real business. He articulated how important it was for underdogs like them to make their own magic happen. He drew parallels to their respective publishing careers, and pointed out how they were both the low men on the totem pole. He banged on the notion that in order to be really successful, they'd both have to claw their way to the top by whatever means necessary.

As Matthew wove his tangled web, it was soon evident he had hooked his fish. Pretty sure the young editor was still crushing on him, Matthew went in for the kill. He suggested they team up to further both of their careers.

Matthew later told me it looked like a match made in heaven. Eric needed a hot property to acquire and Matthew was in search of a publishing home for my thriller. They could discover the new author (me) together and both be heroes. And, as Eric fantasized that a romantic relationship might also be on the cards, Matthew didn't do anything to dissuade him.

Like Matthew, Eric had a lot riding on his first acquisition but he wasn't the sole decision maker at Linton. Matthew had pitched my book as a fresh new take on the thriller genre with a strong, clear, modern voice. He positioned me as an author who would appeal to millennials, a demographic all the publishers were chasing.

Eric read my manuscript the next day and loved it. He passed *The Soul Collector* around to the Linton acquisitions team and got a mixed response. Most people liked it but it wasn't the home run Matthew and he had hoped.

Andrea Cox, head of Linton acquisitions, met with Eric privately to discuss my book's reviews from the team. There had been no general consensus that *The Soul Collector* was a surefire winner. However, most of the acquisitions team was over forty-five and the Linton mandate was to reach a younger demographic. They needed to reach millennials and my book could solve their problem. A millennial himself, Eric was convinced *The Soul Collector* would go all the way to the top of the charts.

Andrea Cox had mentored Eric when he joined the company right out of college. She had a real soft spot for him and he knew it. Though she hadn't read my manuscript, the feedback from her team had given her pause. I was an unknown unproven author with a miniscule social media presence. People in the industry had never heard of me or my manuscript. But she didn't want to shoot Eric down and destroy his entrepreneurial spirit, so she agreed to give my thriller a read on her upcoming extended vacation to the Galapagos Islands.

Not long after, Matthew told me about a dinner he had with Eric. It was at Chez Paris, a popular French place in the meatpacking district. They reminisced about college and marveled at the extreme odds of them both working on a deal together so many years later. Matthew had been a big deal at the university, everyone's party pal and the campus ladies' man. Eric was the opposite. He was shy, thoughtful and quiet and worked on the theater stage crew building sets for the drama club. They only knew each other because Matthew, on a dare from a fraternity brother, auditioned and was cast to play a gangster in a spring production of *Guys and Dolls*.

Though the restaurant was crowded and noisy, Matthew boasted about the huge amount of interest my book was garnering in the industry and wanted to know where Linton Books stood. Desperate to stay in Matthew's orbit, Eric lied. He indicated the feedback had been positive but that his boss, who had the final word, had taken my manuscript with her to Ecuador.

Disappointed the deal wasn't locked up, Matthew learned that day that Andrea was a social media fanatic and on Twitter constantly. Apparently, she had checked out my social media presence and had not been impressed.

The fact was, I was not an influencer and that's what Linton was looking for. If I wanted a green light on my book, I had to start trending. Easier said than done. My life was about to become more complicated but just how much I never imagined.

Chapter 15

A week later, I arrived home after a morning swim at the YMCA. The Medford community sports facility had an Olympic-sized swimming pool and the people who regularly swam there had a whole lot of attitude — pools had rules. Learn them or get out of the freakin' water.

I'm the kind of person who sticks with things and practices whatever it is until I get it. For example, I stuck with writing. I was determined that one day, whatever it took, I would be a published author. I approached swimming with a similar mindset. The first time I got into the pool, I could barely swim a full lap.

As other swimmers breezed up and down the lanes without stopping, I struggled but persevered, which is my nature. Doggedly each day, I added another lap. As my fellow swimmers easily sailed by me in the adjoining lanes, I remained slow and steady and I learned. I wasn't only swimming, I was watching. With my goggles on under the water, I followed the other swimmers examining their strokes and form. I took note of every movement; how far they turned their head and exactly when they took a breath; the flutter of their hand as they pushed the water behind. I observed them kick, counted how long they glided and how far they reached out their arms with each stroke.

After I figured out who was who in the pool, I made a point of picking a lane between the best swimmers. Over time, I got better by mimicking the moves of those on either side of me. After six months of swallowing gallons of pool water, I had worked myself up to half of a mile. I had become one of those annoying people doing lap after lap without stopping.

But one thing I still hadn't mastered was the flip turn. Determined to add that cool factor to my water routine, I went onto YouTube and discovered there's a video tutorial on everything. I spent hours watching swimming videos on how to master the turn and then went to the pool to practice. It took me a long time but I finally got it. Find the mark, forward tumble, face up, push off the wall, flip over onto your stomach and . . . swim. The flip turn only takes three seconds or less to complete but it took me twelve to fifteen hours to get it right.

I approach everything in life the same way including my writing — tenacious, methodical and determined. I pay attention to what other writers are doing, the good, the bad and the mediocre. I read as much as I can, mysteries, literary fiction, romance, thrillers . . . anything that's well done. I'm pretty sure doing my homework was what helped me get an agent.

Home from my swim and feeling energized, I walked through the front door and shouted, "I'm home" to my husband and went directly upstairs to my office. First, I did a quick online check of my recent book sales. When I looked at the numbers, I blinked twice. Was I looking at the wrong page? Sixty-three more copies of *A Burning Desire* had recently sold. In total, since that last explosion, nearly a hundred copies of my arson book had been purchased. Something strange but wonderful was happening.

I checked the sales of my other books. They had also picked up a little. This was notable in a totally great and fabulous way.

Make no mistake about it, a building going up in flames is a terrible thing. But, nobody got hurt as far as I knew, and I couldn't deny it was helping my overall book sales. They say "God works in mysterious ways" and "not to look a gift horse in the mouth". So, I didn't and enjoyed my good fortune.

Downstairs, my husband was having breakfast at the kitchen table while reading the news on his phone, his morning ritual.

"Good swim?" he asked without looking up when I walked into the kitchen.

"Amazing," I said stretching my neck from side to side. "But, in about half an hour my day gets crazy. I've got four interviews and then I—"

"It says on my Medford news app that there was another explosion yesterday," said my husband still glued to his phone, "over in Barrington."

"Another one? A fire too? Was anyone hurt?" I said, already speculating on what it might do for my books. I know, I'm a horrible person but I couldn't help it.

"I don't think so," said Teddy reading from his phone. "According to the article in the *Advocate*, 'witnesses saw something that looked like a Great White shark floating through the air pulling a tug boat. A few minutes later there was a big bang'."

"What else does it say?" I said as I walked up behind him to peek over his shoulder at his phone.

"That's it. The police are still investigating."

I nodded and headed back up the stairs to get dressed for my ten o'clock interview, followed by another at eleven fifteen. An hour later, after finishing my first interview, Teddy stuck his head into my office.

"I'm leaving now. Don't forget, I'm going to be late tonight. Big party at the restaurant, one of those Silicon Alley start-ups spending all their venture cap money on lobster and champagne. Everything has to be perfect. I've got to stay until the end. Don't wait up."

He blew me a kiss and was gone.

I finished my second interview at nearly twelve thirty and started making notes on a resume when my doorbell rang. From my office window, I recognized the car parked in my driveway. It belonged to that reporter, Tommy Devlin. I suspected he was back because of that new shark-drone explosion in Barrington.

When I opened the front door, I was again struck by Devlin's perfect all-American good looks and his two rows of ultra-white teeth. He was handsome and he knew it, which made him less so. There was something smarmy about him which kept me on my toes. Good looks and sleaze are a dangerous combination.

After I expressed surprise at seeing him standing in my doorway, he got right to the point.

"I suppose you've heard there was another explosion yesterday over in Barrington?" said Devlin.

"My husband showed me something about it online this morning."

"Several local people reported seeing a drone that looked like—"

"A Great White shark. I heard about it," I said leaning on my front door. "Let me guess, you think the explosions are connected to my first book."

"It is an odd coincidence," he said looking into my eyes. "Ever wonder if it's one of your readers using your book as a sort of crime handbook or tutorial? You know like an *Arson for Dummies*."

"I haven't thought about it. Besides, drones are everywhere. You can order a drone on Amazon today and have it tonight. As I've already told you, my book wasn't exactly a bestseller, it had a very small universe of readers."

Devlin stared at me, a smirk on his face.

"What?" I said annoyed by the cat-and-mouse game he was playing.

"I have more information than was publicly reported," he said gloating.

As a crime writer, I immediately became more interested in the conversation. "Like what?" I said trying not to sound too eager but I was so curious.

"Messages were left at each of the crime scenes," said Devlin, a satisfied look on his face.

My eyes and mouth went wide at the exact same moment before I could stop myself. He smiled. His words had the effect he intended.

"At the first explosion site in Medford," said the reporter, "the police found a large white rock at the scene. A message in purple or blue crayon was scrawled on it. All it said was, 'How did I do?'."

"How did I do? What does that mean?"

"No idea," said Devlin. "At the second explosion location, the cops found an old wooden plank that also had a message written in purple or blue crayon. It said, 'Did I make you proud?'"

"Make who proud?" I said, my eyebrows knitting together.

"I thought *you* might know," said the reporter.

"What about the newest fire in Barrington? Was there a note left?"

"Yeah," said Devlin looking smug as his eyes drilled into mine. "There was a note written on the back of an old stop sign. It said, 'Did I make you happy?'"

"This is crazy. What does all that mean?"

"Seems to me it's exactly like your plot in *A Burning Desire* — decorated flying drones and buildings going up in flames."

"Except, the teen arsonist in my book didn't leave notes in blue or purple crayon. So we're clear, my thrillers are purely fiction. I can't shed any light on real crimes. The US military uses drones for all kinds of nefarious reasons. Why don't you call the Pentagon and ask them?"

"That's funny," said Devlin. "As a matter of fact, I've already left a message with the Department of Defense for a comment. So, what do you think 'did I make you proud' means?" he asked again, still peering at me.

"I still have no idea," I said and looked at my watch. Another Zoom interview was about to start and I told Devlin I had to go. He left without too much fuss but asked me to keep in touch. Yeah, right. Back upstairs, I looked out the window and watched him leave. Something about him bothered me. I couldn't blame Devlin for his persistence, no one is more persistent than me. I reminded myself that the reporter was simply doing his job. Regardless, I had nothing to say to him.

In my office preparing for the upcoming interview, my mind drifted to the recent explosive events. I had seven minutes until my Zoom session started — enough time to check my book sales, again.

I clicked on my computer and holy moly, another fifty-six copies of *A Burning Desire* had sold. This arson crime spree may have been a terrible thing for the owners of those properties but they were doing wonders for my book sales. I shouldn't have smiled, but I did. Fifty-six copies sold in one day was nothing to sneeze at.

With a few minutes left, I checked Twitter. There were five new posts about the new fire and my book.

> *@CTsally432 "Drone dressed like shark explodes in Barrington CT". I heard there are messages left at the scenes. Anyone think arsonist trying to communicate with author @JillianSamuelsAuthorbook? #A Burning Desire? #Truecrime #arson #explosion #drones #Jaws.*

All five posts said essentially the same thing. Each person posting and reposting believed the explosions were somehow connected to me and my book — the same book almost nobody had read before the attacks started happening. Who the hell was @CTsally432 anyhow and why did she care enough to post about it? Then I saw a meme of an explosion with a caption that said "Boom-Boom Jillian!".

Clearly, there were a lot of armchair sleuths with too much time on their hands lurking on the internet. Platforms like Twitter gave them a place and the means to share any wacky made-up thought, fact or opinion that popped into their noggins.

My life had been reduced to a demented meme. WTF?

Chapter 16

For the next two weeks I put the explosions and fires out of my mind. Instead, I concentrated on my job placements and maintained regular communications with my agent.

"It's still early days. I'm not worried," said Matthew with an air of confidence after I started what-iffing, and playing out worst case scenarios.

"Does it usually take this long? Did you get any feedback from Linton Books?" I said. "Is there anything I can do to help?

"Selling a new author's manuscript takes time. Publishers have to get to know you and your writing. It's a process and a big commitment for them. A lot of money goes into publishing a book."

"But, what if . . ."

"Jillian, I've got it," he said with a fair amount of bravado. "Don't worry. I've got a plan and a few contacts I'm working round the clock. Trust me."

Whenever someone says "trust me" it always makes me *not* trust them. I let out a breath and told myself to surrender. Going with the flow was not typically my strong suit. I reminded myself that Matthew was the expert and I needed to back off and let him do his job. What did I know about book publishing? Absolutely nothing, although I had watched a few videos about it on YouTube.

Eight forty-five a.m. the next morning, my hair still wet from my swim at the Y, I pulled into my driveway. Teddy would probably still be asleep so I headed directly into the kitchen. After turning on the coffee machine, I reached for the phone in my swim bag. There was a text from my neighbor, Sue. Besides Natalie and Teddy, she was one of the few people who had read all three of my books, a true friend.

Did you see Medford Local today? A cell phone tower on south side of town blew up at 7.20 a.m. I still have phone service, do you? Some man here in Medford was walking his dog right before it happened. He saw a small pink hot air balloon with a hanging basket flying above him heading in the direction of the cell tower. It's exactly like your book. Call me.

I googled "explosion in Medford" to see if anyone else had picked up the story. A cell tower was clearly a bigger deal than an empty shed or an abandoned warehouse so I expected there would be some additional press. Sure enough, three other media outlets had carried the story but none provided any additional information.

Checking Twitter, I had eleven new notifications. Some of the same people who had commented on the previous fires and linked them to my books were now tweeting about the cell tower explosion, the connection to my books and me. They all used hashtags like #jilliansamuelsbomb #aburningdesire #dressedupdrone #Silenceofthedrones.

Silence of the drones? Seriously? Then I stopped hyperventilating and wondered if this new story would go viral. If it did, I calculated how many books I might sell. Eleven people commenting on Twitter was hardly a tsunami. Still, something was happening.

I clicked over to my sales dashboard to see how *A Burning Desire* was doing. Sales were up again. Not dramatically, but enough to see that all the negative press was giving my little self-published books a boost out of the abyss. My other two books also showed a slight uptick in sales. My takeaway at the time? Explosions and fires are a bad thing, but not so terrible for selling my books.

It was a little after nine when I made myself a cup of coffee and sat down at the kitchen table to call Natalie. I had to tell her what was going on. A classic overachiever, she was in the office every morning by 7 a.m. before all her colleagues. Her day was half over when everyone else's was starting.

"Only got a minute," Natalie said, her mouth full of something when she picked up my call. "I'm preparing for a big presentation this afternoon, so I can't talk."

"Good morning, how are you, Natalie?" I replied attempting to gently point out her rudeness with humor which went completely over her head.

"I'm pitching a huge piece of business today. If I nail it, my promotion to Assistant VP is a lock. I can only talk for two minutes."

"I'll be brief," I said accustomed to keeping it short when she was at work. "I'm kind of freaking out. Something really weird is happening."

"Be more specific, what do you mean by weird?" she said mildly interested after hearing something was wrong. It might have been my imagination but my BFF seemed to perk up ever so slightly whenever negative things happened to me. When everything was going great in my life, she listened with a modicum of enthusiasm but when my things went off the track, Natalie was riveted but supportive.

"You know how there were three fires in empty buildings near me in Connecticut? Well, this morning, a phone tower blew up right here in Medford."

"What's that got to do with you?"

"The news is saying the tower was hit by a tricked-out drone, like the ones in my book."

"Are you kidding?" she said obviously surprised. "That's insane, Jills. Or at the very least, a huge unbelievable coincidence."

"Exactly. Loads of people on Twitter are posting it's the same as what happened in *A Burning Desire*."

"I don't remember phone towers blowing up in your book. But, the dressed-up drones part I remember and that's bizarre and disturbing enough." There was a long pause. "Although," she said, "any book of fiction will have tons of real life similarities. You just have to look for them."

"What if there is a copycat? What if someone read my book and they're making the same things happen in real life?"

"Why would anyone do that? What would their end game be? I don't see it. Can I be honest with you, Jills?" she said as if she normally sugarcoats everything. "Is it possible you're blowing this whole thing out of proportion? You know how your mind goes. I've seen you take the littlest drizzle and turn it into a monsoon. Don't take it the wrong way, I love that about you. You've got an amazing imagination. That's why you're such a great writer."

"Thanks, but if you—"

"Who would this copycat person be anyway? A crazy fan? Hardly anyone reads your books."

The part about "hardly anyone reading my books" stung, but she was right. To be fair, I didn't know everyone who bought my books. Some of them were strangers.

"There is a silver lining," I said. "The real explosions are impacting my book sales in an extremely positive way. Over the past few weeks I've sold over a hundred and eighty copies. That might not sound like a lot, but for me it's huge."

"Wow. That's a lot of books for a no name author. Good for you, Jills."

Leave it to Natalie to get that little dig in about me being a "no name author", but at least I had her attention. Sometimes Natalie is so predictable. Crimes happening in real life almost exactly as depicted in my book didn't pique her curiosity in the least. But, an increase in book sales, that she was interested in.

"Shit, it's nine twenty," said Natalie. "Don't sweat it, Jills, it's probably just a coincidence. Be happy you're the lucky beneficiary of a bunch of busybodies. Enjoy the ride." Click.

After making myself a cup of tea to calm my nerves, I headed upstairs. Since all my meetings that day were on Zoom, I had to fix my hair, put on a little makeup and get dressed — at least from the waist up.

It was a warmish day and I opened the window in my office a little wider to let in some air. A brown and red wood-pecker about twenty feet from my office window was rhyth-mically pecking on a tree trunk like a metronome. Despite the chaos going on, I forced myself to focus on my work and prepare for the interview I had later that morning.

To my surprise, the morning flew. One job candidate was 'very place-able'. Ka-Ching. With no other calls until later that afternoon, I tackled my overflowing email inbox and checked my messages on my author blog account, *Jillian Samuels Writes*. I had a new email from someone calling them-selves JollyRoger44.

Hi Jillian,
I'm a big fan of your books. Your thrillers really get my pulse racing and I can't put them down. Can't wait to get my hands on your next one.
—JR44

At first, I was flattered. I mean, who doesn't like fan mail? Not that I get very much, if any. Truthfully, I've only received three fan letters. One of them was from my third grade teacher. She sent me a congratulatory note saying she had read my book and that my writing had improved. I guess that was her attempt at humor. Since she'd been my teacher, I decided she didn't really qualify as a fan. The second fan letter was from a librarian at the Medford Library who had always been supportive of my writing. Whenever I took out or returned books, which was often, she'd ask me how my novel was going. Still, she probably didn't count as an actual fan since she also knew me.

As far as I knew, there are no official fan rules but my guess is in order for someone to qualify as a fan, they can't know or be related to you. This message from JollyRoger44 was technically then my first genuine fan letter. Initially, it tickled me and I was pretty excited. I had a real fan — someone who didn't know me personally and liked . . . no wait . . . loved my writing.

But the more I thought about my new fan, the more his or her name rattled around in my head. "Jolly Roger" rang a distant bell. Suddenly, images of ancient ships flashed through my mind but I had no idea why. When in doubt, go to Google. I was right. Turns out the Jolly Roger was the black pirate's flag with the skull and crossbones. My one and only fan self-identified as a pirate?

Later, I was downstairs making lunch as images of the Jolly Roger flag, pirates, sword fights and buried treasure swirled around my brain. Should I have been concerned? Was Jolly Roger an innocent admirer who simply appreciated parrots, treasure chests and possibly the *Pirates of the Caribbean* movie series? Or was he or she a homicidal psycho trying to contact their perceived mother ship? Either way, I didn't think this was the kind of fan I wanted.

I pushed my new admirer out of my mind with no intention of responding. I didn't know it then, but I'd hear from JollyRoger44 again, and things would get even stranger.

Chapter 17

Several days after receiving my "pirate fan letter", Natalie texted me. Her weekend business trip had been canceled last minute. With no social or work plans on her calendar for the first time in months, she generously offered to come up for a weekend visit.

Honestly, I was thrilled. We didn't get to see each other as often as we used to. Not because of my schedule, mainly hers. She was always traveling for work, out with clients or attending some "amazing" event to promote them. But she often said how much she loved getting out of the city and spending a quiet weekend with us in Connecticut. I loved it, too. A weekend of girl time with my best friend always rejuvenated me. I missed her.

On that particular weekend, Teddy only had Sunday off. When I told him Natalie was coming, he promised to make a special dinner for both of us.

"If Teddy's cooking, I'll be there," Natalie had said when I told her. I was so grateful she and Teddy got along. I know other couples where friendships faded away because one partner didn't like the other's friends. That would have broken my heart, but fortunately they got along great. Natalie would take the train up from the city that Saturday and stay until

Monday morning. We'd get plenty of time together, which I desperately needed.

The car windows were open as I drove to the station that Saturday morning to pick her up. The sweet smell of cut grass was in the air. I smiled, took a deep breath and savored the moment.

I entered the tiny Medford station parking lot just as the ancient black diesel train was pulling in. Natalie smiled and waved the second she got off the train. Less than a minute later she was in my car talking non-stop about her clients and her "pathetic" (her word, not mine) romantic life. I'll admit, some of her dating disaster stories were pretty funny. Most of the humor for me had to do with her delivery and the fact that she was so high-maintenance, but didn't know it.

"I'm serious," she said with an exasperated tone, "the only men I meet are perverted losers."

"They can't all be that bad."

"Oh, yes they can. The last guy I went out with brought his pet hamster on our first date, which by the way was our last. He had that disgusting little thing hiding in the breast pocket of his jacket the whole time."

"Eww."

"We met in Central Park to go for a walk and grab a coffee. The whole time we were walking he kept fussing with something inside his jacket. After fifteen minutes, he asked me if I'd like to meet his little friend. I didn't know where that was going and wasn't sure I wanted to. The next thing you know, he's holding a big brown rodent in his hand and introducing me to Pablo."

I laughed so hard as I made a turn around a corner that I nearly side swiped a parked car.

"Trust me. Things are so different now. Being single in New York is brutal," said Natalie so caught up in her own story that she didn't notice we nearly had an accident. "I'm telling you," she said rolling her eyes as she popped a mint into her mouth, "you're lucky you're married. You'd get eaten alive."

"I know," I said, glad I no longer had to play the New York dating game. Natalie's stories were funny but also horrifying.

"Don't get me started on the OB/GYN who wanted me to talk in a baby voice," she said. "The psychological implications of that alone are frightening. I'm so over New York. Up here in Connecticut I can breathe. I'm done with all the big city chaos. Besides, nothing interesting happens in New York anymore."

"That's not true."

"I've already done everything that's worth doing in the city, it's always the same old thing," she said checking her text messages and then her makeup in the car visor mirror. "What time does Teddy get home tonight?"

"Late, not until eleven or twelve, but he left food for us."

"That will give us plenty of girl time," she said with a wicked smile as she pulled a bottle of rosé out of her weekend bag. "I've got a Cabernet in here, too. Party time."

I shook my head. "We're not going to have another one of those nights, are we?"

"Oh yes, we are," she said grinning from ear to ear.

I let out a defeated sigh knowing what the night would bring and that I'd most likely regret it in the morning. Whenever I was with Natalie, I always overdid it. She had that effect on me. She had that effect on a lot of people.

When we got home we devoured the Greek Avgolemono lemon chicken soup that my husband had made for us and made plans to go to a couple of local yard sales. It always struck me as funny that Natalie, who never had a hair out of place and an unparalleled designer wardrobe, loved browsing through other people's old and often dirty junk. Personally, I could take it or leave it but she became visibly excited when she found something she decided was a hidden treasure.

"Look at this," she said holding up a large green pitcher with a small chip in it at our first yard sale of the day. Natalie buying stuff at rummage sales made absolutely no sense. She had a tiny one-bedroom apartment in Manhattan that was already bursting at the seams. She didn't have room to add even a coffee cup let alone the end table I saw her gawking over before she spotted the green pitcher.

"Where would you even put that?" I said walking toward her.

"I could squeeze it in somewhere. Isn't it adorbs?"

After several hours of "garbage picking" we got into the car and headed back to my house. Halfway home, she dug through her large leather bag and pulled something out.

"I bought you a present from the last yard sale," she said. I was about to roll my eyes anticipating some scratched figurine or knick-knack when she produced a cream-colored coffee mug that had "SISTERS" written on it in navy blue.

"I got this for you because . . . you're like a sister to me," she said.

I was touched and got a little teary. For all of Natalie's bluster, deep down she was a total mush. I smiled. "Aww. That was so sweet of you," I said. "I'll think of my 'sister' every time I have a cup of tea."

"No tea now. It's five o'clock," said Natalie's smiling red lips as we pulled in front of my house. "Wine time." If my BFF declared it was vino time, then it was. Once inside she headed directly for the wine glasses in my kitchen cabinet. By five fifteen we were comfortably seated in the living room, our feet up, drinks in hand, a wedge of cheddar and a bowl of chips on the coffee table. Pure heaven.

For the next two hours, we examined and dissected Natalie's galloping PR career and her revolving-door love life. Compared to my quiet domestic existence, her dating adventures and all of their ups and downs were extremely entertaining. I listened and nodded waiting for my turn to speak. There were things I really needed to talk over with her. I wanted to discuss the fires, the police and the reporter. For the first time in a long while, I had a lot going on, too.

After finishing two bottles of wine, Natalie opened a third. Feeling giddy, I took out the cold salmon, quinoa and salad that Teddy had brought home from the restaurant the night before and placed it on the kitchen counter.

"Where's your glass?" Natalie said as she walked into the kitchen. I gladly handed her my empty goblet and she cheerfully went back into the other room to fill it up. We were a team.

"Do you want to eat now?" I yelled.

"Let's try this Cabernet first," she shouted from the living room.

Like I said, our get-togethers routinely devolved into mini bacchanalias. Obediently, I went back into the living room, settled in on the couch next to her and took a sip of the new wine.

"Chin-chin," she said as she raised her glass and took a big gulp. "Yummy. The man in the wine store recommended this one. It's excellent." I took a sip. It was delicious. Natalie wasn't very good at picking men but she was great at picking wine.

As we knocked back the third bottle, I walked her through the myriad of peculiar and disturbing things that had been happening — Jolly Roger44, explosions, fires, cryptic messages and, for good measure, I threw in the creepy postal employee who tried to hit on me whenever I went to mail a package.

"His name is Ned LaGrange," I said.

"He sounds absolutely horrendous. Tell him to fuck off," she said slurring her words and launching into a series of diabolical ways to rid myself of him.

I was a little tipsy, okay drunk, but astonished the usually astute Natalie only focused on the postal worker being creepy. She had missed the most important conversation points — the explosions and messages. I wanted her to zone in on the fact that something super abnormal was going on with my books. Something that was way bigger than me. She only obsessed about Ned. To be fair, Ned was repulsive, but the explosions and fires were far more disturbing than he was. Natalie hadn't picked up on that part of the conversation at all. It was like we were in parallel universes. Then again, I probably should have discussed everything with her before we consumed three bottles of wine.

"We should eat something or I'm going to pass out," I said getting up to get some food and stumbling slightly as I stood. She followed me into the kitchen. We loaded up our plates and headed back to the couch to eat. And that was the last thing I remembered.

The following morning I woke up in my bed with Teddy snoring softly next to me. It was nearly 10 a.m. before I moved a muscle. That's when I felt the wicked headache. I lay still trying to recall the events of the night before. I didn't remember how or when I got to bed. Using my powers of denial, I blamed my hangover on Natalie's bad influence. Teddy stirred and I and slowly opened my eyes. He was staring at me.

"Good morning. Want a little wine with your breakfast?" he said with a goofy grin.

"Oh, my God no. My head is pounding. What time did you get home?"

"Around ten thirty. Thought I was going to spend some time with you and Natalie but you both had already gone to bed. I noticed two empty wine bottles in the trash and another one finished on the counter. Looks like you two had quite a party."

"Tell me about it."

Minutes later my husband bounced out of bed to go for a run leaving me under the covers licking my wounds. Eventually, I managed to put on some clothes and headed downstairs to the guest room on the first floor to wake Natalie. As I walked through the kitchen, I was surprised to see her seated at the kitchen counter, fully dressed, hair and makeup done. She was drinking a cup of coffee and playing with her phone.

"Morning," she said not looking up. "Had some work emails I had to take care of so I got up early. How are you feeling?"

"Why do you look so good?" I said. "I feel and look like shit. You look like you're ready to go to a cocktail party. Did we not drink the same wine last night?"

"We did, but I feel fine. You do look a little pale."

"When did you go to bed?"

"Same time you did, around ten," she said. "Don't you remember?"

I didn't and had a headache and low grade nausea to prove it.

"Did I tell you about the explosions and fires that have been happening around here?" I said, not remembering much of the previous night.

She nodded.

"Don't you think that's weird?"

She nodded a second time. "Of course, I do. I told you that last night, remember? The whole thing is fucking nuts. But, it still could be a coincidence. My advice is don't sweat it, Jills. I doubt it will happen again."

Natalie's last comment turned out to be the most inaccurate prediction of the century.

Chapter 18

I wasn't the only one who had an alcohol-infused night that week. When I called my agent Matthew one morning, just to touch base, he confessed he was hunched over his desk devouring a bagel with cream cheese to soak up the booze in his system. Apparently, he had a late evening the night before involving one too many gin and tonics with an editor. But he assured me, despite his wicked hangover, he was busy sending out follow-up emails on my thriller to all of his publishing contacts.

Given that he had only a single client (me) on which to build his reputation, his honesty about his hangover didn't exactly make me feel confident about him finding a publisher for me. He reiterated how critical it was for him to make big things happen with my book.

"I've got a lot riding on you," said Matthew. "If I don't land this plane, Sanford Weston Literary will probably show me out the door." Then, he stopped talking to pop a couple of Tylenol into his mouth.

For a second, I wondered if my agent had a drinking problem — just my luck. Still, I remained cheerful. "I was just curious how everything's going. Got any nibbles on my novel or heard anything more from Linton Books?" I said, still trying to sound super positive.

He deflected my questions for a minute with a couple of jokes but then got more serious. He admitted he *was* having "a teensy bit of trouble ginning up interest in *The Soul Collector*".

"This year, a lot of the big publishers are sticking with their tried and true authors, those with solid track records," he said. "It's getting harder for new authors to break through. All the agents in New York have been talking about it. It's tough out there, but I'm not a quitter. I'll keep trying."

"Are you saying you're not sure you can sell my book?" I said my heart jumping into my throat. What the hell was happening? I had finally been asked to the prom and when I arrived, no one wanted to dance with me?

"I'm not saying that at all," he said a little too defensively. I detected some irritation in his voice, possibly from my lack of faith and my questioning his abilities. "Rest assured Jillian, I'm still going full steam ahead. I just wanted to be transparent so you understand what we're up against. I told you I'd sell your book and I will. Believe me, I've got a lot more riding on this than you know. You have no idea."

Relieved to hear he was still so committed, I wanted to offer him some help, a crumb to keep him going. I certainly didn't want him to lose interest and move on to another author.

"Matthew, remember when I told you there'd been an explosion and fire in Connecticut similar to events depicted in my first novel?"

"Absolutely."

"There have been more, four in total."

"Seriously? That's really weird but potentially fabulous. Keep going."

"After the first time it happened, there were some posts on Twitter. Pretty soon, my old books started to sell. Since the additional fires, even more of my books are selling."

"How many?"

"A few hundred."

"Shit. When you first told me about this, I thought it was just a coincidence," said Matthew. "But now, multiple times? That's more than a coincidence. What do you think is happening?"

"I don't know. Someone must have read my book and is trying to recreate the plot. But why? They've apparently left notes at the scenes too, just like in my book."

"No shit," said my agent, "this is getting pretty intense."

"Maybe some pyromaniac got inspired by my story?"

"I'll tell you what's inspired, Jillian — book sales," said Matthew becoming increasingly enthusiastic. "Those explosions and fires got people buying your book. This is a fucking goldmine. I just have to figure out the angle and how to work it."

"You think these new explosions will help you sell my new manuscript to a publisher?"

"Are you kidding? Buzz is buzz any way you slice it. Disasters in fiction really happening — people want to read about that. They want to see if it's true and figure out what else might happen. Wouldn't it be nice if we could make the story in your new manuscript come alive, too? Something like that would definitely help me sell *The Soul Collector* to a publisher. They'd eat it up."

"I definitely don't want *The Soul Collector* to become real. Did you forget? One of the primary victims is an author who gets murdered."

"Right," said my agent with a chuckle. "That would be a problem."

He wrapped up our conversation with a pep talk, telling me again to work my social media channels as much as possible. "Every little bit helps," he said as we ended the call. "Remember, it's all about the buzz."

That night, Teddy wasn't working late and brought home dinner from the restaurant for both of us. We sat at the kitchen counter nibbling on some Stilton cheese and ciabatta bread. I took a sip of my Merlot and told my husband about the phone call I'd had with Matthew that morning.

"He thinks the negative publicity from the fires will sell your new book to a publisher?" said Teddy, a skeptical expression on his face.

"He said if the same thing happened with my new manuscript, he'd be able to get me a six figure deal. Of course, we wouldn't want that."

"Why not?"

Incredulous, I stared at my husband. "Because an author is murdered in my book."

"Right. I forgot. But, if it would sell a lot of books, maybe it's something we should consider," he said with a wink and a smile.

I gently punched him in the shoulder and poured myself another glass of wine. Publicity was a good thing, but I wasn't prepared to die for my craft.

Chapter 19

A few weeks later, Teddy caught an early train to the city for a meeting with the investors of the new restaurant. I was home in the kitchen brewing my third cup of coffee and watching the local news on TV. A weatherman stood in front of a gloomy looking map. Connecticut was in for a full week of rain, followed by thunderstorms over the weekend. I glanced out my window. Soon, everything was limp and soggy.

I was about to turn off the TV and head upstairs to my office, but waited to catch the local Connecticut news headlines as they scrolled across the bottom of the screen. I was in full procrastination mode, and stood there an excessively long time watching the chyron news feed instead of preparing for my upcoming Zoom call.

"Parade plans are underway in Waterford," said the announcer.

"School budget has been approved in Derby."

"A litter of cats was found alive and well in the basement of Madison High School." That was the big news? Seriously?

I reached for the remote when another headline flashed across the screen.

BREAKING NEWS: Homeless man found unconscious covered in silver paint near recycling plant in Medford.

I dropped the remote, took a step backward and stared at the TV. According to the news anchor, the unidentified man had been sprayed from head to toe with silver paint. A police spokesperson said a gallon-sized white plastic milk container had been found near the man's body. "How did I do?" was scrawled on the jug with what appeared to be blue crayon.

Once I caught my breath, I moved closer to the TV. That's when I accidentally knocked over my half-full coffee cup. Instantly, milky brown liquid spread across the counter and dripped down onto my just-washed kitchen floor. I don't wash my floors very often so I lunged for the paper towels while processing what I'd just heard.

I had been to that recycling plant and dump a thousand times. In fact, I had taken my garbage there the day before, the same day the man was found covered in paint. The Medford dump is usually deserted. There's a lone clerk who checks people in and out. Usually you had to wait in your car for fifteen or twenty minutes before you saw any sign of him. While I waited for the "dump master" to show up the previous day, I had noticed a strange man hanging around the perimeter of the lot. From the way the man was moving, he looked like he was on something.

But, what really caught my attention from the news story, the thing that caused me to knock over my coffee, was that the man the police found had been spray-painted silver. That's exactly what happened to all the murder victims in my second novel, *The Platinum Man*. Each one was covered in silver paint. What were the odds of that being another coincidence? I started to speculate how soon the police would be knocking on my door again. In my novel the silver bodies were always deceased. The newsman said the police found a man painted but alive. It wasn't exactly the same, but close enough. The news report also said the police were considering whether this would be classified as a hate crime. It wasn't long before I found myself wondering how this new crime would impact my second book's sales. I know, I'm a horrible person but I'm only human.

Adrenaline flowing, I needed to talk to someone fast. Teddy was probably still on the train and he hated talking on the phone in public places, so I called Natalie at work. She picked up with her usual: "I only have a minute.".

"You're not going to believe what happened," I said, barely getting the words out. "Something completely insane is going on."

"You want to talk about insane? My biggest client just put our agency up for review, the woman who highlights my hair broke her arm and isn't taking appointments for three months, and the guy I went out with last night told me he likes to wear pajamas with feet in them."

I tried to get a word in but she was on a roll. "I'm taking my client to Teddy's restaurant for lunch today," she said, not hearing a word I had said. "Teddy promised he'd stop by our table and schmooze for a few minutes. My client is female, forty-four and single. A few minutes chatting with Manhattan's culinary heartthrob will totally float her boat and ultimately mine. I'm counting on your husband's dimples to convince her to renew her contract with my firm. Keep your fingers crossed for me."

"Don't worry. Teddy won't let you down. You know him, he'll lay it on thick. But seriously, something really weird is happening. You know how there were those fires—"

"The explosions?" she said, seemingly not that interested. "We've already talked about that."

"It's something much bigger and crazier."

"Here we go," she said, exasperation in her voice. I knew she was making that eye-roll face she's famous for.

I told her about the news story I had seen on TV. "...and that's exactly what happened in my book *The Platinum Man*. Remember?"

"It's been a while since I read your book. Weren't all the silver people dead?"

"Yes, but—"

"You said this man is alive," said Natalie growing impatient.

"He is, but he was painted silver, just like in my book."

97

"That is kind of weird. What's going on?"

"Right? That's exactly what I thought."

"There has to be a logical explanation. Honestly, Jills, let's not jump to conclusions," said Natalie somewhat dismissively. I heard the distinct tapping of manicured nails on a keyboard and knew I no longer had her full attention. "You know how you get. You take a miniscule thing and blow it up into something gigantic. I love you and it's part of your charm. But from my perspective, the only real similarity in the two situations is the paint. If I remember correctly, in your book, the victims weren't homeless either. So, it's not exactly the same."

"I know it's not *exactly* the same but don't you think—"

"Jills, enjoy the free publicity. Buzz is buzz, regardless of how you get it. You never know, that painted homeless man might increase your book sales the same way the drone fires did."

"You think the painted man is a good thing for me?"

I said this right before she said, "Absolutely," and quickly ended our call.

Holding onto that thought, I ran up the stairs two at a time to get to my computer. Googling "Silver Man Medford CT" I checked the time of the first news report. The earliest one went out on the wires the previous night at 8.52 p.m. I read through a bunch of the other links to see if there was any additional information, but they all appeared to be written from that same original source.

I opened my book sales dashboard to check my recent numbers — and holy shit! During the previous twenty-four hours, I'd sold nine copies of *The Platinum Man*. That's more than I'd sold in the previous twelve months. *A Burning Desire* had also sold three copies in the same twenty-four hours. Even my third book, *Whispers from the Grave*, about a serial killer who marked headstones with knives and later killed the dead person's descendants, also had sold two copies. Until all this stuff started happening, my books barely moved. PT Barnum once said, "There's no such thing as bad publicity."

Clearly, he knew what he was talking about. While the headlines and events were terrible, my books were selling.

I checked the time. Teddy had to be at the restaurant by then so I called him.

"I can't talk," he said when he picked up. "We just had a fire in the kitchen and my produce supplier has been sending me nothing but week-old crap. Can I call you later?"

"It will only take a second," I said. "Please, it's important."

"I've got thirty seconds and then I've got to go."

It occurred to me that my nearest and dearest made very little time for me in my hours of need but I pushed on. "The police found an unconscious man at the Medford recycling plant last night."

"What's this got to do with you or me? Can we talk about this tonight?" said Teddy.

"You don't understand, the man was painted silver, just like in *The Platinum Man*. Isn't that insane? It's happening again, like the fires."

"Stop, Jills, please. You're reading way too much into this. You said the man was unconscious, not dead. The victims in *The Platinum Man* were definitely dead. It's not the same at all. Basically, a man was found with silver paint on him and you've decided it's exactly like your book, but it's not."

"But it was silver paint and—"

"Jillian, don't get all caught up in this. Yes, the silver paint is the common denominator but that's where it stops."

"It's not just me, people on Twitter have noticed. Someone actually posted, "Anyone read Jillian Samuels books?" My thrillers are all coming true. Drones that look like superheroes, men painted silver. #FreakyFriday. #JillianSamuelsAuthorbook. #Whatsnext."

"That settles it. If it's on Twitter it must be true," said my husband.

"All my book sales have picked up, too. Something's happening. Wait until I tell my agent about this. He said we needed some buzz to sell my new book. This absolutely qualifies, it's a whole freakin' hornet's nest."

My husband remained unconvinced and soon cut the call short.

"I've gotta go," he said. "I've got a freezer here that just broke down filled with forty pounds of fish." Click.

Convinced the recent incident might help sell my new book, I called Matthew.

"The crimes up here in Connecticut are the same as what happened in my first two thrillers. Google it," I said. "You'll see."

"I already know," said Matthew. "I was pitching your book to an editor this morning. She did a search on you while I was talking. All the news stories popped up."

"See. Something *is* going on. You think it will help you get me a book deal?"

"It might. I'll milk it for all it's worth."

I probably shouldn't have been so cheerful about my books finally selling as a direct result of other people's misfortune, but I couldn't help myself. I had spent months, years even, writing my manuscripts and then watched them almost immediately fade into oblivion. At last, my little book babies had started to sell and I was their proud mama. I wanted to post something about it on Facebook, but decided it would be tacky. It was one thing if other people posted about the explosions or the Silver Man, but rather unseemly and callous if I did it myself.

After a bit of hard thinking, I came up with an idea. I could create and manufacture other personas on Facebook, Instagram and Twitter. Then *they* could post about my book sales and I could build some buzz for myself. It would have been foolish to not take advantage of these random events, right? When opportunity knocks, you gotta open the door.

While I should have been hunting for job candidates, I spent the rest of the day creating new email accounts and setting up a slew of fake social media personas. By that evening, I had created twelve different identities. Each newly invented person had a full suite of social media accounts including pictures and friends. And, they all had a fascination with me, my books and the bizarre events unfolding in Connecticut.

Chapter 20

By the next day, everyone in Medford was talking about the "Silver Man" case. In a small town like ours, it was huge news. People started calling it a hate crime as further details about the unconscious man trickled out. Everyone had an opinion.

Our town recycling facility is situated in a wooded area next to the Medford garbage dump at the north end of town. It officially closes at 5 p.m. After five, it's occasionally a hangout spot for local teens. Why kids congregate at a dump, I'll never know.

From what I gathered from the active Medford grapevine, at 6.40 p.m. on the night the man had been found alive, a couple of male teenagers on bicycles climbed over the seven-foot tall, locked fence to "have a look around". Erected mainly to keep out animals like deer, fox and coyote, the fence also kept people from leaving their garbage without paying their town disposal fees.

That evening, the two young men climbed over the fence and wandered around. They had apparently picked through dumpsters hoping to find something they could sell online. After rummaging through dozens of bins and finding nothing of value, they started to leave when one of them spotted another full dumpster in the back of the lot. Minutes later, the kids discovered what looked like a dead body and called 911.

At 7.10 p.m., a patrol car was dispatched. The first police officer on the scene determined the man was still breathing. Minutes later, the "Silver Man" was taken away by an ambulance. Detectives Brodsky and Marino arrived as the emergency vehicle was leaving and were briefed by the patrolman.

Because the victim was covered in silver paint, the officer had been unable to make an identification. The victim had no ID, but the cop thought he might be George Argos, a transient who had been moving around between New Haven, Harwich and Medford for months. According to the officer, Argos occasionally checked into city or church shelters but never stayed for long. A serial drug user who often hung out in empty lots or buildings, he slept wherever he could find shelter. According to the EMTs report, the man painted in silver was whacked out on something pretty heavy duty and hadn't regained consciousness while in their care.

According to the local gossip, the detectives interrogated the teenagers, learned nothing more and warned them to stay out of the dump. Almost dark, the two detectives pulled out flashlights and did a complete walk around of the perimeter to make sure there weren't any other victims.

Finding nothing, they headed over to the local ER. After conferring with the attending doctors, the detectives were informed the "Silver Man" was in a coma, possibly a drug-induced one. The victim had a large contusion on his head which could have happened from falling and hitting it on one of the numerous concrete slabs at the dump. When the ER nurses were able to get some of the paint off of the man's face, they recognized him. The victim was George Argos; the cop at the dump had been right.

Argos had been in that particular ER many times before. Like restaurants, ER's have their regulars. Mr Argos apparently had what you might call a "season's pass" to their emergency room. According to the *Medford Local* newspaper,

Argos was in there every other month for drug and alcohol related issues. The ER doctors thought it likely his injury was self-inflicted given his intoxication levels. If Argos tripped and fell, he would have gone down like a dead weight and could have sustained the injury on his head. With nearly fifty years on the police force between them, Detectives Brodsky and Marino didn't rule out an assault. Regardless of how the original injury happened, everyone in town agreed on one thing: someone else had covered Argos in paint and left him to die.

According to MedfordLocal.com the next morning, Argos was awake and talking and insisting on leaving the medical facility. The hospital staff called the police and Brodsky and Marino were soon in the building. *Medford Local* also reported Argos was missing two of his upper front teeth and questions remained as to why he was at the dump at all. It was also reported that EMTs had found used needles and empty drug packets in Argos' pockets. From the tone of the article, it sounded to me like the cops were more interested in finding out how the man had sustained a head wound, lost teeth and got covered in paint rather than his drug paraphernalia. The big question people kept asking: was Argos assaulted or did he have an accident? The cops wanted to know if there was someone dangerous lurking in Medford and so did everyone who lived in town.

I wouldn't have known anything more about Argos than what I heard on the news if it weren't for a chance encounter with two ER nurses who had taken care of him. I was on an excessively long and slow checkout line at my local Stop and Shop. The two nurses who took care of Argos had just gotten off of a twelve-hour shift and were yapping like they were alone on a mountain top versus in a crowded supermarket. So much for patient confidentiality.

"I'm tellin' you, Louise. I've seen a lot of weird things in the ER," said the first nurse as she loaded her groceries onto the belt. "That guy with the silver paint was totally freaky. He had on ladies thong underwear . . . backward."

According to the pair of Florence Nightingales, when the detectives, Brodsky and Marino, arrived in Argos' room, the patient had a large bandage covering the front of his forehead and a few remnant flecks of silver paint still on his face.

"I tried to get all that paint off of him," said the second nurse, "but some of those little suckers wouldn't budge. I had silver paint all over my hands and in my hair when I got home last night."

According to the chatty nurses, Argos deflected the detectives' questions and at one point went so far as blaming a drunken Tooth Fairy for his missing molars. He apparently told the cops he "had spent most of his life high and remembered very little from the past twenty years".

"That Silver Man wasn't giving anything up," said the first nurse as she stuck her credit card into the machine. "He's a tough one but he'll live."

I read about the story and the two detectives in our local newspaper, and recognized the officers' names. They had been the lead investigators on one of the biggest Connecticut abduction cases in recent memory: the disappearance of college student Anabel Ford. The young woman had gone missing nearly five months earlier. That missing persons/kidnapping case had been covered both locally and nationally by the media. Anabel Ford was pretty, blonde and pre-med which is probably why the coverage was so intense and widespread. She made for good copy and her pretty innocent face drew in viewers as it splashed across TV and phone screens. Despite Marino and Brodsky's valiant efforts over many months, the missing girl had still not been found. General consensus: Anabel was probably dead. Not long after the Ford case went cold, Brodsky and Marino were reassigned to the "Silver Man" case and entered then into my life.

Both Brodsky and Marino had joined the police department in their early twenties. When I met them they had been partners for over eighteen years, often finishing each other's sentences. Now in their mid-forties, they handled homicide, missing persons, drugs and arson. From what I could tell, they took their jobs very seriously.

Total opposites, Brodsky was all business and no nonsense. I did my homework as all good writers do. Brodsky was born in Russia; his family had emigrated to the United States when he was only fourteen. Despite thirty-two years of living in America, he still carried a slight Russian accent. Over the months that followed, I noticed his accent got stronger when it suited him. I gathered that when he questioned an uncooperative witness, suspect, or me for that matter, he affected the persona of a Cold War KGB interrogator, or a Putin FSB acolyte. A well-built reasonably good-looking man with a tough guy patina, he had thick black hair, equally black eyes and apparently based on a few of his comments, worked out at a local boxing gym. Divorced twice, he had two teenaged sons that he adored.

Marino came across as an easygoing jokester. I learned later it was a clever facade. He was genial but more than capable. Raised in a hardscrabble Italian neighborhood in the nearby city of New Haven, Marino spent most of his youth hanging out in the streets. By the time he turned fifteen, he'd already been involved in a string of petty crimes and a few more serious ones.

His high school partner in crime was then arrested for stealing cars and wound up doing time in prison. Young Marino was supposed to be boosting BMWs with his friend that night. Only dumb luck saved Marino from the same fate and spared him a stint in the joint. That night, Marino never met up with his friend because he was home with food poisoning. While his best friend was being cuffed and read his rights, Marino was puking into a toilet and crying out for his mother. After that night, Marino found himself at a fork in life's road.

It was a cautionary tale he often told (he even told me), and joked about that string of events that changed the course of his life. "If it weren't for that undercooked chicken-parm hero I ate at Lombardi's Pizza that day, I would have been doin' five to ten upstate. After my friend got arrested, I went to see Mr Lombardi, the owner. That unsanitary bastard and his filthy hands was the only thing that kept me out of prison. I thanked the old man, but I didn't shake his hand."

After his narrow escape from incarceration, Nick Marino decided it was time for a significant lifestyle change and signed up for the New Haven police department. "I figured I'd rather join the cops than spend my life being chased by them, I'm not that fast a runner."

Twenty-four years later, Marino still lived in the same neighborhood in New Haven, only now with his wife and teenaged daughter. He was well liked around the department for his good humor, even occasionally lobbing a macabre joke at a crime scene.

I do a ton of research for my thrillers. From what I've read, crimes come in waves: a change in the weather; the lunar cycle; or even the holidays. The pattern is often the same. Everything's quiet for a while and then the shit hits the fan at the same time. If you ask a cop, they'll tell you every couple with marital problems goes at it on the same night. Gang members burglarize and ransack stores and drug dealers unload all their bad stuff on the same weekend. The next thing you know, emergency vehicles race around trying to start life in hearts that have stopped beating. I follow all local crime news as fuel for my writing. You never know where you're going to get a great story idea. Other than the Anabel Ford investigation, however, which I may one day write about, things around Medford were usually quiet and peaceful. Given what was going on, it appeared my quiet period was over.

I was upstairs in my home office trying to close an employment deal when a gray sedan pulled into my driveway. The car stopped and I looked down from my open window. A police medallion was sitting on the front dashboard. Through my window I could hear a police radio droning faintly inside the car. Two dark-haired men were in the front seat talking loudly. I could hear every word they said.

"I'm telling you, Brodsky, Pepe's Pizza in New Haven is the best. Better than in Napoli. My mother, God rest her soul, fed me Pepe's pizza before I got baby food," said an Italian-looking man talking with his hands as he got out of the driver's side.

"You've never been to Italy," said the shorter but brawnier man with what sounded like a Russian accent as he opened the passenger door and got out. "How would you know what's the best pizza?"

The tall Italian man appeared stunned, tapped his heart twice with two fingers and did the same to his head. "Because I know it in here and in here," he said as he let out a hearty laugh and walked around to the other side of the car holding a paper coffee cup. He opened the lid, looked down and smiled. "Looks like a pine tree to me. I love when they make pictures in the steamed milk."

Brodsky squinted at his partner with a look of such disdain that it made me giggle. "Why do you need drawings in your coffee?"

"Tastes better with pictures," said the Italian with a smile.

At that point, I'd had enough of the cheap dinner theater performance in my front yard and shouted down to them from my window.

"Hello? Can I help you with something?"

The Russian with the thick neck pulled something shiny out of his breast pocket and held it up.

"Medford PD," he said holding up his shield. "I'm Detective Brodsky and this is my partner, Detective Marino. We're looking for Jillian Samuels."

"That's me."

"We'd like to ask you a few questions," said Brodsky.

"About what?" I shouted.

"If you could come down for a few minutes, it would be easier," said Marino.

Curious but pretty sure their visit had something to do with the drone situation and maybe the Silver Man, I went downstairs, opened the front door and asked to see their badges up close. You can never be too careful, there are home invasions all the time. Their badges looked legit (not that I'd ever seen a detective's badge before or would know if it was real or not). I stepped outside and closed the door behind me. The one with the thick neck, Brodsky, did most of the talking. They were investigating the string of explosions and fires. They said they were also looking into a possible assault that had left a man unconscious and covered in silver paint.

I sized the two lawmen up pretty quickly — writers do that. We absorb, assess and process every piece of information. From the minute I met Marino, I knew he had a big heart. His partner Brodsky on the other hand, was more forbidding though clearly smart, intuitive and focused. In my estimation, as a team they evened each other out. They were an in-the-flesh "good cop-bad cop" duo — no play acting, but the real thing.

"From what we understand, both the explosions and the Silver Man assault have strong similarities to plots in your books," said Brodsky looking at some notes. He asked me if I knew anything about the crimes or if I had any theories on who might be responsible.

"I only know what I saw on the news and on Twitter," I said, shaking my head.

"Can you think of any reason someone might want to recreate the scenes from your books?" said Marino.

"No," I said. "Believe me, the whole thing has been freaking me out. But to be clear, they're not exactly the same. In my books, people *died* in the fires and the victims found covered in silver paint were also dead. No one's died, right?"

"Not yet," said Brodsky in full deadpan. "We'd like to keep it that way."

Chapter 21

When Eric Shaw's boss returned from her "life affirming" trip to the Galapagos Islands, she called him into her office. As promised, she had read my manuscript while she was away. Bottom line — she thought *The Soul Collector* was good but didn't love it. Over forty-five, Andrea had been in the book publishing business a long time. While she suspected my novel might resonate with twenty-something readers, she wasn't ready to pull the trigger. Linton Books had become pickier about which properties they acquired. And, I didn't have any star power or influence on social media.

That was the opening Eric had been waiting for. As luck would have it, in the weeks since Andrea had left for South America, my social media following had increased significantly. Eric walked his boss through the latest developments with my older books, the number of new followers I had, and my dramatic increase in interactions on Instagram, Facebook and Twitter. He showed her robust Twitter exchanges and pictures posted from Connecticut news sites about the fires and explosions. Because it appeared my books were actually coming true, it aroused conspiracy theories and public interest had ratcheted up nicely.

Together, they scrolled through various sites and found numerous posts about me, drones and explosions, along with plenty of speculation regarding the real life connection to *A Burning Desire*. Surprised to see I had ten times more followers than before she left for vacation, Andrea agreed to give my book a second look.

Once Eric had his boss hooked over the drone fires, he shared the news about the homeless man covered in silver paint. Trying to spin his own conspiracy theory in order to get his boss on board, he mentioned how "a man covered in silver paint" was exactly like the murders in my second book, *The Platinum Man*. He added that I lived in Medford, the same town where some of the crimes had occurred.

That last tidbit got Andrea's attention. Eric showed her how Twitter had gone nuts after enough people connected the real drones and Silver Man to my books.

After thirty minutes of social media surfing, Andrea agreed I had a small groundswell of interest that appeared to be growing. Her biggest concern was that my notoriety wouldn't last. Publishing is a slow business. If they acquired my book, it would be over a year until it was published. Interest in my books would surely wane as the crimes faded away.

She was not convinced, but didn't want to crush her young editor's entrepreneurial spirit. After a serious conversation about the ramifications of failure at an early stage of his career, she finally gave Eric the thumbs up to acquire *The Soul Collector*. She reminded him it would be his neck on the chopping block if it tanked. If that happened, she'd have to move him out of acquisitions and into an administrative role. And, that's the fairytale story of how my little thriller was acquired by Linton Books.

If *The Soul Collector* ended up a failure for Linton, Andrea knew it wouldn't break the bank given the paltry amount of marketing money they were going to invest. Eric wondered if he had made a terrible bargain. Soon, all his negative thoughts disappeared as he shared the good news with Matthew.

As Eric explained the details of the acquisition to my agent over the phone, Matthew's ebullient reaction made it all worth it. Heartily congratulating each other on their first book deal, they made lofty and elaborate plans on how to send my little thriller into the bestseller stratosphere. Eric promised to secure multiple audio and foreign rights deals and Matthew, film options and the associated merchandising — aka extra gravy money. They discussed high-profile author blurbs and testimonials for my book and how they were both on their way up.

Matthew's next call was to me. I sounded like a giddy teenager on a first date when he told me the news. My book was really happening and would be published by one of the hottest publishing imprints in New York. Linton Books had earmarked a publication date just over a year away. He told me it would be a fast and tight schedule so they could capitalize on my current social media popularity. Work on my cover would start in a few weeks. Game on. I was dancing on air.

The following evening, Matthew told me he took Eric out for a celebratory dinner at the lively Chez Paris eatery. They shared one toast after the next and Matthew gave Eric his undivided attention. I had heard all about the "crush" thing between Eric and Matthew. It's not something I would have done, but I wasn't going to tell Matthew how to run his business. That night, my agent gave Eric renewed hope there might be a relationship path for the two of them. That's exactly what Matthew wanted him to think. He figured he'd keep Eric on the hook by doling out just the right amount of flattery and sensuous glances without ever stepping over the line. By the end of that night, though his career was hanging in the balance, Eric was sure he had made the right decision in acquiring my book.

Several rounds of wine later, Matthew underscored how they both had a lot riding on my book's success. Not wanting to leave anything to chance, my agent had a plan and was looking for Eric's full support. Once again, I learned about all of this much later, long after my book came out. Matthew's plan was risky, but from his point of view, totally necessary and he wondered if Eric was willing to do whatever it took?

As he unpacked his unorthodox scheme, Matthew admitted it would require bending rules, and maybe even breaking a few. Though not fully kosher or even legal, my agent was committed to doing whatever was needed to accomplish the mission. While it wouldn't be easy, Matthew convinced Eric if they worked together, they could absolutely make it happen.

Blinded by his feelings, Eric took only a moment to consider what the handsome agent had suggested and immediately signed on. Once the partners in crime had struck a deal, Matthew laid out his unethical plan in step-by-step detail. Together, they would make *The Soul Collector* the bestseller of the year.

Chapter 22

A few weeks passed and all the pieces for my new novel were moving in the right direction. My agent and editor appeared to be doing everything possible to make my book a success. The book cover was in development in the Linton art department and on a Zoom call I got my first set of edit revisions from Eric.

When I opened the edit document during our meeting and saw all the mark-ups on my manuscript, my face must have fallen.

"Please don't worry. It's coming along fine," he said noticing I was suddenly quiet. "All of the suggested changes are only to help your book be better. Remember, we're all on 'Team Jillian'. Our goal is to make your book the best it can be. You've got to trust me."

"I do," I said trying to regain my composure and forced a smile. "You and Matthew have been great."

"Matthew's an amazing guy. You're very lucky to have him as your agent. Did you know he and I went to college together? I'm sure it won't surprise you to learn he was very popular on campus. Everyone had a crush on Matthew."

That's when I realized my agent had sold my thriller to Linton Books because of a college connection. Not because my book was great or even good, not because Matthew had deep connections and pull in the industry. If my agent had not gone to school with Eric, would I have had a book deal? I was spiraling again instead of focusing on the positive. I told myself, it really didn't matter how my book got to Linton. All that mattered was that it did. Soon, *The Soul Collector* would be out in the world and I'd be on my way up — at least that's what I thought at the time.

In the spirit of collaboration, I did my part on social media by posting and engaging with anyone who was interested. From the day I signed with Linton, I made it my business to become a proficient Instagrammer, TikTok maven and Facebook junkie. I posted on Twitter and Instagram daily. I "liked" everything, and "followed" everyone. I joined an obscene number of online book clubs and reading groups and became active in all of them. The life of the literary party, I was all in. Whatever it took, I was willing to do it.

My very supportive husband promised to give out some of my older books at his restaurant in the days leading up to the book launch. The American Bistro attracted a lot of local celebrities. Teddy had easy access to all those New York tastemakers. He and I cooked up a plan where he would take pictures of his high-profile customers holding my books while at the restaurant. He'd text the photos to me and in real time I'd post them on Instagram and Facebook. Sometimes he'd even get a video of the people and within minutes, I'd have it up on TikTok or Book Tok. Everything working together created additional awareness of my book and the "Jillian Samuels" brand. Naturally, I kept my agent apprised of everything I did. I was a team player.

Double bonus — the owners of Teddy's restaurant also agreed to let me do a book signing the week my new book came out. Yippee! I was doing everything humanly possible to make my book a success. Despite all my efforts, as time passed and the explosions and homeless Silver Man stories turned into yesterday's news, all social media activity on my channels took a serious nosedive.

"I checked your Twitter feed yesterday," said Matthew during our weekly phone call. "What's happening? You've had almost no interactions all week. As we get closer to the launch, you've got to step it up, Jillian. Linton Books is watching everything we do. We've all got a lot riding on this."

FFS. Like I don't know that? Frustrated, I rattled off the litany of things I'd done that week to promote my brand and the book.

"No one said it would be easy," said Matthew with little empathy. "You've got to turn on the gas as we get closer to your pub date. Linton needs to see that your brand has long-term viability. What you do now will dictate how much money they spend on promoting it. If they decide it's not going to be a hit, they'll put as little muscle and money behind it as possible. You don't want to disappear right out of the gate, do you?"

I rolled my eyes. How could he ask me that question? Of course I didn't want to "disappear right out of the gate". I didn't spend over a year of my life writing the damn manuscript so it would vanish on week one. But, I'm also not a magician. The truth is, you can't *make* something "go viral", it either does or it doesn't. Many have tried and many have failed.

"Do you have any suggestions," I said, trying not to sound too bitchy, which was how I felt.

He told me to keep pushing and said that he also had a plan of his own in the works. That was a relief because I was freakin' out of ideas and exhausted from all the posting and pandering I'd been doing. At the end of the day, all my self-promoting had hardly made a blip. Tweet this, retweet that. I was absolutely nowhere and seriously frustrated.

To keep my sanity and my body from completely deteriorating, I dragged myself out of the house. I had a few errands to do and planned to take an afternoon Pilates class at my regular studio. As I drove through the center of town, I glanced up into my rearview mirror. It looked like that same green SUV which had been following me was two cars behind. I pulled over so I could get a better look and maybe catch the license number. When I did, the SUV made a hard right and disappeared. At that point, I was convinced someone was definitely following me. But who, and more importantly, why?

A ball of unhappy energy was sitting in my throat blocking my airwaves and my stomach was churning when I arrived at the Zen Pilates Center. I waved to my regular instructor, laid out my mat and took my place on the floor to stretch.

The music started. The entire forty-five minutes, I struggled and checked the clock every few seconds to see how much longer I'd have to endure the torture. I sipped from my water bottle often trying to regulate my body temperature, which was apparently set to extremely hot.

When the music finally stopped, the instructor told everyone how "amazing" we were. Clearly, she hadn't been watching me. I slowly dragged myself off of the floor and saw her walking toward me.

"You okay, Jillian? You seemed kind of out of it today," she said, casually flexing her perfectly toned arms. I looked down at mine. Despite the years of classes, my arms had no definition whatsoever. It struck me as rather unfair and I tried not to hate her.

Surprised that my anxiety was so obvious to my instructor, I did what anyone would do in that situation. I lied. "I didn't sleep at all last night. There was a noisy owl outside of my window who wouldn't shut up. I probably only got three hours."

"That'll do it. Sleep is the most important gift we can give to ourselves," she said smiling like the Dalai Lama as she walked away all sinewy and sculpted. "See you next class."

"Whatever," I muttered to myself as I picked up my yoga mat. Grabbing a coconut water from the machine, I headed over to the post office to mail out some employment contracts. They absolutely *had* to go out that day or nobody would get a job offer and I wouldn't get my commission.

As I drove over there, it crossed my mind that I might have to interact with the creepy postal worker who regularly hit on me. I was so not in the mood for him that day, but the packages had to go out.

Pulling into the parking lot of the tiny Medford post office, I groaned when I saw the lot was nearly full. It would be crowded inside and I had to get home for a conference call with a new client. Sure enough, when I entered the building there were two extremely long lines. Although, one was significantly shorter than the other.

Given my time restraints, the logical thing would have been for me to stand on the shorter line. The problem was, that shorter line led directly to Ned LaGrange, aka demented postal worker who had the hots for me. The longer line was serviced by a very pretty female with a warm smile and rows and rows of long skinny braids tied up on the top of her head. Judging from the length of the line in front of her window, it was evident that Pretty Braids was the more popular choice. Everyone in town who frequented the post office knew about chatty Ned LaGrange. Most people were willing to wait on the longer line for Pretty Braids in order to avoid a conversation with Ned.

For those reasons, I usually opted for the longer line on my weekly post office run, but this particular day, I didn't have the luxury of time. Gritting my teeth, I let out a breath, shook my head and reluctantly got on the line that led directly to Ned. I braced myself for our inevitable unpleasant interaction. Not only was Ned's line shorter but it moved more quickly because people tried to avoid any type of chit-chat. That didn't stop Ned from trying to engage each person with borderline inappropriate humor or sharing overly familiar observations. Most said as little as possible and left as quickly as they could.

When the person in front of me completed their transaction, it was my turn. I gulped and walked slowly toward Ned as if walking a gangplank, a pirate's sword at the base of my spine.

"Jillian Samuels, haven't seen you in the old USPO for a while," said Ned in a sing-song voice. He rolled up his sleeves ostensibly for me to see his bulging muscles through his pasty white blue skin. "What-choo been up to lately, Jillian?"

"Working. In fact, I have a business call in a few minutes so I'm in a bit of a rush," I said handing him my packages. I gazed past him, convinced if our eyes met, I would probably turn to stone or something even worse.

"You've got your workout clothes on, looking good. You been pumping, Jillian? I'm an LA Fitness rat myself. Over there every night, lifting weights," he said flexing his bicep again. "Gotta stay in shape if I'm gonna keep up with all the ladies buzzing around at the gym. You know what I mean?"

My stomach lurched as the conversation made me nauseous. "I just took a Pilates class, and I'm in a rush to get back for a conference call," I said, immediately regretting sharing any personal information.

"I was just thinking that you look like you're in really good shape, Jillian. You go to that Pilates place in the town center?" he said slowly checking me over from top to bottom. Kill me now, I thought as the hairs on the back of my neck stood up and a quiver went down my spine.

Moving painfully slow as always, Ned chattered about his workout routine and a few of his romantic conquests at the gym. "There's three times more ladies at the Medford LA Fitness than men. I have my hands full over there. You know what I'm sayin'?"

I looked at my phone. "Oh, my God, is it two o'clock already?"

"That means I'm off the clock in a few hours," said Mr Big Stuff smiling at me with his little yellow teeth. "You know where I'm heading? Right over to the gym to give my pecs a workout. You should join, Jillian. I know the manager really well. I could score you a discount. Once you're a member, I could walk you through all the machines. I'll get you pumping the big weights in no time."

"Thanks, but I'm good," I said grabbing my receipt and bolting toward the exit. I felt very unsettled. Ned LaGrange knew way too much about me — my address, my husband's name, where Teddy worked, where I got packages from, and where I sent them. He knew I took Pilates and what studio in town I went to. As I got into my car, I glanced over my shoulder. Ned was standing by the front door of the post office waving at me through the glass while flexing his right bicep. Ick. You can't make this stuff up.

Chapter 23

Agitated from my interaction with Mr Post Office, I drove along the vacant, country roads toward home. Despite my best efforts to put them out of my mind, my thoughts shifted back to the random fires and the silver homeless man. Those combustion events had fundamentally changed the course of my writing career. For the first time ever, my books were selling. Who could have predicted any of it?

As I turned onto my street, a fellow swimmer from the pool called. She had seen new posts on Twitter about me and my books. Apparently, another homeless man had been found painted silver in Barrington. Only this time things were very different — the man was dead.

"Was he murdered?" I said still sitting in the car in my driveway.

"All it said was the man was found dead," she said. "That's all I know."

I thanked her and raced to my desk just in time for the conference call with my client. As soon as it was over, I jumped onto my computer and opened Twitter. Scrolling through all the recent postings, I found quite a few comments linking the dead painted man in Barrington to me and my books. Over thirty new posts speculated on all sorts of conspiracies, while others made callous and snarky jokes. Someone suggested I was a follower of Satan. WTF? These random crimes and their tangential connection to me had taken on a life of their own. Granted, they were all terrible events. However, I couldn't deny that other people's misfortunes had created real momentum for me and my books. I shouldn't have been happy given the circumstances, but I was.

I combed through all the posts about the new dead man to see how he died but there was very little written other than he was found dead. It wasn't clear if he had been murdered. Then, I checked my book sales for the week. Up again. Yippee! I was about to call Matthew to give him the good news about the new "dead" and possibly "murdered" Silver Man when I noticed I had a voicemail.

It was from Tommy Devlin, the reporter who had stopped by my house. He wanted to write a feature story about the recent string of crimes and how they appeared to mirror events in my books. He wanted to know what I thought about the latest development, and if I believed any of it was connected to me.

I looked at my book sales numbers again and did some financial cartwheels in my head. Net conclusion: crime in general was bad, but these copycat crimes had turned out to be great for my business. Natalie always said, "Better they're talking crap about you than not talking at all." Those posts were absolute crap based on nothing concrete, but I decided to surrender to the universe and be happy about the free publicity.

To keep my PR momentum going, I called Devlin back. After ten seconds of small talk, he revealed that his police sources believed the dead man was most likely murdered.

"Oh, my God. How was he killed?" I said.

"They didn't tell me much," said Devlin, "only that the injury to the back of the man's skull couldn't possibly have been self-inflicted."

"Maybe he fell down like the other silver man?"

"The police have ruled out an accident. The victim was found in a large grassy area. There was nothing hard in the vicinity that he could have hit his head on," said the reporter matter-of-factly. "According to my sources, the dead guy had a pretty significant head wound. They said it looked like someone hit him repeatedly with a pipe or something like that. Apparently, the back of his skull was smashed in. His brains were all over the place."

I gulped. "Oh, my God. That's awful."

After hearing that revolting tidbit, I agreed to meet Devlin the following day at a local coffee shop in Medford. Then, I called my agent and told him about the second silver man, that he was dead and possibly murdered.

"Dead? That's great. This is exactly the kind of thing I was talking about," said Matthew. I couldn't see his face but from the tone of his voice I could tell he was smiling. "Some people wait a lifetime for a bluebird to fly in their window and it never comes. You know how lucky you are, Jillian?"

"I don't feel very lucky," I said slightly appalled by his glee. "Why is all this happening?"

"Don't look a gift horse in the mouth. Just run with it. I'll let Linton Books know about this significantly fabulous promotional development. A dead body might motivate them to put more money behind your launch."

"You think?"

"I'll let senior management here at the agency know what happened, too. When they hear about all the intrigue and chatter on social media, they'll all get on board with your book."

"They're not on board now?" I said.

After an awkward silence Matthew spoke. "They love your book, but you're a new author so some people here are taking a wait-and-see approach."

"What does that mean?" I said, my eyes narrowing.

"All the stuff that's happening currently is great, but your pub date is still far away," said Matthew. "By the time *The Soul Collector* comes out, this dead Silver Man saga will be ancient history. We've got to find a way to keep the copycat story alive until your book comes out."

"I'm doing an interview with a reporter tomorrow," I said. "He wants to do a feature story about me, my books and everything that's happened."

"Awesome. I'll bet we can get the Linton PR team to put something out when that story runs. From now on, we embrace conspiracy theories because that crazy shit sells books."

"A man died, Matthew," I said, surprised by how openly he celebrated a tragedy.

"I know and it's very sad. But remember, selling a lot of books isn't going to make him undead."

That was the moment I realized my agent was a cold-blooded opportunist. He had one agenda — make my book hit the top of the charts. I technically couldn't fault him for that. And, while he sounded a bit callous, deep down I knew he was probably right. What do they say? Every cloud has a silver lining. These random crimes could be the difference between my book soaring into a movie deal or ending up in a sale heap in a bookstore basement.

Matthew said he'd call Eric and tip him off to the steady groundswell of interest in my books and the recent development — a genuine dead body. He'd convince Eric that the dead man news story was picking up steam and ripe for some kind of promotional opportunity.

After over twenty-five years at Linton Books, Andrea Cox knew a potential blockbuster scenario when she saw one. Their PR department was instructed to stay on top of the Connecticut crimes and draw a strong dotted line to me whenever possible. With my book launch still many months away, they agreed to keep the salacious side story alive for as long as possible.

Now that there was an actual murder victim attached to my books, I wondered if it would be a game changer. It was tricky. How could I leverage what was happening to sell more books without appearing insensitive or worse?

Whenever confronted with a problem, I tended to get cerebral. I would look at things from every angle ad nauseum and turn inward. My husband was the opposite. No matter what was going on, Teddy always remained levelheaded, calm and tactical in a crisis. He prided himself on being the one person in the room who never lost his head. That's probably why he was so good at running a big New York City restaurant kitchen. From the stories I'd heard him tell, all kinds of insanity and drama happen behind the scenes in restaurants. If the chef doesn't keep it together, the kitchen falls apart — fast. Teddy would know exactly what my next move should be. Unfortunately, that night, he wasn't due home until after midnight so I had to wait.

Because of his crazy hours, we'd practically been living separate lives for a few years. The restaurant business is a total late-night affair. I'm not complaining. He was in the restaurant business when I met him, so I knew what I'd signed up for. Usually, I was asleep when he crawled into bed every night. In the mornings, I would get up early and he'd sleep in. We'd try to have a late breakfast together before he left to catch the train to New York. I knew our incompatible schedule wouldn't be forever. Once both of our careers were where we wanted them to be, we'd be together all the time. We had a plan.

When Teddy got to the restaurant and started the lunch shift he became incommunicado — full stop. Between lunch and dinner, he did all of his planning — ordering supplies, changing menus, etc. During the early part of the dinner period, he supervised the kitchen, tasting old and new dishes to make sure they were perfect. If everything in the kitchen was running smoothly, then, and only then, he'd change into a clean white shirt, comb his thick wavy hair and mingle on the restaurant floor with the customers. He knew exactly how to lay on the charm as he greeted his adoring public. I'm not a hundred percent sure, but I always thought he liked the social part of work more than the actual cooking. Bottom line: Teddy enjoyed attention.

Connecting with his customers was what he did best, and the dining public lapped it up. At first, Teddy was surprised by all the fuss and was even a little shy when it happened. Over time, I noticed he began to enjoy it. When some little foodie website put him on the list of "Big Apple's 10 Culinary Hotties", I watched his head nearly double in size. I couldn't blame him, I would have been the same. With a lot of teasing from friends and family, we were fortunately able to keep his feet on the ground. Still, there was no question that Teddy's star had risen dramatically since we met. I was really proud to be his wife. They say, behind every great man there's a woman. I liked to think that my support of him contributed to his success.

On paper, things were moving in a positive direction, but sometimes it felt like Teddy and I were on separate paths. Both of us were going in the same direction but we were alone on the journey. Teddy's glamorous New York City life was so removed and different from the quiet writer/headhunter's life I led in Connecticut. Occasionally, I had pangs of insecurity and wondered if my husband would get bored with me. I wasn't flashy or loud, I was just me — a woman who worked from home and wrote thrillers in my pajamas. When my books finally started to sell, I thought it put us on a more even playing field.

When I signed with my agent, somehow it evened things out between Teddy and me. I wasn't competing with him, but having the agent meant I also had a shot at a big time career and my star was on the rise. I think relationships need some parity to keep things running smoothly. It might have been my imagination, but I could have sworn Teddy became more interested in my writing career *after* I signed with Matthew. Before then, it was always me bringing up my books at the dinner table. But once I'd signed, Teddy became very curious about publishing and my writing process and wanted to talk about it all the time. Naturally, that made me happy. I loved talking about my stories and characters. Things were finally happening for both of us — New York's hottie chef and his wife, the bestselling American novelist. That sounded pretty good to me.

I didn't know it then, but smooth sailing was a long way off. Before my ship pulled into a safe harbor, a lot of shit would hit the proverbial fan.

Chapter 24

Later that day, my friend Sue, the same person who had messaged me about the dead man, called me from her car. Weeks before, I had ordered Florida oranges from her church fundraiser and she wanted to stop by and deliver them. I told her to pull around to the front of the house and I'd meet her there.

When I opened my front door, Sue was standing there holding a large straw basket that said *FLORIDA* on it in big orange letters. After handing me the container of fruit, she waved a bright yellow piece of paper in front of my face.

"This was sticking in your front door," she said looking at it more carefully. "Hard to miss a flyer that's school bus yellow. Looks like it's from one of those door-to-door religious groups. I get them at my house, too. Haven't seen those people around in a while, but if they're at your house, they'll be at mine in no time."

I knew the group she was referring to. I couldn't remember what their religion was, but they were always nicely dressed and extremely polite. Twice a year they appeared at my house. Sometimes I'd talk with them, sometimes I hid. If I wasn't in the mood to be cordial, I'd play possum when the bell rang and hide in my room quietly until they left. I wasn't always up for discussing my spiritual health with strangers who likely stood on morally higher ground than I did.

"Thanks," I said taking the yellow pamphlet from my friend's hand. I glanced down at the bold headline and read it out loud. "'You too can be saved.' Good to know," I said with a laugh. I studied it further. Beneath the headline were additional inspirational words of wisdom. "'The one slow to anger is better than a mighty man. Proverbs 16:32.'"

"They're obviously not talking about me," said Sue, chuckling as she walked toward her car. "When somebody ticks me off, I go from zero to a hundred in two seconds."

As she pulled out of my driveway, I shut my door and tucked the yellow paper into my pants pocket. Then, I texted my husband.

Wake me when you get home, I need to talk to you. Things are heating up. XX

The appearance of a dead body had definitely taken the stakes up a few notches. It would be late when Teddy got home but I couldn't wait until his next day off to talk. There was too much going on for me to handle it alone, and I needed his counsel. We were a team and well suited to one another. Whenever I started spinning, Teddy maintained a sober voice. He was the yin to my yang and why we were so perfect together. We balanced each other out.

Three glasses of wine with dinner while waiting for my husband to come home had probably been a bad idea. Groggy, I had fallen asleep on the couch not long after I ate. Just after midnight, I woke from the sound of the garage door opening. I jumped up, grabbed my wine glass and the empty bottle and stashed them in the kitchen.

"You're awake," he said surprised to see me as he closed the basement door.

Yawning, I walked toward him and gave him a kiss. "You smell good," I said nuzzling into his neck. "How do you smell so fresh after working in a hot kitchen all night with all that garlic, onions and oil?"

"I wash with soap after my shift. You should try it sometime," he said letting out a laugh. "You don't want me coming home smelling like halibut and onion soup, do you?"

"No, I do not," I said tightening my arms around him, feeling the contours of the muscles in his back.

"Now, I'm all yours. What did you want to talk about?" he said pouring himself a glass of red wine.

"Another body painted silver was found in Barrington," I blurted out.

"Are you kidding?"

"And, the man was dead."

"Dead?" said Teddy. "He was definitely painted silver?"

I nodded, satisfied by his surprised reaction. Lately, he had been so wrapped up with his own stuff. Now, for the first time in weeks, I finally had his complete attention. Murder will do that.

"Terrible," said my husband shaking his head while scrolling through the news story on his phone.

"I probably shouldn't say this but . . . there is a bright spot. Every time there's another incident, the sales of my books increase."

"The question we have to ask is — who's doing this and why?" said Teddy as he took another sip of his wine and furrowed his brow. "Do you ever wonder if the person behind this is trying to send you a message? Or, what if it has nothing to do with you at all. Maybe it's some nut with no imagination who accidentally stumbled across your books and is using them as their playbook."

Teddy reached for the pile of mail on the kitchen counter. Not wanting to lose the floor, I quickly pulled out the yellow flyer from my pocket and handed it to him. "This afternoon, Sue delivered those Florida oranges I ordered. She found this paper stuck in our front door." He examined the wrinkled yellow pamphlet and then turned back to me with a confused look on his face.

"Are you trying to tell me you've found religion?"

"Flip it over," I said. "I didn't see the message at first. After Sue left, I was about to throw it in the garbage when I noticed some handwriting on the back."

Teddy turned the pamphlet over.

"I will fear no evil, for you are with me; your book and your words, they comfort me. Psalm 23:4"

"Some kind of religious proverb," he said as he looked up into my eyes. "What do you think it means?"

"I don't think it's a random spiritual message at all. I think it was meant specifically for me. You know notes written in purple or blue crayon were found near the bodies of both men covered in silver paint."

"But the writing on this pamphlet is in black pen," said Teddy.

"I know, but it's still weird. Stuff is happening from my first and second books, right? Now, today, I get this note talking about my 'book and my words'."

"I'm not convinced this pamphlet is connected to the other stuff. Maybe the people going house-to-house put personal notes on all the religious materials they leave. I'm sure there's a rational explanation."

"That's exactly what they say in a movie right before a giant butcher knife goes into someone's stomach," I said. "All I know is the police and the press are stepping up their investigation. Whether I like it or not, they think there's some connection between the real crimes and my books."

"I'll tell you what," said my husband reaching for a new bottle of Cabernet and pouring himself a half glass. "I'll call the police tomorrow and see if I can get to the bottom of everything."

"Would you?" I said reaching for his glass and taking a sip.

He nodded. "Don't worry. I'll sort things out. By the way, I meant to ask you, did you meet with your agent in Medford this morning?"

I shook my head. "In Medford? No, why?"

"I could be completely wrong. I only met Matthew twice, and briefly. You and I went to his office to pick something up once. Another time he came to my restaurant and I went over to his table to say hello. Still, I could swear it was him I saw getting off the northbound train in Medford as I was getting on the southbound. He was with another guy about the same age and they were both carrying large shopping bags. I assumed you had a meeting with him."

"I'm sure if he was in Medford for another reason he would have been in touch," I said wondering what that was all about.

"I'm probably wrong," said my husband. "It might not have been him."

"What did the other guy look like?"

"I didn't notice. It was only for a split second as I got on the train. Could have been someone who just looked a lot like Matthew."

"I guess," I said but it gave me pause.

"Now, I've got some news for you," said Teddy sitting down next to me.

He looked serious so I sat up straight on my kitchen stool.

"Plans for the new restaurant are moving along at a good clip," he said. I nodded and reached for his wine glass a second time. "There have been some positive new developments . . ."

As he animatedly talked, a big smile stretched across my face. Seeing my husband with so much enthusiasm about the new restaurant was contagious. At that moment, I loved him so much that I thought I was going to burst. Both of our careers were finally in sync and we were moving forward together. Teddy would soon have his own restaurant and I, hopefully, an international bestselling novel.

He finished telling me all the details about the new space and I leaned over, put my arms around him and gave him a big kiss. Our future was so bright that night, I never imagined everything would change from one single phone call.

Chapter 25

After finishing a morning phone interview, I answered outstanding emails and reviewed Tommy Devlin's bio on the *Connecticut Advocate* site to prep for my afternoon meeting with him. There was a homepage story about another tricked-out drone made to look like a hot pink and purple pig with angel wings. The flying pig had been seen soaring over Medford the previous day. No explosion or fire, just a pig. I chuckled to myself, apparently pigs *do* fly.

According to the article, at least ten local residents had seen the airborne pig overhead. Because of the previous explosions, every person had called the police immediately. But before the cops arrived, the pink and purple pig crashed into the side of a covered bridge and landed on some rocks below. Some truant high school boys fishing off the bridge recovered the drone. No explosives were found.

I checked social media. Sure enough, the Twitter minions were already on it and posting about the pig drone, and noting it was a dud. All I knew was it got me and my books back into the social media conversation. I even picked up a dozen new followers that day. While I was reading through all their wacky comments and conspiracy theories, Matthew called.

"You're practically famous," he said when I picked up. "Did you see all the new activity on Twitter about you? Things are moving along nicely. A drone that looks like a flying pig, gotta love that."

"Thankfully, this one didn't blow up and no one was hurt."

"All I care about is getting your name out there. Buzz is buzz is buzz."

"I guess. By the way, were you up in Medford yesterday?"

"Me, no. Why would I be in Medford?"

"Teddy thought he saw you get off the train. Must have been someone else," I said.

"I've got one of those faces. People think they see me all the time. Besides," said Matthew, "if I was in Medford, I would have definitely stopped by to see my favorite client."

I think "only client" would have been more accurate, but I let it go. We spoke for a few more minutes and then Matthew ended the conversation with his usual "keep your foot on the gas pedal".

Later that day, I purposely arrived early at the Daily Grind coffee shop for my meeting with Devlin. After ordering my customary black coffee, I surveyed the room. The walls were made of cheap wood paneling meant to resemble the inside of a barn. There was a small wooden table with two metal chairs by itself in the far back corner. Perfect. It would be difficult for anyone to overhear our conversation from that location. I sat down at the table to wait for my "date".

At 2.45 p.m., the journalist from the *Advocate* opened the door of the shop and walked in. He was on time. I appreciate punctuality and he scored a few points with me. I studied him for a second before he saw me. If I'm being honest, Devlin was as handsome as my husband, but with a completely different look and vibe. Teddy was Mediterranean swarthy and sexy while Devlin's looks were more traditional and Northern European. Devlin looked like a model from a discount men's clothing ad. At first blush, his classic features seemed quintessentially all-American. After a second look, I detected an element of sleaze, something I'd noticed about him before. I couldn't put my finger on what it was, but it was definitely there. Once I noticed his smarminess, I couldn't stop seeing it. Bottom line — I didn't trust him.

Standing inside the doorway, he looked around. I waved and he flashed his perfect white teeth which I had always suspected were veneers. He walked toward me with the confidence only one with an inflated ego would have.

"Thanks for meeting me," he said putting his brown leather backpack on a nearby chair. "Can I get you anything?" I shook my head and he went to the counter to get a coffee. Minutes later, seated across from me stirring a latte, his baby blues searched deeply into my eyes. He knew the effect he had on most women, but I wasn't most women. His questionable charms were not going to work on me. I had already found my prince and wasn't in the market for another. But as he continued to look me over, I was surprised to find myself blush. What was that all about?

"What kind of stories do you cover?" I said attempting small talk in order to regain my composure.

"Right now I'm working on the explosions and fire story as well as the Silver Man assault and murder investigation. For the last few months I'd been covering the disappearance of Anabel Ford. You must have heard about her, she was all over the news. She's the local Dover College student who disappeared a few months back."

I nodded. Everyone in Connecticut knew about that case, it had been the lead story forever and her face had been splashed across the news nightly for months.

"Sad case," said Devlin. "Each day that passes, the police say it's less likely they'll find her alive. Multiple police departments, CT state police and the FBI have all been involved. After all that manpower, nobody's got nothing."

"I've been following the story. She went missing after a fraternity party, right?"

Devlin nodded. "According to witnesses, Anabel had been at an off-campus party and had been drinking — a lot.

Somehow, she got separated from her friends and ended up leaving on her own. She never made it back to her dorm. There haven't been any new leads since a day or two after she went missing."

"What about the CCTV footage?"

"None of it showed anything useful. All the tips that came through the hotline were investigated but turned up nothing. It's like she vanished into thin air. I've interviewed her family a few times trying to get the word out. They're out of their minds with grief and anger. She had her whole life to look forward to."

"It's a terrible story. I feel so sorry for her family."

"Since the news on Anabel Ford has slowed to nothing, my editor reassigned me to a few new stories, yours being one of them."

"Hold on," I said leaning back in my chair. "Let's get one thing straight. This is not *my* story. I have no idea why, but someone is recreating scenes from my books and using them to act out some sick live-action play. I have nothing to do with any of it. Are we clear?"

"I'm sorry. I wasn't trying to imply that you're involved in any way."

For some reason, that reporter made me nervous. He was good. He started out slow and friendly, making the conversation seem totally casual. But soon his questions came in rapid fire and none of my answers quenched his thirst. Clearly, Devlin liked to get to the bottom of things and wouldn't stop until he got the full story. He'd be disappointed, because I had nothing for him.

"Why do you think all this is happening?" said Devlin.

"How would I know that?" I said, irritation creeping into my voice because I had already covered this with him and the police. "Once I put my writing out into the world, anyone can read it and what they do with it is out of my hands. Technically, I'm a victim in this whole saga, too."

He nodded and took a beat. "Have any strangers contacted you about this story? Any unusual interactions or requests?"

"No. Well, maybe. I'm not sure, but I think someone left me a cryptic message."

That's when I told him about the yellow pamphlet with the handwritten proverb that my neighbor found on my front door.

"Couldn't that proverb simply be referencing the power of the Bible?" he said a little dismissively after I repeated the proverb a second time.

"What if it's a message from the killer, like the ones found written in crayon at all the crime scenes?" I said.

"By any chance, do you have that pamphlet with you?"

I smiled, reached into my bag and pulled out the crumpled yellow paper. I pride myself on always being buttoned up, thorough and prepared. I knew if I mentioned the pamphlet, he'd want to see it. I try to anticipate things and not get caught off guard. Devlin flashed his perfect teeth again as he took the paper from my hand. He carefully examined it, as I had expected he would.

"'I will fear no evil, for you are with me; your book and your words, they comfort me'," he said reading the note. A puzzled look crossed his face. "Psalm 23:4." He shook his head. "It could be a personal spiritual message or . . ."

"Or?"

Devlin held up a finger and picked up his phone. "When in doubt, Google it." After a few seconds he looked up and smiled. "I think I found something." He pointed to the yellow pamphlet on the table. "What's written there on that paper, that's not Psalm 23:4. The real verse is 'I will fear no evil, for you are with me; *your rod and your staff*, they comfort me'. 'Rod and staff' in the note were changed to 'book and words'. Jillian, you have good instincts. This might be a twisted personal message from the killer to you."

Chapter 26

That same day, like dogs digging for an elusive bone, Brodsky and Marino drove to my house for a surprise visit. I was where I always was, in my home office hunting heads. As usual, my office window was open because the room was always so hot. Even on the coldest winter days, it was an oven.

I heard tires on the gravel in my driveway and then saw a blue compact car pull up in front of my house. I peered out from the side of my window blocked by a curtain so the inhabitants of the vehicle couldn't see me. At first, I didn't know who it was until the big Italian got out followed by the Russian. Brodsky, in particular, was a hard one to forget with his black eyes that looked directly through to your soul. There was no mistaking him. He had a neck as thick as a telephone pole.

Marino stood on the driver's side, looking down while rubbing his left hand.

"I can't get this damn silver paint off," he said holding up his left palm to show his partner. He then wiped his left hand vigorously on his right sleeve.

"Now you made a stain on your jacket," said Brodsky. "Why do you always wipe your dirty hands on your clothes."

"Because I don't have a plush terry-cloth towel in my pocket," said Marino, grinning and wiping his hand on his sleeve a second time. "As I was saying before you interrupted me, in my opinion, the new murder, the homeless guy, and Argos, and all those fires connect right here with Jillian Samuels."

I was stunned. The cops suspected me? My mouth dropped open but I remained out of sight and continued to listen.

"You think she's involved?" said the Russian.

"Nah. But, she may have an enemy who's trying to make it look that way. Somebody could be setting her up?"

"It's possible," said Brodsky.

"An obsessive book fan?" said Marino. "Maybe someone who gets off turning fiction into reality. Loads of people lose their identities over certain books and movies. Think about the millions of people who dress up like Harry Potter. Or the crazies who go to Star Trek conventions as aliens. Maybe this is some kind of fandom thing?"

"Let's go have a chat with Ms Samuels," said Brodsky closing his car door. "Now that someone is dead, we've got to turn up the heat. Maybe a murder on the table will trigger her memory."

Obviously, I wasn't supposed to hear any of that and I was a little insulted. Those detectives thought I was holding something back. Why would I do that? I raced down the stairs to the kitchen, turned on the electric kettle, and grabbed a mug and a tea bag to make it look like I had been in the kitchen all along.

When the doorbell rang, for a split second I considered pretending I wasn't home like I did when those missionary groups came a-knocking. I did have a work report due to one of my clients in a few hours so I could justify not answering the door. After a few seconds of internal debate, I decided it was my civic duty to give the police a few minutes of my time. They were just doing their job. If I were them, I'd want to talk to me, too.

"Detectives," I said as I opened the door with a forced smile, "what brings you here?" Obviously, I knew why they were there. I write thrillers.

"It appears there's been another reenactment from one of your books," said Marino.

"I heard about the man in Barrington," I said. "A friend saw something on Twitter and called me. Then I saw a report on the local cable news. How are you so sure it's related to my books?"

"There are now too many coincidences to ignore the possible connection to you," said the Russian. "If it was only the two people covered in paint, it could be anything or anyone. The perpetrator could have read your book *The Platinum Man*, liked the concept of spray paint, but that's where the connection to you would end. However, there have also been explosions from superhero drones and subsequent fires as depicted in your other book *A Burning Desire*. This leads us to conclude there is a strong connection to you. Two of your books, two different sets of crimes which now includes one homicide."

I sighed, the Russian had a point. "But why would someone go to such lengths? If it was to get my attention, they had that after the first explosion. Look, I write thrillers. What if . . . what if the intended victim all along was the man who was just murdered. Maybe all the other events were meant as a distraction or a smokescreen to throw the police off the trail?"

"That's one theory we've considered," said Marino. "That's why we need your help."

I invited them into my living room with the intention of being as accommodating as possible, which was a slightly selfish decision on my part. Occasionally, I need police procedural information when I'm writing my thrillers. I figured if I was helpful to them, when I needed an inside cop perspective for my novels, they'd return the favor. A little quid pro quo never hurts.

I had barely taken my seat on the couch when the detectives fired off a slew of questions. It took me a little by surprise when I realized I was being interrogated. In a weird way, it was kind of exciting. "Was there any real-life inspiration for your characters or plots? Did you ever collaborate with anyone on your books? Do you have any enemies?"

I never considered the possibility of enemies before. Do most people take inventory of their life and keep a list of enemies, I wondered?

"I don't know," I said in all honesty. "I've never thought about it. I suppose there are people who don't like me, but hardcore enemies, I don't think so. I'm a pretty simple person."

"Anyone ever threaten you?" said Marino.

I shook my head. "I lead a really quiet life here. It's just me and my husband, although we're thinking about getting a dog. I have a few close friends in the city and a couple of acquaintances up here. I don't know too many people in Medford. Truthfully, Detectives, I'm kind of an introvert."

They continued peppering me with questions. To almost every one, I answered emphatically, no. Frustration was written all over their faces.

"Ms Samuels," said Marino, "let's take this in a different direction. Has anything odd or disconcerting happened to you personally in the past year or two?"

Well, that was the hundred-million-dollar question. Anything disconcerting happen to me? Yeah, like all the time. "Where do I begin," I said. "There's this creepy mail-man named Ned LaGrange who flirts with me in a stalker kind of way whenever I go to the post office."

Marino wrote down Ned's name. "What's your gut on LaGrange?" he said. "Is he focused only on you or does he bother other people, too? What I'm getting at, is he danger-ous or lonely?"

"I don't know," I said shaking my head as images of Ned's fleshy face flashed in front of my eyes. "I suppose he could just be sad. As far as Ned acting that way with others, frankly, I'm not sure. I don't stick around the post office long enough to observe him. When I finish mailing my packages, I'm out of there. I only mentioned him because you asked if anything strange had happened and Ned LaGrange is off the charts bizarro."

I told them about the yellow religious pamphlet with the proverb found in my door. They made a note but didn't appear too interested in that. Tough crowd. I was glad I had saved the best nugget for last — Jolly Roger44.

"Someone sent me an email through my author blog," I said. "They called themselves JollyRoger44." I shared the details of my super fan pirate with the detectives.

"Don't misunderstand me. I love it when people like my books, but Jolly Roger's praise was a little over the top. I'm not Hemingway . . . although, I'd like to be," I said with a little chuckle trying to lighten the mood.

"Hemingway killed himself," said Brodsky matter-of-factly. "You don't want to be him."

"I didn't mean it that way. I only want to *write* like him," I said qualifying what I thought had been a cute joke. The Russian clearly had no sense of humor.

"Interesting moniker, Jolly Roger," said Marino perking up. "I'm a history buff. Did you know the origin of the Jolly Roger is—"

"The skull and crossbones flag used by pirate ships," I said jumping in. "I know."

Brodsky's eyebrows went up. Finally, a human reaction from the man.

"The pirate is something we should follow up on. Can you send us those emails and give us that religious pamphlet?" said Brodsky. I nodded. "Anyone else you can think of?"

"This may seem stupid but, I think a green SUV has been following me around town," I said.

"How often have you seen it?" said Brodsky making a note.

"Four or five times."

"A lot of people drive green SUV's. Did you get the license plate?"

"No."

"We'll look into it."

I nodded wondering if he meant it and stood hoping they picked up my signal that it was time to wrap up. "I hate to toss you out but I've got a report due this afternoon. If you have any other questions, you know where to find me. Hope I helped."

As they stepped out onto my front walk, I called out to them. "Do you really think there's a connection to my books or is this social media conspiracy theory overdrive. You know how the stupidest things spread on the internet."

"There's no doubt there have been a peculiar series of events. Only time will tell," said Brodsky as he opened his car door and got in. Clearly, a man of few words.

"We'll be looking into things. It might simply be a terrible coincidence," said Marino with a half-smile as he opened his car door, "or not."

* * *

The following Monday, I raced home from my morning yoga class in order to make my regular 11.15 a.m. weekly Zoom call with Matthew. I deliberately took an 8 a.m. class so I'd have time to do a few errands on my way home. One of my stops was unfortunately the post office. I absolutely had to send a registered letter to a client which meant I couldn't put it in the mailbox. I had to go inside the federal building.

When I pulled into the parking lot, it was empty. I did a little happy dance inside my head. If I could be in and out of the post office in ten minutes, I'd have time to take a shower and dry my hair before my session with Matthew. I wanted to look nice for him, to reinforce he'd backed the right horse.

Inside the post office, there was one line with only two people on it. Pretty Braids was the only employee on duty. Ned LaGrange, usually perched right next to her, was nowhere in sight. I let out a sigh of relief and evaluated the postal needs of the two people standing in front of me. Based on what they held in their hands, I calculated exactly how much time they would take at the window. One had a small box. That looked quick unless there was a surprise transaction, like picking up held mail. That might extend my time there.

The second person in line was holding nothing. That made her a total wild card. I checked the time as Wild Card Woman stepped up to the window. I couldn't hear what she said but her hands were moving fast. She must have been explaining something complicated because Pretty Braids squinted at her and shook her head. It was clear from PB's body language there was some confusion and she turned her head and called for backup. A moment later, Ned LaGrange stepped out from the back room and up to the counter.

After conferring with PB for a minute, Ned apparently solved her problem and stepped up to the adjacent window ready for action. Open for business, Ned beckoned to me with a big yellow tooth smile. His eyes ran over every inch of my body as I walked reluctantly toward the counter.

"Mornin' Jillian. Haven't seen you in a few days. Wearing workout gear, I see. Lookin' good. Been to Pilates again, I suppose?"

"Yoga."

"Yoga's supposed to be really good for you, lengthens the tendons. I prefer the weights myself. I like to sweat it out," he said opening the top button of his uniform shirt so his brown curly chest hair was visible. Eww. "Where do you take yoga, maybe I'll try it. Bet those classes are full of ladies, right? Don't get too many pumped-up guys like me in there. But hey, there's always a first time for everything."

I started to hyperventilate. "I'm kind of in a rush, Ned."

"Sure, I get it, no problemo," he said as he processed my registered letter. "By the way, I've been reading your books. Good stuff."

"You're reading my books?" I said trying not to let my revulsion show on my face. "How did you know I wrote books?"

"I know lots about you, Jillian. You come in here all the time sending packages and shipping things out. Postal workers know a lot of things. I'm reading *Whispers from the Grave* right now. I already figured out who the killer is. I should have been a cop. I'm good at solving puzzles. Really cool book though."

I mumbled a half-hearted "thank you", grabbed my receipt and bolted out the door to my car. I shuddered thinking about Ned LaGrange, resident Neanderthal, reading any of my books. The thought of his beady lecherous eyes looking at my beautiful words was so unsettling.

Chapter 27

Several weeks passed and the police continued their investigation of the "Silver Man Murder". Given my weird connection to the case, I found myself checking the news several times a day. I couldn't help it. There had been no arrests that I was aware of. The local news station reported that Argos, the unconscious man, and the dead man whose name I didn't know, had both been heavy drug users. The local and state police were working together but had turned up zilch. Occasionally, there were tiny mentions online about the case. From a writer's perspective, the story arc wasn't moving forward at all.

Life goes on for everyone and it's no different for law enforcement. With new crimes to investigate each week, the police rarely contacted me. I remembered a few years earlier, an extremely attractive mother of six in Bakersfield CT went missing, her face was plastered all over the local news and made the national news, too. That missing mother was a top headline for weeks. Her husband was soon the prime suspect. It's always the husband or boyfriend, isn't it? Silver men who used drugs weren't nearly as sexy as a hot, wealthy, thirty-nine-year-old woman with six kids who vanishes.

Her story dominated the news for weeks until they found various parts of her body in a dumpster in New

Haven. Before they arrested her husband, (like I said, it's always the husband), he took a swan dive off a New York City skyscraper. Case closed.

The Anabel Ford story had also been front page news for months, but with no new developments, she only made the news once in a while. Like Anabel, the Silver Man Murder mystery had gone from a bold print headline to a back page mention.

* * *

I'm not going to lie; the fires, assault and murder had been good for my book business. Now that none of it was in the news, my literary star was falling and it stung. Only a few weeks before, I had been a trending topic of conversation all over social media. A month later, nobody was interested and sales of all my books slowed to almost nothing.

By then, it was only my agent, the Linton Books PR lady and me who were keeping the Jillian Samuels' brand out there. I had been so close to having a viral moment, I could practically taste it. When the public interest shifted, I was left floating adrift. With my book launch still many months away and public interest dead, Matthew and I discussed strategy for "our little problem" each week on our Zoom catchups.

"Your buzz on Twitter and Instagram is flat," said Matthew, his bedside manner leaving something to be desired. "We've got to pump it back up."

Apparently, writing a damn good thriller accompanied by an actual dead body and a murder investigation was not enough. "I've been tweeting and posting until my fingers bleed," I said. "I've followed and liked a gazillion people. I don't know what else to do."

"We face this problem every time we launch a new book. Everyone's vying for the same eyeballs. Unless a publisher spends boatloads of money or something crazy happens like that Silver Man, it's nearly impossible to break through."

"So, what do we do?"

"We need something out of the box that will have real impact. I'm having dinner with Eric from Linton Books tomorrow night to brainstorm. By the way, Eric mentioned he wanted to go to the American Bistro. I tried to get a reservation but they were booked for the next three weeks."

"I'm sleeping with the chef. I'll take care of it," I said with a fair amount of bravado. As soon as we hung up, I called Teddy and begged him to find a table for "*my* agent and *my* editor". I wanted to show Matthew that he had backed the right horse. I was someone who could make things happen.

When Matthew arrived at the Bistro that night, Eric was already seated at a table sipping a martini. The two traded industry gossip before getting down to brass tacks. As they went through the timeline for my launch, each man revealed their own anxiety about the future success of *The Soul Collector*. (Matthew told me much later after everything went down, how he and Eric had both stuck their necks out to acquire my book.)

Halfway through his meal, Matthew spotted Teddy doing his nightly rounds. He pointed him out to Eric explaining that the handsome man in white, who looked like an Italian movie star, was my husband. I guess Teddy did me proud that night. The next morning, Matthew called me first thing and raved about how "wonderful and charming" Teddy was.

"Why do you think I married him?" I said as I let out a little girlish laugh that I regretted the moment I heard it come out of my mouth. I was a lot of things but girlish — no.

"I think Eric has a little crush on your husband," said Matthew. "After Teddy went back in to the kitchen, Eric spent the rest of the night talking about him and asked me all sorts of questions."

"Teddy has that effect on everybody," I said, proud my husband had successfully greased the wheels for me. Whenever I had a traffic ticket or wanted to return something that had been marked final sale, I sent Teddy. Nine times out of ten, they'd give him the refund or cancel the ticket. I often wondered what it must feel like to exude all that effortless charm and have doors swing open. It had to feel good. I had to settle for being charming by proxy.

I think Teddy's charisma had a lot to do with his success as a chef. He's a great cook but there are loads of great cooks out there. Why did Teddy become a darling of the New York restaurant scene? In my opinion, it wasn't only his duck breasts with apricot chutney or his braised short ribs with burgundy gravy. It was the whole enchilada.

Chapter 28

As my pub date for *The Soul Collector* inched closer, my fear and excitement was palpable. Instead of securing job placements and making money, I paced around my house half the day obsessing about the launch. I had my heart set on a bestseller and it didn't look like that was the way it was going to go.

Natalie had offered to come up to Connecticut and spend the weekend with me. A visit from her was exactly what I needed to take my mind off everything. Natalie would mainly want to talk about herself which would keep me from obsessing over my book. Plus, Teddy was working the whole weekend so she'd be around to keep me company.

It was Natalie's busy season and we had barely spoken more than a few words in weeks. She and I planned to take a few long walks at a nearby park to have a much needed catchup.

It was only after she arrived that I found out something had happened. After a two-week relationship with a man who worked in the New York City mayor's office, gorgeous Natalie had been dumped. My BFF was not accustomed to getting blown off by anyone, especially a man, and was looking for some serious props. I offered her my home, wine, chocolate and as many yard sales as she wanted. A fair exchange for both of us, she had my sympathetic ear and I got my BFF's company for the entire weekend.

That Friday night, while Teddy was in the city working the dinner shift, Natalie and I had the house to ourselves — exclusive girl time. Teddy and Natalie got along great but the dynamic was different when it was all three of us. Truthfully, I looked forward to it being just Natalie and I that night. We'd have an old-fashioned slumber party, just like we used to.

I picked her up at the train station and we went directly back to my house. Comfort being king, we immediately put on our pajamas. I lit a fire as Natalie assembled an excessively large cheese platter for our night of debauchery. It didn't take long before a second bottle of white wine was open and Natalie was jabbering about one man after the next. We argued over which mindless Netflix movie to watch. I finally selected one we had both seen, so we could talk and not have to pay attention to the plot. Then, we got down to business. I honestly couldn't count the number of times Natalie and I had created this same scene.

When we were both single and living in Manhattan, our respective tiny studio apartments were a few blocks away from each other. We'd sleep over the other's place, some-times two or even three times a week. We'd make popcorn and watch movies, do our nails, and most importantly share secrets. Boyfriends occasionally got in the way, but despite those romantic entanglements, we always managed to carve out time for us. BFF's forever.

Her visit to Connecticut that weekend underscored how much I had missed that. With me married and living in the country and Natalie down in the city leading her glamorous single girl life, our sleepover parties had become few and far between. As we got older, it became harder to schedule our visits. No more spur of the moment crashing on each other's couches. We were all grown up and I provided her with a proper private guest room on the first floor of our house.

Settling back on the couch as the fire roared, a wine glass in our hands, we started light talking about our comings and goings the previous few weeks. Natalie's chatter centered around work, annoying clients and her terrible string of boyfriends.

"I'm telling you, Jills, it's a freakin' man jungle out there. It must have something to do with all their testosterone, because I'm convinced men are insane," said Natalie taking a big gulp of wine. "I mean it. They're seriously twisted. I always thought once they got into their thirties they'd grow up. But no, they still act like egotistical hormone-driven powermongering tools. I'm thirty-five years old and these assholes are still playing the same games they played in high school. I am so done."

Even now, I can't believe I'm saying this, but I actually felt a little sorry for her. When I first moved into the city after college, socializing in New York was fun. Swipe here, swipe there. Read profiles, send cute and clever messages. Flirt. But, after a while, looking for a partner became an unpleasant job. Before I met Teddy, I also was done, fried, finished and over it. I'd been off the market for a few years now, but I had a good idea how my friend was feeling and tried to tell her.

"You don't understand, it's completely different now," said Natalie stretching out her legs in front of the fire. "I'm literally exhausted. You're lucky you found someone like Teddy and you don't have to put yourself through it anymore. I'm so jealous of you."

The glamour puss of the universe was jealous of me? How was that possible? Natalie had one of the most coveted PR jobs in the city and men routinely fell at her feet. Her designer wardrobe lacked for nothing and most important of all, she had a head of hair that rivaled no one. Her long, thick, wavy, dark chestnut brown hair was so goddamn glorious she could wash it, wrap it wet in a towel and go to bed without drying it. In the morning, she'd shake her hair out and look like a model in a shampoo commercial. The woman didn't use a blow dryer ever because her hair dried perfectly on its own. What normal person's hair does that? I had to

150

juggle multiple tools and hair products in order to style my limp strawberry blonde hair. Even then, I achieved spotty, often unsuccessful results. All Natalie had to do was bend over, flip her hair back, run her manicured fingers through it and voila! She was jealous of me? Don't get me started.

"Give me a break," I said staring at her. "You're the one with the incredible life. You'll find the right person. Remember, you went out with Teddy before I did. I was lucky I got your leftovers."

"The timing wasn't right for Teddy and me. I had too much going on back then."

"Maybe you should slow down and be more selective about who you go out with," I said. "Stop jumping from one guy to the next or you might not see the right person when he's standing in front of you."

Natalie stopped moaning and looked at me with a flicker of awareness in her eyes.

"Jills, what if I already met the right person and we missed each other?" she said. "What if I didn't give that person a chance?"

"I'm sure that didn't happen," I said reassuringly, wondering if there was some truth to it. She did go out with a lot of men and became bored with each relationship within a short period of time, sometimes days — sometimes hours. But if she hadn't dumped Teddy so publicly and quickly, he and I would have never gotten together. Given that, I guess I should be grateful for her erratic and fickle ways.

"Do you know how lucky you are?" she said pouring herself more wine. "You've found what we're all looking for — a home, a partner and a little money in the bank."

"Home and partner, yes, but not much money in the bank," I said. "Remember all those 'sure thing' real estate investments Teddy and I got involved in over the last few years?"

Natalie nodded.

I filled her in on some of our "financial mishaps" that had left us with a fair amount of debt. Soon, she changed the subject and we spent the next two hours dissecting Natalie's disappointing romantic entanglements. Eventually, even she grew bored with the boyfriend topic and shifted gears once again. "So, how's everything going with your new book?"

"I wanted to talk to you about that. Things with my book are moving along," I said, "but more strange things happened this past week."

Sensing something juicy, Natalie's eyes lit up and she leaned in closer. "Really? Like what?"

"Remember that radiologist I met online a million years ago, before Teddy?"

"The doctor who liked you to wear high heels in bed?" said Natalie. "The one who lived with his mother?"

I nodded. "Out of the blue, he messaged me on Facebook last week."

Natalie's mouth dropped open. "Why didn't you tell me?"

"I tried to. You were 'busy'," I said making air quotes, feeling a little smug.

"I would have made the time if I knew it was something that critical," said Natalie. "You know I'm there for you night or day."

"Anyway, he sent me a message. We had this little private texting thing going back and forth — you know, kind of joking around about old times. I found out he's married and has a kid. I told him I was married, too. Then he said he saw my pictures on Instagram and Facebook and that 'time had been extremely kind to me' and that I 'looked fantastic'."

"Here we go. They're all the same."

"Then he said, it would be great to reconnect and would I like to meet up in the city for a drink or two."

"No," said Natalie finishing her glass of wine and reaching for the open bottle.

"That's when the wheel came off the cart for me. I wondered if Mrs Radiologist knew Dr Radiologist was inviting old girlfriends out for drinks. I responded with 'you always were a total dirt bag which is why I ended it with you. I'm getting off this train now'. Then, I blocked him permanently."

"This is what I'm talking about," said Natalie. "Another pathetic cheating loser."

"A couple of days later, I started getting weird messages through my author website saying things like 'I'm your biggest fan' and 'can't you give me a hint about your next book. I'm dying to know what it's about'. The messages kept coming. There were probably twenty in total."

"Who needs fans like that? You think it was the radiologist?"

"I don't know," I said, the wine suddenly hitting me. "I could handle that. But what if it wasn't him? What if it was the same person who left that religious pamphlet on my front door? Remember, I told you about that."

Natalie nodded.

"Whoever left that yellow pamphlet knows where I live."

"It sounds sketchy. You need to be careful and make sure you lock your doors. Up here in Connecticut, your nearest neighbor is so far away they won't hear you if you scream. That's why I like living in New York. If I sneeze, my neighbors know it."

Natalie's comment about my neighbors not hearing me scream wasn't the least bit comforting. We had already knocked off several bottles of wine. I was about to respond to her comment when we heard the motor of the garage door opening below us. Teddy was home.

Minutes later, he joined us. I was pretty buzzed but didn't protest when he poured us all another glass of wine. More alcohol was probably the last thing I needed that night, but I was already too far gone to make a better, more adult decision. I greedily took the full glass and sat back on the couch. I was a little tipsy and with my two favorite people in the world. Everything felt right with the world, until it didn't.

Chapter 29

The next thing I remembered was waking up the following morning in my bed with a wicked hangover. Teddy was already up and I smelled coffee brewing downstairs. I looked over at the clock. It was nearly 10.45 a.m. I never slept that late, not ever. In serious pain, I chastised myself for drinking so much with Natalie — again. I shouldn't have tried to keep up with her. Talk about a hollow leg, she's got a hollow body. She barely weighs a hundred pounds. And still, I've seen her do shots for hours and it never seems to affect her.

I dragged myself out of bed and staggered into the bathroom. My reflection in the mirror caused me to gasp. To say I looked like shit was an understatement. I splashed cold water on my face, brushed my teeth, popped two Tylenol into my mouth and headed slowly down the stairs holding the handrail because my legs felt a little wobbly. It wasn't my proudest moment.

"Look who's up?" said Natalie looking perky and fresh sitting at the kitchen counter. Her eyes moved to her phone.

"How are you feeling?" said my husband as he flipped a mushroom omelet in a pan.

"Fine." I said, pouring myself a coffee.

"You look a little pale," said Teddy dishing the eggs out onto three plates and handing one to me. "Eat this. You'll feel better."

I sat down and put a forkful of omelet into my mouth. What that man could do with a simple egg was incredible. It was rich and salty and exactly what I needed. I looked over at Natalie still glued to her phone. "How are you feeling?" I said as I took another bite.

"Me? Totally fine," she said looking up at me. "God, you look white, Jills. Do you remember Teddy and I walking you up the stairs to bed last night?"

I shook my head as I sat on my kitchen stool of shame. "This only happens when *you* come up for a weekend," I said trying unsuccessfully to shift the blame for drinking too much onto my best friend.

Natalie rolled her eyes. "I didn't pour the wine down your throat, Jills."

"Did I say anything stupid?" I said. "Anything I should regret?"

"You were fine," said Teddy chuckling while placing a piece of buttered toast on my plate. "I wanted to run an idea by both of you. You know my food empire dream, right? My first step, the new restaurant is already in play. But that's only the start. I want to go bigger."

Teddy stepped away from the stove to take center stage in the middle of the kitchen. I sat back, I could tell he was going to go on for a while. "I'm thinking," he continued, "T. Samuels food trucks all over the country. Maybe I'll use my real family name and call it 'Samaras the Greek'. I'd franchise them and at the same time they'd provide exposure for the T. Samuels brand. I've been looking into it and found a manufacturer and a vendor who can do the job."

"That's a great idea, Teddy," said Natalie before I had a chance to weigh in. "Food trucks are so hot right now, they're everywhere. It's the future."

I didn't think it was a bad idea except for the fact that it would require a lot of money upfront. We were already behind the eight ball trying to fund his new restaurant and now he wanted to add food trucks? My head started to throb again.

"I was thinking Greek street food. That's what everyone wants these days," said my husband, his eyes on fire. "I'd put together an edited menu of six to ten items and I'd supply my franchisees with product and preparation technique. One day there could be hundreds of T. Samuels trucks on the road. What do you think?"

I didn't want to be a buzz kill after Natalie had been so positive. But it was easy for her to be supportive, she didn't have to come up with the money. "I think it's a great idea, but don't you have enough on your plate right now?" I said. "You're already working eighty hours a week."

"To the victor go the spoils," said Teddy with a grin. "If I want to go global, I've got to have a global vision."

I smiled and nodded at him thinking he was overreaching but said nothing negative. He had neither the bandwidth nor the finances to start a food truck business. I kept my mouth shut and instead picked up my phone to check my email.

Combing through tons of spam, I spotted a message in my inbox that had been generated from my author website. I didn't get too many of those. It turned out to be from JollyRoger44 — again. Like all his/her other emails, it was brief.

Who dies in your next book, Jillian Samuels? Everyone's DYING to know.

I gasped. Teddy and Natalie both looked at me.

"What's wrong?" said my husband.

"I got another email from JollyRoger44," I said handing my phone to him. He shook his head as he read and passed it to Natalie.

"This is so messed up," I said. "If JollyRoger44 is behind all the copycat stuff, what does he want? I'm walking on eggshells waiting for something terrible to happen."

"Maybe it's just a friend playing a sick joke?" said Natalie.

"No way. My friends know what I've been going through," I said wringing my hands. "No one would do something like that. Besides, any semblance to a joke ended right after that dead man turned up covered in paint. I've got a freakin' pirate stalking me."

Chapter 30

I tried to get my head back into the recruiting game. We still had bills to pay despite the many distractions. Dwelling on my books and the surrounding drama only made my anxiety flare up. My job placements had dwindled to almost nothing and my supervisor Audrey had been on my back. The truth was that I was so preoccupied with my books, the crimes, the police and all the other crazy stuff that I had almost no ability to focus on anything else.

I had just finished a Zoom interview with a very attractive woman with an Ivy League degree — Ka-Ching. Combing through my job assignments, I noticed two of my clients were looking for salespeople with Ms Ivy League's qualifications. I wrote a kick-ass introduction outlining the woman's accomplishments, attached her resume and crossed my fingers. For the first time in weeks I stayed focused on my work. I had a totally normal morning — until my phone rang.

"How's it going, Jillian?" said Matthew. "Less than a year to go now. Getting excited?"

I groaned inside my head. My once productive morning was about to be hijacked. Of course I was excited, but there were so many other emotions I was also feeling.

"Who wouldn't be?" I said. "Can't wait. Tick-tock."

"We're still getting occasional pickup from all those copycat incidents but I'll be honest, it's fading. Where's a fresh dead body when you need one, right?" said Matthew who then laughed at his own joke. My agent was once again proving to be a rather cool customer with only one agenda: book sales. "You know how the news cycles run, hot one day, cold the next. Keep posting stuff on social media."

"I don't know what to post anymore. I'm completely tapped out of ideas."

"Just tweet something like, 'so creepy when the stories in my books came true. I feel like I'm being stalked'. *#realitybites #stalker #thriller #terrified*," said Matthew.

"I'm not going to do that. Publicly posting about having a stalker is like asking someone to stalk you. Besides, I may already have one." That's when I told him about JollyRoger44. You would have thought I'd handed him a winning lottery ticket.

"I love it. You've been holding out on me, Jillian. JollyRoger44 is fantastic. I mean, not good for you, but great for feeding the Twitter beast. Use it. You obviously have a rabid fan. You know what we call that? PR platinum. I like the pirate angle, too. You should post a bunch of pirate memes or some pictures of parrots. Arrgh!"

My front doorbell rang and I peered out of my upstairs window. A car I didn't recognize was in my driveway. "Matthew, I've got to go, someone's at my door."

"Keep the momentum going," he said. "We've all got a lot riding on you. None of us can afford to have a lackluster launch. It would be publishing suicide."

After several sharp knocks, I ran down the stairs and opened the front door. Detectives Marino and Brodsky were standing on my steps "Can we come in, Ms Samuels?" said the Russian. "There's something we need to go over with you."

I nodded and led them into the living room.

"A couple of maintenance men were cleaning up the grounds at the cemetery in North Medford. They found a large knife sticking out of a lily plant sitting on the grave of a Walter S. Loomis."

"A knife?" I said.

"Mr Loomis died in 1957. The knife was stuck through a laminated card that said, 'You're Next'. Any idea who might have put the knife and note there?"

"Why would I know that?" I said squinting at him.

"We've gone through all of your books," said Marino. "This knife in the cemetery thing appears to be right out of your third book *Whispers from the Grave*. At this point, a pretty strong pattern has been established connecting you to a whole lot of crimes and it's giving us some concern."

I didn't like the direction the conversation was going and felt I needed backup. I told them I had to cancel a conference call that was about to start which wasn't true. I asked them to wait in the living room while I ducked out the back door and called Teddy.

By some miracle, my husband answered. I started speaking in rapid fire. "Teddy, those two detectives are here again. They found a lily plant and a dagger in a grave at the cemetery in North Medford. There was a laminated card with it and they think I had something to do with it."

"Slow down. A dagger in a grave? This is getting way out of control," said Teddy. "What the hell is happening?"

"Can you please come home now?" I whispered. "Please."

"I can't. We have a huge corporate party here tonight. I won't get home before eleven thirty, maybe even later."

"But . . ."

"I've got to go. I promise, I'll be home as soon as I can," he said. "And Jills, make sure you lock all the doors and windows. You'll be all right. Love you."

"I love you," I said.

Trying to maintain a semblance of composure, I went back into the living room and sat down. The two cops stared at me but said nothing. Clearly, they were waiting for me to speak.

"Do you think someone is stalking me?" I said in a half-whisper.

"It's hard to say, but something's going on," said Brodsky. "I think you need to take this whole thing more seriously. The fact is, we're not sure where this is headed or if and when it will stop. Someone has zoned in on you and they're not letting go."

"With the recent developments," said Marino, "there's no doubt the common denominator is you. All the crimes loop back to your books."

The detectives shared the details of the new graveyard vandalism case with me. When they were through, they asked me the question I'd been expecting: did I have any connection to Walter S. Loomis, the dead man in the marked grave?

"I've never heard of Loomis. But I agree with you, whoever's doing this is using my three books as a blueprint for their sick agenda," I said as I paced around my living room like a caged cat. "If you've read my books then you know what comes next. A descendant of Walter Loomis is in grave danger. I would suggest you find out if Mr Loomis has any children or grandchildren. It could be anyone . . . a niece, a nephew or even distant cousin. His family needs to be warned."

"I haven't finished reading *Whispers from the Grave* yet," said Marino writing something in his notebook. "Why does your killer do it? And, what happens at the end of the book?"

"All the murders in that book are completely random. The killer sticks a knife into an unknown grave and weeks or sometimes even months later, a grandchild or some far-flung relative of that person is murdered," I said. "Sometimes the grave is as much as a hundred years old and the murder victim many generations removed. The challenge for the police in my novel was that there were so many potential victims to vet and warn. The cops didn't know where to start. If Walter Loomis died in 1957, unless he was an only child and a monk, there could be hundreds of descendants, all of whom are possible targets."

Brodsky looked at his partner and tipped his head toward the door. "Sounds like we're going to be busy."

"If you think of anything else, give us a call," said Marino as he and his partner stepped out the door and onto the front walk. "And Ms Samuels, make sure you take your own security seriously. We don't know how far this person intends to go. Lock your doors when we leave. Better safe than sorry."

As he opened his car door, Brodsky suddenly turned around and looked at me. "I don't think we ever asked you this before. Are there any other books that we don't know about?"

"I've only self-published three."

Brodsky let out a breath. "That's a relief," he said.

"But, I do have a new thriller that will be published by Linton Books coming out the last week of February next year."

"What's it called?" said Brodsky.

"*The Soul Collector.*"

"What's that one about?" he said giving his partner a weary sideways glance.

"It's the story about a serial killer who opportunistically murders people in different creative ways," I said. "He pushes people from high places, strangles, stabs, hits and runs, whatever presents itself."

"A regular jack of all trades," said Marino running his hands through his hair.

"I guess you could say that," I said.

"But your new book isn't out yet. No one's seen it, right?" said Brodsky. "Whoever's behind all these crimes wouldn't have been able to read that one to get any ideas. How many people know what your new book is about?"

"Loads of people could have seen it. Possibly hundreds," I said. "Before I landed my agent, I sent synopses and copies to dozens of literary agencies. When Sanford Weston Literary took me on, a bunch of people from their agency read it and passed it around to who knows how many. Then my agent shopped it to tons of publishers who also would have read it. I have no idea how many people have actually seen it. Once my new publisher acquired *The Soul Collector*, everyone from editors to publicity to the art department has had access to it."

Brodsky nodded. "Lock your doors. I have a feeling things are heating up. You don't want to be collateral damage."

Chapter 31

As soon as the detectives pulled out of my driveway, I did exactly as they and my husband had instructed. I locked all the doors and windows in the house. I even engaged the deadbolt on my front and back doors, something I never ever did during the day. We only deadbolted when we went to bed at night.

With my house locked up tighter than a bank vault, I went back to my desk and powered through my outstanding job requisitions for a couple of hours to take my mind off the situation. Despite my determination to stay focused, I found myself wondering if the discovery of the dagger at the gravesite would have any impact on my future book sales. It dawned on me that the only way it would, is if the public at large found out about it. A knife found on a sixty-year-old grave wasn't exactly newsworthy. The only way anyone would learn about it was if I told them. So, I posted a few provocative comments about the grave on Twitter, Facebook and a few other assorted places. Then, I posted a picture of a dagger on Instagram. Don't judge, free publicity is free publicity. And, as my agent often said, "pure gold".

Over at the *Connecticut Advocate* offices, Tommy Devlin was still looking into "my case" and called me. After a few salutations, he shared his observations and lingering questions — like before all the shit started happening, how my thrillers had been relegated to the Amazon book dungeon. Which to be fair, was kind of true. Before the drone explosions started, my books ranked well over four million, which in book speak is really bad — terrible actually. But, after the crimes began, when people started buying copies of my old books, my book ranking jumped into the Amazon top five thousand. Devlin thought the movement of my older books was odd and a little suspicious. Although he repeatedly said he didn't think I had anything to do with it. He said the whole thing bugged him. After so many months of digging, the ace reporter couldn't get a handle on why any of it was happening or who was behind it. He'd even read all three of my thrillers to gain better insight and came to the same conclusion as the cops. Someone was carefully recreating the scenes from my books for some unknown reason. Whoever was behind it was extremely precise and stayed true to my book's exact narrative. I agreed with Devlin but pointed out he was missing the why?

"For what reason would someone do this?" I said. "What would their motive be? Who benefits?" As a thriller writer, those are the questions I would ask — I'm just sayin'."

After we hung up, I thought about it. There was one person who benefited mightily from all of it — Devlin. He had covered the story from the beginning and secured front page headlines in his newspaper and website, not to mention syndication. Things had been going great for him when he was covering the Anabel Ford disappearance. With no new developments in the Ford story, he was back writing copy about missing dogs and lost car keys. Then the drone fires started, he was off the races again. Between my copycat story and the Anabel Ford disappearance, Devlin had made quite a name for himself in Connecticut. My hunch was he wanted to keep it that way.

Through the Medford grapevine, I had heard Devlin also desperately wanted back into cable news. Word on the street was that he had been regularly communicating with old colleagues at CNN. What can I say? Medford's a small town, people talk, others listen. I'm a listener. The way I heard it was, Devlin was angling to cover the whole copycat story for CNN — but as a CNN New York Metro reporter and eventually an anchor.

During our phone conversation, Devlin had asked me if I'd sit down for a longer exclusive interview. I was about to say no when I heard Matthew and Natalie's voices reverberating in my head — "bad publicity is better than no publicity". So, I agreed to the interview.

Later that afternoon, the reporter rang my bell. I still didn't fully trust him. Something about him was off-putting but I couldn't put my finger on it. At our first meeting at the coffee shop, he came off as confident but that day at my house, I detected smugness rather than confidence. I knew his type. He was the person who'd put himself first in any situation including marriage, which is probably why he didn't have one. I wasn't convinced he'd listen to what I had to say or tell a fair story. He was obviously looking for a sensational headline to attach his name to. I was merely a stepping stone toward his greater career goals. I reminded myself of that when during the interview he acted like he really cared about me and my family. Devlin only cared about Devlin and getting his story. I kept that front and center and didn't let my guard down for a second.

Despite my misgivings, I let him into my home and into my living room. Before I had taken my seat, the man with the perfect fake teeth started firing questions at me. Cornered with no way out and not trusting him in the least, I answered each one with as little detail as possible. I didn't want anything to come back and bite me later. My sense was, he would twist any story to make it a headline and elevate himself regardless of who got hurt. Devlin wore his ambition on his sleeve illuminated by neon lights that said, *I LOVE ME*.

"Ever cover a story like this before?" I said, making small talk, hoping our interview wouldn't take long.

"Nope. This one's as bizarre as it gets. The good news, it's crazy enough to sell lots of newspapers and that's all the owners of the *CT Advocate* care about. Interested consumers mean more advertising dollars in the corporate piggy bank. This copycat story has all the makings for a documentary series if you ask me. CNN does them all the time. You should think about it."

Ahh. The plot thickened. That's what he was after. He didn't want to just cover the story. He was using me and the whole case for his grand re-entrance back into CNN with a big documentary deal. Clearly, the man with the perfect hair had a lot riding on the outcome of the investigation and much to gain. I wondered if the police had taken a serious look at him as a possible suspect. I made a mental note to mention it to Brodsky and Marino the next time I heard from them.

From the time the incidents started, I had been trying to maintain a low profile. It was Devlin who was constantly dragging me into the limelight. As I sat there, he peppered me with questions and I responded with one-word answers.

"Is something wrong?" he said glaring at me after my ninth monosyllabic response.

"I'm concerned if your paper runs a series about the killer, it will only add fuel to the fire." I said. "Did it ever occur to you that your reporting could trigger a new crime?"

"On the contrary," he said with measured sincerity. "This story has been running on social media without any help from me. My organization shining a light on it might actually lead to catching the person or people responsible. Trust me, someone out there knows something."

I stared at him. He was so transparent. He didn't care if his interview with me encouraged additional crimes or put Teddy and me in danger. He was only after his story and where that would take him. In fact, he probably hoped we were in danger — bigger headlines for him. That way, he'd finally score his prime time anchor job at CNN. Then it occurred to me, was I any better than Devlin what with all my postings on Twitter? Was I as big an opportunist as the reporter?

"Since we last spoke, do you have any new theories on who might be behind the crimes?" said Devlin.

I shook my head and rolled my eyes. In my opinion, that was an amateur question for a supposedly experienced journalist. Obviously, if I knew who did it, I would have already told the cops. I wouldn't wait around for a second rate reporter to ask me the million dollar question to jar my memory.

"Nothing comes to mind?" he said again as if a little prod from him might unleash a torrent of critical information.

"Like I've said from day one, I have no idea. This all came out of nowhere."

"Can we go over the timeline again of when the events from your books started happening. Maybe you've missed a connection to other things in your life that you haven't thought of?"

Despite the fact that I was pretty sure I had already told him everything, I replayed the timeline of my book publishing career up and until the whole mess started.

"We're in agreement. The sales of your books grew substantially after the fires started," said Devlin.

I let out an aggravated sigh. "Look, we've been over this. A bunch of obsessive people on Twitter with nothing better to do started posting conspiracy theories and my books started selling. It's that simple and that's all I know."

"How did you feel about that?"

Who the hell did he think he was, a freakin' therapist?

"How would you feel?" I said. "Honestly, at first, I was thrilled my books were selling, who wouldn't be? On the other hand, someone was committing crimes and using my books as their blueprint. Obviously, that was disturbing. Those are normal reactions, wouldn't you say?"

Devlin nodded as he took notes.

"At first," I said, "the police thought someone set the explosions and fires for financial gain, maybe insurance money or something like that. Another theory was that the culprit hoped to throw the investigation off track by copying things in my books in an attempt to send the police in the wrong direction. We all wondered if it was to hide another crime."

"I see. So, the intended crime might not have happened yet? Clever. If that's true, it's a very long game they're playing."

"The police don't tell me everything, but I believe they're also looking at the owners of the three properties that caught fire. As far as I know, nothing unusual has turned up yet."

"Interesting," said Devlin scratching the back of his neck. "Arson to get a big payout makes sense. But, when you add in the two victims painted silver, one of whom is dead and now the knife at the grave, it's not so straightforward. Also, did you ever wonder why all the crimes happen in the vicinity of you, the woman who wrote the books? Why not in Chicago or Miami?"

"I have no idea," I said tired of his questions.

"We've got one dead body and the potential threat of another based on the note and knife at the graveyard. This perpetrator has moved pretty far afield from setting small utility sheds on fire, wouldn't you say?"

Oh, my God. Yes, Devlin, I *would* say that. I would also say the whole thing is fucked up. Instead, I only nodded and very obviously checked the time on my phone. He ignored my clear signal to wrap it up which pissed me off. "I've got a few more questions for you," he said.

Letting out a loud exasperated breath, I sat back sullenly on the couch. I had agreed to talk to him and was stuck. I reminded myself that if this interview ginned up some publicity for my book and kept my agent and publisher happy, it would all be worth it.

"You have another book coming out," said Devlin looking at his notes.

"That's correct."

"You're not self-publishing the new one like you did with the others?"

"No," I said smiling for the first time since we started. "*The Soul Collector* is being published by Linton Books, a very reputable independent publisher."

"I've heard of them. Congratulations. That's a big step up for you. Three books that didn't sell and then you get an agent and a big book deal. Nice."

"I was very lucky," I said wondering where he was headed with that last loaded comment. Was he insinuating I might have had something to do with the whole mess? He didn't know the answer, so he was pointing fingers at anyone and anything. I wondered if he should be pointing at himself.

"Let me ask you something," said Devlin. "When did you get your book deal with Linton Books? Was it before or after the first drone explosion?"

What was he implying? His questions annoyed me but I stayed cool even though I wanted him out of my house. Channeling my inner calm, I shrugged it off and tried to reconstruct the exact timeline and answer his rude question. "I believe two of the fires happened *while* I was looking for an agent. I think I remember telling Matthew about the drones shortly after we met. But I'm sure the fires occurred before I had a deal with Linton Books."

"I see," said Devlin still taking copious notes which irritated me further. "How about the unconscious man, Argos, the one painted silver? Did he turn up before or after you got your agent?"

"I believe Mr Argos was discovered *after* I had signed with Sanford Weston Literary."

Weary of the inquisition, I made a firm comment about needing to get back to work. He finally took my cue and stood up.

"You've certainly given me some food for thought. I still have a lot of work to do on this story," he said. "Would you mind checking the exact timing of your book deal with Linton as it relates to the murder victim and get back to me?"

I nodded and rolled my eyes as he turned and walked toward the door.

"Got any more theories?" I said as he stepped outside onto the front walk.

"I'm still in the fishing mode. I've been doing this a long time. It's always a convoluted mess in the beginning. Eventually, the pieces start to come together. Most of the time, it boils down to one thing. 'Follow the money'."

With that last provocative comment Devlin abruptly turned and walked to his car. I closed the front door and locked it. It was the middle of Teddy's work day, and I wasn't supposed to call him unless it was an absolute emergency, but I did anyway. He didn't pick up so I texted him and waited a few minutes. All I got was an automated 'can I call you later?' text. I hate those.

I thought about Devlin's last question: when the second victim was found dead. I looked at my calendar. That man was definitely discovered *after* I signed with Matthew. Was that a weird coincidence or a harbinger of something more sinister?

I opened the practically empty fridge to see what I could cobble together for dinner that night. How ironic, I was married to a chef and there was nothing to eat in our house besides cereal, pesto and capers. Hungry, with no other options, I drove to the Medford Town Market to pick up something for dinner.

While stopped at a red light, a green SUV sped through the intersection. It looked just like the car I'd seen following me before. When my light changed, I made a hard left, and eventually caught up to the SUV but stayed behind at a safe distance. I didn't know what I was dealing with.

I tailed the car for a few miles until it turned into a big strip mall parking lot and pulled into a space. I parked in a spot two rows over, turned off my engine and ducked down in my seat. The driver's side door opened slowly and a man got out. His back was to me and he was wearing a long-sleeved black shirt.

Scrunched down low in the driver's seat, I peeked up a few times trying not to be seen. The man in the SUV walked around to the rear of his car, opened the lift and pulled out a duffel bag. When he turned around I gasped. Holy shit!

It was freakin' Ned LaGrange and he had a white skull and crossbones splashed across the front of his shirt. Was my mailman JollyRoger44?

He locked his car, swung his bag over his shoulder and walked directly into LA Fitness. Before I pulled out of the lot, I drove past his car and took a picture of his license plate. Get this — he had a vanity plate that said *UR MYN*.

Chapter 32

A little after ten thirty that night, Teddy was in our kitchen making himself a sandwich. When I went downstairs and saw what he was doing, I laughed to myself. My very important, sought-after New York chef husband was making himself a peanut butter and jelly sandwich with a glass of milk for dinner.

"What?" he said smiling as he looked up at me and bit into his PB and J.

"You're very adorable, you know that?" I said as he bit into his culinary masterpiece.

We made small talk for a few minutes. Teddy didn't like to be ambushed when he got home from work. So, after what I considered an acceptable period of chit-chat time, I launched into the details of my meeting with Devlin. When I finished, I waited for my husband's response.

"What do you think he meant about 'following the money'?" I said.

"I don't know. It's just an old catch phrase?" said Teddy through his last mouthful of food. "You've heard it before, follow the money."

"What money?"

"I guess the reporter was trying to figure out who would benefit most from your thrillers going viral," he said while pouring himself another glass of milk.

"But, my books didn't go viral. The explosions and fires only made a tiny ripple on Twitter. I'd hardly call that viral."

"You sold more books, didn't you?"

"Not enough to make it worth burning down three buildings."

The two of us kicked the can down the road a little further, but gained no more clarity. With nothing more to discuss, Teddy changed the subject.

"This afternoon, I met with the new restaurant investors and the entire marketing team behind T. Samuels. It's really happening, Jills. If things go the way they hope, they're going to open a second and a third T. Samuels in Las Vegas and Miami within the next three years. After that, there would be six or seven more in other major metros — it's the beginning of the empire."

It sure sounded like plans for the opening of T. Samuels were moving at a fast pace. The restaurant's space design had been approved and the remodeling work had already begun. I asked Teddy when I could see it. After comparing calendars, he invited me to meet him in the city the following weekend to have a look.

"Wait until you see the place. Our designer is a creative genius. He's doing some unbelievable things with the space. T. Samuels will be completely different from other restaurants. We're going for casual chic modern, that's what people want these days — nothing too pretentious or formal. Customers want a relaxed dining experience but they also want something unique and special. Our designer calls our vibe Caz-Chic, short for Casual Chic."

"Caz-Chic? Is that a thing?"

"I have no idea, but it is now," said Teddy all smiles. "On another note, their business manager asked me how much I planned to invest. I've been looking all over for places to borrow money where interest payments won't kill us. I haven't found any good options yet. We can't screw this one up. This is our big chance. But I'm still not sure how we're going to pull the money part off."

"What about taking out another mortgage on our house?"

Teddy shook his head and reminded me we didn't have any equity left in our home. I remembered then that we had borrowed against the house a few years earlier when he got an insider's tip on a hot stock. The stock didn't pan out and we lost a ton. I had forgotten about that. We also took a hundred thousand out of our house to invest in a digital marketing company. It ended up being a house of cards and we wound up selling our shares at a loss. We were out seventy-five thousand dollars on that one. It had looked like a sure thing and I didn't blame him for losing the money. At the time, I thought buying that stock had been a great idea, too.

"I need at least five hundred thousand dollars to invest in T. Samuels," he said, his brow furrowed.

"Does it have to be so much? Couldn't you invest a hundred thousand? That would still be a big investment."

"Putting *only* a hundred thousand into a restaurant with my name on it is hardly worth it."

"But it's something. If you think about it . . ."

Teddy's phone rang and he walked out of the room to talk to one of the investors. I was about to explain my rationale for a lower dollar investment and put forth another suggestion but never got the chance.

I went upstairs to soak in my tub using my favorite orange blossom bath balm. Before I got in to the warm soapy water, I lit the matching orange blossom scented candles. The smell reminded me of a trip my mother, sister and I had taken to Florida when I was a kid. I hadn't been there in years. Given the financial situation Teddy had just outlined, it didn't look like we were going on any vacations in the near future. If I wanted to smell orange blossoms, a trip to Florida was not in the cards. I'd have to make do with candles and bath balm.

Dimming the lights in the bathroom, I climbed into the big oval soaker tub and tried to dream up a way to get the money for my husband. I was in charge of my mother's finances. She still had some money left, but it was all earmarked for the assisted living facility she lived in. I couldn't touch that. I'd invested her money in the stock market and had been getting decent returns. But, if the market took a dive, I was screwed. If Mom's money ran out, she'd have to come live with us. Given our jobs and the possibility of children within the next couple of years, neither Teddy nor I were prepared for that.

I tried to relax in the citrusy-sweet warm bath water, and was soon in my happy place fantasizing about my future publication day. Matthew had said that *The Soul Collector* had "bestseller written all over it". A bestseller would solve everything. We'd have enough money to take care of my mother and invest in Teddy's restaurant. A runaway book hit would change everything. Sure we wouldn't get the money he needed for a while, but if we knew it was coming, it would be the solution to all of our problems. I said a little prayer right there in the tub and submerged my head under the water believing it would somehow seal the deal.

The next morning over breakfast, while Teddy played around with his phone, I floated the idea of using the profits from my future book to invest in the new restaurant.

"What kind of money are we talking about?" he said putting his phone down suddenly interested.

"You know I got that thirty-thousand-dollar advance that I put in the bank. Matthew thought I might earn another two hundred thousand if he can make the foreign rights deals happen. He told me one of the other agents got thirty-eight translation deals for one of their clients. He thinks he can do the same with mine. But we won't know until the book comes out."

Teddy leaned forward. "Another two hundred thousand? You never told me that."

"I'm pretty sure I did. You've been so preoccupied."

"Two hundred K would be amazing. That would make all the difference."

"Matthew says it's all about the buzz. It's not the half a million you wanted, but it's still a lot. It would give us enough money for a decent stake in the new place."

I saw the wheels turning in Teddy's head. I had struck a chord. Suddenly, my little writing hobby had taken on new meaning for him.

"In that case, what can we do to help your book take off?" he said. "We need something really big and headline grabbing."

I rattled off what little I knew about book marketing. My agent and publisher had both said that book promotions were often a crapshoot. Even people who had been in the publishing business their entire careers couldn't definitively say why one horse pulled ahead of another.

"Look what happened with my first few books. I self-published them and no one read them. After a little chatter on social media about those stupid fires and suddenly my thrillers start to move. Maybe we need to create some more noise around *The Soul Collector*, something that will get people talking, posting and tweeting. When you start trending, sales happen."

"How do we get you and your book to 'start trending'?" he said, furrowing his brow again.

I searched the recesses of my brain for an answer and then it came to me. "It's so obvious. We already have our own secret weapon — Natalie. The woman is a master of public relations. If anyone knows how to create excitement around a brand, she does."

We called Natalie and put her on speaker.

"I'll do what I can," she said after I explained our problem. Within seconds she shifted into her trademark PR high gear. "We need to come up with a scathingly clever angle to break through all the extraneous clutter and noise. At the same time, we don't want to step on the toes of your publisher who may have their own publicity plan in the works. We've got to work in tandem with them, that's critical."

When we finished the call, Teddy and I smiled at each other. When it came to publicity, Natalie Bloom was a heat-seeking missile. If she was on the mission, my book's success and the investment money were practically in the bag. If things went as planned, Teddy would soon be able to lay the first brick of his "restaurant empire".

Chapter 33

A few weeks later on a Friday afternoon, I got a call from Brodsky and Marino. They had some questions and wanted to talk to Teddy and me down at the police station.

"It won't take long, Ms Samuels," said Brodsky over the phone, his Russian accent fully engaged, "we just need to go over a few details. It's important."

"I've already told you everything I know."

"We'll talk more when you get here. We've got some issues we need you and your husband to clear up."

I hate it when people are so obtuse. Since Teddy was off the following Monday, I told Brodsky we'd see him then. First thing Monday morning we arrived at the Medford police station and were brought into a conference room by the front desk officer.

Lost in our own thoughts while we waited for the detectives, I noticed Teddy looking at his watch seven or eight times and emitting a few sighs.

"We've been waiting for almost fifteen minutes," he said. "This is my only day off in weeks and I'm spending it at the police station. What do they want to talk to us about anyway?"

"They didn't say."

As if on cue, the door of the room flew open and the two detectives marched in. After exchanging greetings, the cops got down to business. "As you know, we're trying to find out who's behind the random crimes that appear to be connected to your books," said Brodsky. "The first few fires were peculiar but no one got hurt. Then Argos, the first man painted silver turned up. When at first it appeared he may have fallen and hit his head, we were cautiously optimistic. However, when the second silver-painted victim turned up dead from clear blunt force trauma, this became a homicide investigation. That's serious."

"We've added people to our investigative team and would like to get a list of all of your contacts," said Detective Marino picking at a white stain on the lapel of his blue sports jacket. "I'm talkin' about old friends, romantic relationships, business colleagues, groups or clubs you do or did belong to, and any religious affiliations."

As the two lawmen talked, I took in their words and body language as only a thriller writer would. That's what writers do. Marino and Brodsky couldn't have been more different. When the Russian talked, it felt like he was about to toss you into a gulag. I envisioned him spending his evenings doing shots of vodka while sipping borscht. Truthfully, I found him a little scary. Marino on the other hand was a stereotypical "New Yawker" type Italian cop: friendly, sloppy and seemingly a nice guy.

"I take some local exercise classes — yoga, Pilates and swim at the Y. I'm also a member of several writing groups, although I haven't been to any of those recently," I said keeping my eyes on Marino because Brodsky made me nervous. From Teddy's body language, I thought the Russian put him on edge, too.

"You think there could have been some professional jealousy with someone in one of your writing groups?" said Marino.

I shook my head. "I doubt it. Most of the people in the groups weren't published authors. Many were still working on their first manuscripts. Some only had an idea for a book. Everyone was at different stages. Although, now that I think about it, I guess I was one of the furthest along in my writing."

"Someone could have been envious of that. Ever have any arguments or unpleasant exchanges at these groups?" said Marino.

"You get all kinds. Occasionally, there were disagreements but none with me that I recall. Most people were friendly, collegial and supportive. I can't believe it was anyone from those groups." I said. "They're a pretty tame bunch."

"Someone blew up several buildings, spray-painted two men, possibly assaulted one and killed the other," said Brodsky. "That same person has also threatened the descendants of a man who died in 1957. We've got to find out who that person is before something else happens and someone else gets hurt."

When he put it that way, I saw his point.

"We're going to investigate everyone you've been in contact with over the past ten years," said Marino, "and we need you to provide names." I nodded and started writing.

"Let me be very clear, we're way past thinking these acts were random," said Brodsky. "Someone has a master plan they're executing. We believe the person behind these crimes is smart, organized and on a mission. What that mission is, we don't know yet. But, we will find out."

While I wrote down all the names and phone numbers I could think of, the detectives pummeled Teddy with questions about his employees and customers and if there had been any workplace issues or problems with staff or diners. Teddy said "no" to everything. Then, they gave him some paper to write down his contacts.

"These are all the authors' names I can think of," I said handing Brodsky the yellow legal pad with my list. "Half of the people are women in their seventies. I think you're barking up the wrong tree."

"I like to bark," said Brodsky taking the list from my hand.

"What about your other activities?" said Marino looking at me. "Can you think of anyone who ever bothered you or made you feel uncomfortable?"

I thought for a moment. "There was a male Pilates instructor who was a bit too handsy."

Teddy shot me a look. I had never mentioned it to him because it was nothing. But I could tell from my husband's expression, it was going to become something after we left the police station. "He's gone now, anyway," I said quickly, sorry I'd mentioned it. "He left the studio last year."

"I'll need a name," said Marino. I wrote down the instructor's name and tried to think of any other possible contacts that would be relevant.

"I did get a message from an old boyfriend on FB instant messenger not too long ago," I said.

"You didn't tell me about that," said Teddy with an accusatory stare. I knew then an argument was definitely in our future.

"It was nothing. Jason reached out to me. A few messages went back and forth between us, and that was the end of it," I said. "It was completely harmless. Besides, it's not him, he's a doctor."

"You know how many doctors are in jail?" said Brodsky writing something down. "Anyone else?"

Before I could stop, the words I had promised myself I would not share based on my total lack of evidence tumbled out of my mouth. "Did you ever talk to Ned LaGrange? I think I've told you about him before."

"Who the hell is Ned LaGrange? Why do you know all these men, Jillian?" said my husband pushing his chair back from the table making a loud screech on the wooden floor. "Sounds to me like you have an extremely busy social life while I'm in the city working."

"Ned is no one, Teddy," I said attempting to calm him down.

"He's apparently important enough to mention to the police . . . twice."

My husband was obviously taking his testosterone out for a test drive.

"Ned LaGrange works at the Medford post office," I said to Teddy. "He's a federal employee and personally offensive on so many levels. When I mail a package, he flexes his muscles and attempts stupid, flirty, small talk. I only mentioned him because the detectives asked."

"But, you *did* mention him," said Brodsky examining me, his bushy black brows knitted together.

"Anything else?" said Marino.

"It's probably nothing. That green SUV that I thought was following me around town could be Ned's." I didn't tell them about his license plate or his skull and crossbones tee shirt because it sounded stupid. Ned hadn't actually done anything — yet.

As soon as I stopped babbling, I felt Teddy's eyes drilling into the side of my head. We were definitely going to have an argument, possibly as soon as in the police station parking lot.

"Medford is a small town." said the Russian. "One is bound to cross paths with the same vehicles from time to time. Mr. LaGrange lives here in Medford. Could it just be a coincidence?"

"I guess so," I said, sorry I'd brought it up. Truthfully, I had no specific evidence against Ned. "I'm probably over-thinking things."

"Maybe," said Brodsky giving his partner a look. I wondered what that look meant.

After they finished with me, they went through Teddy's list of contacts. I could already tell by my husband's body language that our ride home wasn't going to be fun.

Finally, it appeared the detectives were wrapping up. "Anything else," I said with a tinge of impatience in my voice. "We've got a million things to do today."

"Ms Samuels," said Brodsky, "my sense is you're not taking this seriously. The fact is, you are at the center of this whole investigation and have no explanations for anything."

When we got into the car neither Teddy nor I said a word. Brodsky had tried to blame me for being oppositional and unhelpful which had irritated me. Teddy was obviously pissed off I hadn't told him about my old boyfriend getting back in touch. Honestly, it was so insignificant I didn't think to mention it. I only told Natalie when I'd had a few too many drinks that evening we got together. I was very happily married and Teddy should have known that. He should trust me. I've never given him a single reason not to.

"Are you going to say anything?" I said as he drove silently through town.

"You said it all. What do you want me to say?"

"This is ridiculous. Are you seriously jealous of an old boyfriend who sent me a message on Facebook?"

"That's not the point."

"What was I supposed to do, not respond to him?" I said getting more annoyed.

"Yes."

"Fine. The next time an old boyfriend reaches out, I'll ignore him."

"Good."

"You're acting like an idiot."

"Seems like you've had conversations with all sorts of men," said Teddy with a tone I didn't like.

"Pull into the post office right now," I said my voice getting louder. "I want you to get a good look at Ned LaGrange so we can put an end to this. If Ned sees you, maybe he'll stop flirting with me."

"Then you *were* flirting?"

"Give me a break, Teddy. Ned LaGrange is awful. I only go into the post office to mail packages for work. He talks to me. What am I supposed to do?"

Teddy and I were on the verge of a major fight so I insisted he accompany me into the post office under the pretext of buying stamps. Once my husband got a look at the weirdly over-pumped mailman, I was sure his misplaced jealousy would be put to rest. Then, we could get on with our one day together in weeks.

When we walked into the post office it was a familiar scene. One very short line waiting for service from Ned, and a super long line in front of Pretty Braids' window.

"See, it's just like I told you," I whispered as we joined Ned's shorter line. "Nobody wants to interact with Ned, not even the men. Most people wait on the longer line for Pretty Braids."

When it was our turn, we stepped up to Ned's window.

"Jillian, haven't seen you around in a few days," said Ned, a smarmy grin plastered on his white fleshy face, red splotches growing on his cheeks. "What's cookin'?"

"Hello, Ned. I need twenty stamps, please."

"That's all for you today," he said suspiciously eyeing my husband standing a few feet behind me.

"Ned, I'd like you to meet my husband, Teddy."

I could swear the blood drained from Ned's face because he suddenly looked paler than normal.

"Nice to meet you," he mumbled as he gave my husband a long once over. "Your wife is one of my favorite customers. She's a great writer, too."

Later, when we got into the car, Teddy waited before turning on the ignition.

"Well?" I said.

He started to laugh. "You win. The man is horrendous, a throwback to an earlier version of human."

I leaned over, kissed him on the cheek and let out a relieved sigh. The stupid fight was over — everything was back to normal. I hated when we argued, especially about dumb things. Ned LaGrange was not worth fighting over.

As we pulled into our long driveway, I wondered about Ned. What if his pathetic sad sack routine was just a cover? Maybe he *wanted* people to think he was an idiot? Then, he'd be the last person anyone would suspect. It could be his weirdness was all an act? If it was, he had definitely perfected it.

Chapter 34

The minute we arrived home from the police station, the detectives called.

"Did we forget something?" I said when I heard Brodsky's monotone voice on the other end.

"We have one more question for you" he said. "You told us you have another book coming out, *The Soul Collector*, correct?"

"That's right."

"Can you give me more details," he said. "That day at your house you told us a little, but I'd like to hear more specifics on the story. It might help with our investigation."

Before I opened my mouth, I knew what I was about to say was going to shock him. "Remember I told you the book is about a serial killer. The man enjoys killing but only does it at opportunistic moments. He has no set pattern, no pre-plan to kill. He wakes up each morning, goes out into the world and if a murder opportunity presents itself, sometimes he goes for it, sometimes he doesn't. It's the not knowing part he finds exciting. Each kill is always an unexpected yet pleasant surprise. He never knows when a kill is coming and that's what he loves the most."

"You have a vivid imagination," said the Russian.

"Because none of the crimes or the victims are related to each other or the killer, it becomes a huge source of confusion for the police. They can't get a handle on the killer because there's no pattern or motive. But actually, there is. His motive is the pleasure, the pure fun of the phantom kill."

"In your new book, how do each of your victims die?" said Brodsky.

"The first victim is standing alone on an elevated train platform. It's late and dark and there's no one around. But actually, there is. The killer, on his way home from a movie is standing behind a cement pillar watching the approaching train lights as they come up the tracks. This is a local station and the train that's coming is an express. It won't be stopping or slowing down. As the train passes through the station at top speed, the killer steps forward and shoves a middle-aged dentist into its path."

"My mother always told me never stand too close to the edge of the train platform," said the detective. "I guess she was right."

"The next victim is a young woman on a bicycle. It's 6.30 a.m. and the killer is driving to work. The woman is riding in the bike lane as the killer comes up behind her. She's a kindergarten teacher and four months pregnant. He only finds out she was pregnant later when he reads about her death in the newspaper. As he drives, he checks ahead for any oncoming traffic and then looks in his rearview. It's early, there's no one else on the road. Adrenaline rockets through his body and his breath quickens. He smiles — a perfect kill scenario. Stepping down on the gas pedal, he does a sharp swerve into the bike sending the woman flying into a tree. She dies at the scene. He keeps going, a grin on his face, thinking what a great start to my day. So you see, the police never get a handle on the killer because of the randomness of the crimes. His motive is not connected to the victims at all, it's connected to the opportunity."

"Are those the only two murders in the book?"

As I formed a response, I envisioned the surprised look on Brodsky's face when I answered. What I was about to say was going to stop the burly Russian in his tracks.

"The third and final victim is a woman in her thirties, a moderately successful author of thrillers. She has been experiencing writer's block and drives to a small state park in the mountains about forty minutes from her home to get some inspiration from nature.

"It's a beautiful warm fall weekday morning when she arrives at the remote hiking area. She's packed a lunch and plans to spend the afternoon drinking in the surroundings. She hopes a day in the woods will unplug her creative juices and enable her to write freely again."

I stopped for a second to recall the details of the story. It had been a while since I had written it.

"Anyway, the author pulls into the tiny parking lot at one end of the park. There are only three other cars there. She smiles thinking it unlikely she'll run into other hikers. She doesn't want to talk to anyone that day. She wants to be alone, that's the whole point of being there. She takes a free map from a wooden stand at the entrance and looks it over. There are several marked nature trails and she selects the loop that takes three and a half hours. The trail is marked with orange signs and described on the map as the most scenic of all the hike options. She plans to stop for lunch in a spot the map says has amazing views."

"I have a feeling I know what's coming," said Brodsky without emotion.

"It's not what you think," I said. "Anyway, the author grabs an extra water bottle from her trunk, puts it in her small backpack and heads out. The leaves have started to turn yellow and she's in awe of the spectacular scenery. Every fifteen minutes or so she comes to another opening in the forest with a magnificent view. Two hours into her hike she arrives at her favorite scenic spot, Juniper's Vista. She sits on the edge of a large rock overlooking the green and yellow valley below.

"The sun is shining as she unpacks her sandwich and settles back to enjoy her lunch with Mother Nature. After thirty minutes of meditation she stands to take one last look before continuing on her hike. That's when *he* comes upon her."

"The killer?" said Brodsky.

"Yes. He went to the park for the same reason she did. He wanted a day out in nature to soothe his tortured soul. When he arrives at the same scenic spot, he recognizes it as an 'opportunity', and quickly puts on his baseball hat and sunglasses.

"Standing on the rock looking out with her back to him, she hears something rustle from behind and turns. He waves and smiles as he approaches."

"He's going to push her over the cliff," said Brodsky.

"He greets her and tells her he doesn't have a trail map and that he's lost. He asks if he could look at her map. While standing on the edge of the large precipice, she takes out the paper and examines it. While she explains what direction she thinks he should go in, he leans forward and pushes her right over the edge."

"What a way to go."

"When he looks down, her mangled body is sprawled in a thicket far below and he smiles. Taking the extra water bottle out of her pack, he takes a swig and whistles as he walks back along the trail."

"So, the third victim was killed by a fall," said Brodsky.

"No."

"No?"

"Somehow, the woman lived and is found the next day by a park ranger and airlifted to a hospital. She ends up surviving," I said. "She was very lucky."

"If she was truly lucky," said Brodsky in his familiar Siberian deadpan, "she wouldn't have been pushed off the mountain in the first place. But wait, you said all the victims in your book were killed, this woman lived."

"She lived, but not for long," I said. "She was in the hospital and then in rehab for months. Eventually, she recovers and resumes her life writing books. After all the news coverage of her being pushed off the cliff and her months of recovery, the cops never get close to catching the assailant. Eventually the press and law enforcement move on to fresh cases.

"The killer however does not move on. He can't get that woman out of his mind and is determined to finish what he started. This was the first and only time one of his kills didn't take, and it drives him crazy."

"Sounds like he was already crazy."

"He learns everything he can about her. He finds out she lives alone and goes to her home one night, breaks in and strangles her to death. Then, he dumps her body into a full bathtub."

"Why a full bathtub?" said Brodsky.

"To get rid of any fingerprints."

"And the killer?" said Brodsky. "What happens to him?"

"Never caught. The book ends with him coming upon another fantastic kill opportunity."

Chapter 35

Time passed and things stayed quiet — no new crimes were recreated from my books. Sadly for me, without any fresh salacious headlines or social media posts, public interest in my books waned. Though Brodsky and Marino were still investigating the "Silver Man Murder" and I occasionally heard from them, the case and I appeared to be yesterday's news. Even Devlin hadn't contacted me for a quote in a long while. My fifteen minutes of fame appeared to be over.

In the meantime, my agent told me he and my editor met regularly for lunches and dinners to discuss real time strategy for my book. Matthew had once alluded to the fact that he thought Eric had a little crush on him and that he, Matthew, knew just how to play it.

"He'll do anything I tell him," said my confident agent on one of our weekly calls. "Don't worry. I've got this."

It was at one of their dinners that Eric dropped the bombshell. After many months, senior management at Linton Books decided I didn't have enough star power or social media following. They were pulling back on the marketing budget and only spending the bare minimum on my launch.

Matthew had always anticipated a budget cut as a possible scenario but had hoped it wouldn't happen. Now that it had, he told me he would implement plan B. I didn't get the details, but I got the impression his strategy teetered on the wrong side of moral, ethical and legal. Matthew told me he had shared his plan B with Eric and the editor had signed on. Together, they were committed to making my book a hit — no matter what. Honestly, I didn't want to know how, I was just glad they had a plan.

* * *

Meanwhile, the new T. Samuels restaurant plans had gelled and Teddy was working twenty-four seven. He hadn't had a day off in months. The demands of the new venture were overwhelming. At the same time, he still had all his responsibilities as head chef at the American Bistro. My husband was essentially working two full-time jobs which meant there was no time for me. He was at the new place on his days, nights and mornings off from the old place. He left before dawn and returned in the middle of the night long after I was asleep. I worried he was going to get sick.

Fortunately, the restaurant's investor group had a corporate apartment in Midtown that Teddy could use whenever he needed. I even stayed there with him one night. His schedule had become so hectic that I started traveling into the city once a week just to have lunch or dinner with him. If I didn't do that, I would have never seen him. It was only temporary, but still, it kind of sucked.

One Sunday, I took a train into the city to meet Teddy at the new restaurant so he could show me around. A few electricians were up on ladders but otherwise, not much other activity. The place was shaping up and my husband beamed with pride as he walked me around the space showing off a little.

"It won't be like this forever," he said as we left the site to grab a quick sushi lunch. "Things will calm down soon, I promise." Teddy had carved out exactly sixty minutes for us to eat and then he had to get back to meet with some suppliers. Calling it a crazy time was an understatement. I missed him and had felt like a single person for the longest time. I was lonely in Connecticut all by myself and had started feeling a little resentful.

"I can't wait until you have only one job again," I said as I dipped my salmon roll into some soy sauce. "When the new restaurant opens, what if you're stretched even thinner?"

He assured me I was worrying needlessly and that soon everything would fall into place.

"You'll see. Everything will be great. My main concern right now, is finding the investment money so we get a piece of the action. If I don't, I'll be working my ass off for other people for the rest of my life."

"Is it that important? Can't you be happy with having your name on it?"

"No. If the restaurant is going to have my name on it, I want a bigger piece of the pie."

"But what if—"

"I know I can get my hands on about sixty-eight thousand right now but the interest rates are terrible. I don't want to do that. If your book does as well as you say it will, that would give us another hundred thousand or more. I talked to the investors and they'll allow me to put in my share of the money over a set period of time. I can pay them back when your book hits the charts and we're more liquid. Then, I'd have a substantial stake in the business. Remember, we've got to get in on the ground floor. This is only the first restaurant of many and next year . . ."

As I listened to Teddy opine about the future of his restaurant empire, I felt a little sick. Our whole future was now riding on my book's success. My husband was counting on me for the cash and that was a lot of pressure. If *The Soul Collector* was a hit, it could literally make his dreams come true. I didn't want to let him down.

When our lunch hour was up, I kissed him goodbye and walked to Grand Central Station to catch the train back to Connecticut. While waiting in the cavernous historic terminal, after promising my husband the world, I texted Matthew to reassure myself things were still on track.

Checking in. How are things going for the launch? Everyone still pumped for my book?

Since it was Sunday, I didn't expect to hear from Matthew until the next day. I was surprised when he texted back five minutes later.

Everything fine. All under control.

I let out a relieved sigh. Thank God someone had something under control because I certainly didn't. By the time I got home it was 4.15 p.m. and my house was eerily quiet. Feeling a little lonely and sorry for myself, I tried to FaceTime with Natalie and thankfully she answered right away.

"Hey stranger," she said as she puckered her lips. "What do you think of my new lip stain. It's called Jungle Baby Rose."

"It's so you," I said. And it was, too. Natalie had at least five hundred different lip products all in different shades of red.

"You should try this color. The salesperson told me it looks great on everyone," she said.

Not me, I thought. Red isn't my color. My complexion is fair and peachy and my hair color isn't dark enough to pull off red lips. Whenever I tried it, usually at Natalie's insistence, I wound up looking like Pennywise the clown from Stephen King's *It*. Not the look I was going for.

"Why are you all glammed up?" I said noticing she was in full makeup, wearing her best blue-green cashmere sweater and favorite pair of dangly gold earrings.

"I might as well tell you, but you're not going to like it. I'm going out with the Mystery Man tonight."

The Mystery Man was a sore spot between us. He was someone Natalie had been seeing on and off for years. Every time she had another breakup which was practically monthly, she'd fall back into the arms of her Mystery Man. She called him that because he was married and she fiercely protected his privacy.

"You're my BFF, if I was going to tell anyone who he was, I'd tell you," she had said years before when she first started seeing him. "But he made me promise never to tell a soul. My lips are sealed."

That was a first. Natalie's lips were never sealed. Truthfully, I didn't care who he was. I was more disturbed that she had no compunction about being a home wrecker. I also thought she was wasting her life with someone who was already taken. Every time she went back to him, I tried to convince her it was going nowhere, but she never listened.

"I live in the moment and right now, the Mystery Man fills a void," she had said on more than one occasion. "We have fun together. What's so wrong with that?"

There were so many reasons it was wrong and I tried to explain them all. She didn't want to hear it. Natalie was an enigma. She cut corners and didn't play by the rules but at the same time, being with her was like being on a wild fantastic ride. Even Teddy liked her, but agreed she was probably headed for disaster.

"Natalie jumps from one guy to the next," he had said once. "She doesn't know what she wants."

I agreed. My BFF was chasing something dangerous and I worried about her.

Chapter 36

My final edits for *The Soul Collector* had been completed. The cover, acknowledgments, bio and front of book quote were also finished. Eric and the other Linton people had been a dream to work with and seemed happy with my revisions and input. My agent appeared optimistic and there was nothing more for me to do except hurry up and wait. I had gotten very good at that.

Both Matthew and Eric encouraged me to keep my foot on the social media gas pedal, so I did. After the Silver Man Murder, and that interview I did with Devlin, which wound up getting a fair amount of pick up in the media, I was able to use both of them to promote myself on Twitter and Instagram. The reality was: dead bodies sell books. That worked for a while but as it had in the past, once the media spotlight faded, interest in me diminished significantly. After all my struggles with publicity, I had newfound respect for what Natalie did every day. With nothing new to crow about, I started making up stuff for my posts. I got pretty creative spinning gold out of straw.

Alone in my home office one afternoon, I gave up trying to convince a candidate to accept a job offer when he informed me he had just accepted another position. Fuming,

I ended the call just as my doorbell rang. I looked out the window. Marino and Brodsky's car was parked in front of my house. Cranky after losing a big recruiting commission, I actually warmed to the distraction of a police visit.

I wondered if they had new information or if there had been a breakthrough in the case. My publicity well had run dry and I needed some fresh material for a *Soul Collector* post for Instagram and Facebook. Something new and juicy would make my agent, editor — and husband for that matter — very happy.

I led the two detectives into my living room and had a moment of déjà vu.

"Been a while," I said sitting in my favorite chair as they both took a seat on the couch.

"Let me get straight to the point," said Brodsky doing another perfect impersonation of a KGB agent. "A knife stuck through a note, written with a Midnight Blue Crayola crayon, has been found stuck in the ground in a cemetery in Harwich. It was on the grave of a Nicolo DiPaola who died in 1978. We need your help."

"I've never heard of Nicolo DiPaola," I said.

"We've done a deep dive into all your books, Ms Samuels," said Marino popping a tiny white mint into his mouth and offering me one, which I declined.

"We've known each other for a while now, Detective, please call me Jillian," I said.

"All right, Jillian," said Marino. "In your *Whispers from the Grave*, the killer leaves a note on headstones, right? The first note says 'Eeney Meeny Miney Moe, very soon you'll have to go'. Correct?"

"Yes, Detective. The serial killer in my book left cryptic rhyme riddles for the cops. Why? Did you find another body?"

"Not yet," said Brodsky. "We'd like to prevent that from happening. In your graveyard book, how exactly did the killer select his victims?"

"My killer was into genealogy in a major way. He was a card carrying member of Ancestry and every one of those

DNA sites. He was obsessed with it. To choose his victim, he'd go down to a town hall and randomly pick the name of a dead person. Then, he'd research that individual and find out everything he could. Once he located their grave, he'd find and study all of their descendants using genealogy. Sometimes the dead person had hundreds of living relatives, other times only a handful. With so many potential victims and so many avenues to chase down, the killer had the police in my book running in circles. The cops were never able to pinpoint the victim before the killer struck again. Some of the people murdered didn't even know they were related to the man in the grave.

"Nicolo DiPaola died more than forty years ago. He could have dozens of descendants," said Marino to his partner.

"How old was he when he died? Was he married with children?" I said, the thriller writer in me trying to be helpful.

"He was seventy-two," said Brodsky. "He had been married with four children, twelve grandchildren and as of today, thirty-two great-grandchildren, none of whom he ever met."

"We have no doubt now that the killer is absolutely mimicking plot lines from your books," said Marino. "We're trying to prevent another murder. Is there anything you can tell us about the psyche of the killer in your book and why he'd choose one descendant over another?"

I shook my head. "Honestly, no. That probably makes me a lazy and shitty writer but I never delved into that question. My killer just picked a person randomly. I never got into the reasons why."

For the next few weeks things were quiet — no new bodies. Of course if one had turned up, my editor, agent and the Linton Books marketing department would have done somersaults. Meanwhile, I was a nervous wreck as the clock ticked toward publication day. Pretty soon it would be plain to everyone if I was a good writer or simply a pathetic desperate hack. Everything that mattered to me was riding on the success of this one single book. Everything.

While I was at home obsessing, Teddy continued working crazy hours. He had lost weight and had dark circles under his eyes. I was worried about him. And, he was still counting on me and my future book sales to fund his restaurant dream. On more than one occasion, I reminded him that writing a bestseller was akin to a winning lottery ticket, there were no guarantees. He didn't want to hear that and told me to be more positive.

As time went on, things became a little tense between us. For weeks at a time, we barely saw each other. When we did, we often argued. My recruiting business, which was a straight commission job, had taken a serious nosedive because of all my distractions. I had barely made anything the previous two months and Teddy and I were way behind in our bills. That contributed to us being at odds with each other. They say financial problems are the number one thing to tank a marriage. I couldn't let that happen to mine.

One weekday night, I waited up for him until nearly 1 a.m. because I hadn't seen him in days. I'll admit he looked exhausted. A little voice in my head told me it probably wasn't the best moment to throw a whole bunch of stuff at him. But, we were partners and I told myself there was never a good time. I didn't want him to be surprised. I wanted him to know my recruiting work wasn't going well and that I hadn't closed any contracts for quite a while.

"This is a bad time to not be making money," Teddy finally said after hearing me out. "Every penny counts. You've got to try harder. Stop ruminating on every little thing. This is our make it or break it time. If we don't do it now, we're screwed."

"How do I focus on employment contracts when bodies are turning up and the police pop in every other week? There's also been talk of pulling back marketing on my book. You're down in New York City making crème brulée and dreaming about your 'restaurant empire', while my world is falling apart."

"Once again, you're being overly dramatic."

"I've got a lot of pressure on me from my publisher, too."

"It's always about you, isn't it?" my husband shouted as he got up and walked out of the room.

I thought his comment was really unfair. It was a little like the pot calling the kettle black. Teddy was the showboat, not me. He was the one *New York Magazine* called a "Culinary Rising Star". It was his name that would be on a marquee over a hot new Manhattan eatery, not mine. Nobody was lining up to talk to me or put my name on a building. Did he forget I was the one holding down the freakin' fort?

Between my new book, the explosions, the dead body, knives in graves and my marriage in a not happy place, I was barely holding it together. Exercise was the only way I got through it. Whenever I felt stressed and out of sorts, I drove straight to the Medford YMCA for a relaxing swim.

One early evening during peak time, I arrived at the pool. There was only one unoccupied lane. I grabbed it. The minute I got into the pool and felt the silky water around me, I was immediately rejuvenated. Weightless, floating and gliding, I swam to the end of the lane, rolled forward, did a somersault, pushed off the wall, flipped over and headed back in the other direction. After about twenty laps, stopping at the shallow end to take a drink of water, I heard a voice in the lane behind me.

"That you, Jillian? I thought I recognized you under the water."

Startled, I spun around and lifted my goggles.

"I've been watching you. You have great form," said Ned LaGrange smiling with those teeth that looked like barley. "Swim here a lot? I just joined."

I could not believe it. That pool was my safe place, where I went to decompress. I started to hyperventilate and mumbled something about how late it was. I scrambled out of the pool, grabbed my gear and started to walk away when Ned shouted to me.

"Hey Jillian, next time we're at the pool together, if there aren't enough lanes we could share one. I'm totally cool with that."

That's when I was convinced Ned LaGrange *was* stalking me. But what would I tell the police? If I told the cops he was a stalker because he had a shirt with a skull and crossbones, a license plate that said UR MYN and did laps at the YMCA, they'd think I was nuts. At that point, I had no concrete evidence so I said nothing more to Teddy or the police. Maybe I should have but technically, Ned hadn't done anything wrong. Even so, he was on my watch list.

Chapter 37

Early on a weekday morning, my phone rang in the bed-room. I couldn't hear it because I was in the shower. But Teddy, who was sitting on our bed, saw my caller ID said "Medford PD" and answered it. A minute later, he tapped on the glass shower door.

"You'd better get out and get dressed," he said. "There's a problem."

"What now?" I said naked, dripping and feeling vulnerable.

He handed me a towel and explained that Detective Marino had called. Something terrible had happened. A man's body had been found floating face down in Fern Lake over in the neighboring town of Barrington, CT. The dead man's name was John Mercer and he was a master plumber and carpenter.

"What's that got to do with us?" I said as I dried my hair briskly with a towel.

Teddy explained what he had been told. Apparently, Mercer was the second cousin of Walter S. Loomis, one of the graves that had been defaced with a knife and note in blue crayon. That morning, a group of middle-aged walker-talker women were on an early morning trek on the path around the lake. One of them spotted Mercer's body floating face down fifty yards from the shore. The victim's abandoned row boat was found floating out in the middle of the water. According to several people who knew Mercer, he went fishing at that location regularly.

"You realize what this means, don't you?" said Teddy, visibly agitated and a little snippy. "This is right out of *Whispers from the Grave*. What the fuck is going on, Jillian?"

"I don't know," I snapped, as I put my wet hair up in a towel turban. "How many times do I have to say that?"

Teddy's face went red. "This has got to stop now," he said loudly. "I've got too much going on. I can't deal with all this insanity."

He had too much going on? Seriously?

"I'm at the epicenter of this whole nightmare," I shouted. "You go off to Manhattan every day to manage your *empire* and I'm left here dealing with all this shit."

Surprised by my outburst, he stared at me. Neither of us spoke, knowing if we continued, the conversation would only go downhill. After a minute-long stand-off, I broke the silence. I was always the one to give in first. After years dealing with my father's rages and my sister Camille's vitriol, I had learned how to be the peacemaker. My husband didn't like to admit when he was wrong — ever. I usually sucked it up to preserve the harmony. It was no big deal and honestly, we didn't fight that often.

"I'm sorry," I said. "I'm just really stressed out. I can't even wash my hair without getting bad news."

"You'd better get dressed. The police will be here in twenty minutes," he said coldly as he walked out of the room.

My head pounded as missiles came at me from all directions. First it was crazy things with my books. Then my husband not talking to me. And now, the police were breathing down my neck. Even on the recruiting end, my boss had started asking questions.

"Your numbers are significantly off this quarter, Jillian. Last quarter was bad but this one's worse," said my manager,

Audrey, the day before while going over my projections on the phone. "What's going on with you? Doesn't look like you're going to come close to hitting your number. Is something wrong?"

Well, let's see Audrey. Maybe fires, explosions and death have impacted my usual sunny disposition? I didn't say that to her, but I sure wanted to. I normally keep my professional business separate from my personal life. I promised Audrey I had lots of irons in the fire and told her she shouldn't worry.

"I'm on it. The next few months will be a job placement bonanza," I said with a little too much enthusiasm. It was a total lie, but that's what she wanted to hear.

With the police on their way, my morning had once again been hijacked. I smoothed my hair back into a pony tail and put on my favorite, slightly worn, gray yoga outfit. I could squeeze in a yoga class at lunchtime if the detectives didn't stay too long. I promised myself to have them in and out in less than an hour. Then, I'd spend the rest of the day looking for great job candidates and get Audrey off of my back.

The doorbell rang sooner than I had expected. Now Teddy was in the shower so I ran downstairs to answer the door. To my surprise, it wasn't Brodsky or Marino. It was Tommy Devlin. That man had uncanny radar always appearing right after something terrible happened.

"Good morning," he said while casually leaning on the door frame. "Sorry to drop by so early unannounced but I was hoping to get a statement from you for the *Advocate's* morning feature. We're live in about two hours."

"I'm sorry but I can't talk to you right now," I said closing the door until something stopped it. I looked down, it was Devlin's foot.

"You probably haven't heard but—"

"I've heard," I said, rolling my eyes thinking the press are bloodsuckers. "The police called a few minutes ago. I'll save you some time. I don't know anything and I have no comment. Now, if you'll please move your big fat foot out of the way I—"

"But, surely you can see that . . ."

Oh, my God. Devlin was practically forcing me to slam the door on his toes, which I really didn't want to do. I'm not a naturally rude or violent person and work hard not to be impolite even when it's warranted. Natalie on the other hand, can turn on a dime if someone looks at her the wrong way. For a split second I wondered if I should set Natalie up with Devlin. He was good-looking enough for her and they appeared to be cut from the same cloth.

As I was trying to decide whether to injure Devlin's foot or fix him up with my best friend, the detectives' car pulled into my driveway. The cavalry had arrived.

"If it isn't Tommy Devlin," said Marino as he got out of the driver's side. "Bad news travels fast."

"Doing my job."

"How about you let us do ours," said Brodsky closing his car door and walking toward us. They were like gladiators preparing for battle, each one sure of their own justification and might.

"I already told him, I have no comment," I said facing the detectives.

"We've got police business, Devlin," said Marino popping a stick of cinnamon gum into his mouth. "You'll have to speak to Ms Samuels another time."

"Come on, it will only take a minute and I really need a quote for—"

"You're on private property," said Brodsky moving closer and getting into Devlin's personal space making the reporter bristle. "The lady would like you to leave."

"You never heard of freedom of the press, Brodsky? I guess they don't have a free press in Moscow, right?" said the reporter with a smirk.

I saw the impassioned look on Brodsky's face. Devlin was tangling with the wrong cat. The Russian was bigger, stronger, had a badge, gun and backup. What had started as a morning meet and greet had turned into a cockfight. Clearly, it was time for a woman to step in.

"Enough. Detectives, please come inside," I said firmly. "Mr Devlin, call me later this afternoon. At that time, I'll make a statement on whatever the police say I can. Fair?"

Devlin nodded and headed to his car as I directed the detectives into the living room. Teddy, who had missed the whole altercation, came bounding down the stairs.

"Where have you been?" I whispered while taking my husband's hand and following the two policemen down the hall. "We almost had a rumble on our front steps." Once seated in the living room, the detectives briefed us on the new homicide. The victim found in the lake had suffered "a catastrophic injury to the head". Marino said at that point they had no significant leads or suspects. It was obvious they were frustrated but I was also getting a weird vibe from them.

"Your books are still at the center of this case," said Brodsky eyeing me suspiciously.

Honestly, I was a little taken aback. Only moments earlier Brodsky had stood up for me with the reporter. Now he was staring at me like I was Jack the Ripper.

"I get it. You can't solve these crimes, so you blame me," I said.

"That's not what he meant," said Marino trying to smooth things as he shot his partner a look. "Obviously, someone is using your books to make a point. We were hoping there might be some detail you'd forgotten that could be of help."

"If my wife knew anything, she'd tell you," said Teddy jumping to my defense. "Jillian is flawlessly law abiding. She even pays her parking tickets the day she gets them. Who does that?"

After twenty minutes of questions that I'd already answered, the detectives left when it was evident I had nothing new to add. Minutes later, after my husband and I both apologized to each other for our early morning outbursts, Teddy left to catch the train into the city. I went to my desk and plowed through a pile of resumes. After a few productive hours, I uncovered some good prospects and was feeling rather proud of myself. I was about to reach out to one of them when Matthew FaceTimed me.

"Did you hear about the dead guy they found floating in a lake near you in Connecticut?" said my overly enthusiastic agent. "The police think there's a connection to your books. How good is that? Things are heating up again, Jillian. Now, we've got two bodies. You gotta love this."

"I don't know anything about it," I said thinking Matthew shouldn't be so happy about a murder.

"The news story I read said the guy's name was Mercer and he was related to Walter S. Loomis, the man who had the knife stuck on his grave. Jillian, this is unfolding exactly the way it did in your book. Don't you see? This is our golden ticket. We have to make the most of this development and milk it for every drop. Your new book comes out fairly soon. Now is the time to get on Twitter and tweet up a storm. The conspiracy theory idiots will eat it up and, hopefully, buy your new book on pre-order."

"I'm a little uncomfortable doing that," I said. "Someone died, Matthew. You want me to promote my book by exploiting a man's death?"

"Absolutely, one hundred percent. Are you kidding? Strike while the iron's hot."

"What about the man's family? Don't you think posting on Twitter to sell books is kind of insensitive, cruel even?"

"Not at all," said Matthew throwing his moral compass right out the window. "The man is dead. Using his demise to promote your brand won't change his condition. He's beyond help at this point. Trust me, you can't buy this kind of publicity. Be happy. Most authors would kill for this."

On some level I knew he was right. I had checked out Facebook and Twitter right after the police left. A ground-swell of traction about me had already started on all the social channels. It wasn't huge yet, but it was enough to impact book sales.

"I guess I could mention it," I said. "I could tweet about how eerie the similarity is to my books."

"Don't be shy. I guarantee you the Linton Books publicity team will be all over this. It's a gift from the gods."

And, there it was. My agent was actually overjoyed that a corpse had been found in Fern Lake. He didn't even try to hide his glee. I was fighting a losing battle. My publisher, my agent and even my husband and best friend were all on the same page. At the end of the day, my brand and my books were finally getting noticed, so I surrendered.

"Okay," I said as I looked into his eyes on my phone screen. "If you really think it's the right thing, I'm onboard. I'll blog about it and post it everywhere I can."

"Trust me," said Matthew with a grin, "this is the way to go. You're going to have a bestseller if it kills us both."

An hour later Devlin's name popped up on my phone. I groaned. Clearly, I wasn't going to get any more recruiting done that day. Devlin said he wanted to interview me for a weekly news segment he did on a local cable TV channel.

I wasn't inclined or prepared to make a TV appearance, but I could see the opportunities it presented. To get him off the phone, I told him I'd think about it. Immediately after, I called Teddy to ask him what he thought. On the one hand, it seemed inappropriate for me to go on TV in the middle of an active murder investigation. On the other, there was no denying a TV segment would be fantastic publicity for my new book. My call went straight to Teddy's voicemail. I looked at the time, he was probably in the middle of the dinner prep.

Frustrated, I texted Natalie, who was at the airport about to board a plane and couldn't talk. I really needed to speak to someone about whether or not to do this TV appearance. I tried my neighbor, Sue, the one who had first alerted me to the crimes on Twitter. She also didn't pick up.

Shifting my attention back to my day job, I sifted through a pile of resumes and returned a few phone calls. Ninety minutes later Teddy called back.

"Where have you been?" I said. "I need to talk to you."

"Jills, I run a huge kitchen. I can't always stop and pick up personal calls."

"There's something important we need to discuss."

"What's going on now?"

I told him about Devlin and the TV interview and how I wasn't sure if I should do it. He was quiet for a moment before he answered.

"TV exposure would be great for promoting your new book," he said. "On the other hand, it could also fuel the fire for more crimes or invite additional copycats."

Additional copycats? That terrifying notion hadn't occurred to me. "You think there could be other crazy people out there who want to get in on the action?" I said in a whisper.

"I probably shouldn't have said that," said my husband. "On second thought, keeping something in the dark only makes it scarier. Maybe if we shine a light, the cockroaches will scamper out and we can find out who's behind it. Going on TV is your chance to set the record straight. You tell them you don't know how or why any of this is happening, because that's the truth."

"But what about the copycats?"

"Jillian, a TV interview would be monumental publicity for all of your books. Who knows what kind of national pick up your interview with Devlin might get. Think how many books you might sell. This is too good an opportunity to let pass."

After Teddy's counsel, I called Devlin and agreed to sit down with him the next day. I arrived at the studio a bundle of nerves. During our twenty- minute taped discussion, Devlin acknowledged that I was also a victim. Saying that on a public forum was huge. Finally, I had some vindication. My novels had been appropriated by some lunatic who put me in the position of having to defend myself and my work.

As it turned out, the Devlin interview was picked up in syndication and a slew of stories about me appeared in newspapers, magazines and websites all over the country.

A few days after the interview aired, Matthew called me.

"I've got some great news for you," he said. "Because of all the recent press, Linton has increased the promotion budget for your book launch by three hundred percent. We've got real momentum now."

"That's amazing," I said feeling relieved, as a smile spread across my face.

"They've been watching your backlist too, and noticed the old books have been moving. That's a clear indicator of your vitality."

"After everything that's happened, it's hard to believe it's all finally working out," I said, letting out a relieved breath.

"I don't want to give you false hope, but I heard from Eric this morning that Linton Books management thinks *The Soul Collector* now has the potential to be a mega hit. I'm talking blockbuster. Do you understand? Jillian, you're going to make a ton of money."

Chapter 38

After two dead bodies had been found brutally murdered in the same part of the county in less than a year, the citizens of southwestern Connecticut were justifiably jittery. Weeks after Mercer's death in early November, several police departments within the county, including Medford, had joined forces with the city of New Haven and formed a regional task force. Marino and Brodsky, who had been working the case the longest, led the team. Finding and stopping the person or persons behind the murders, ostensibly inspired by my books, was their number one priority.

Right after Mercer's body was found in the lake, Linton Books pushed the sensational headlines hard and used them to promote my new book on social media. In the process, I picked up a significant number of new followers all of whom expected me to weigh in on a daily basis. Ugh. Both my agent and editor kept tabs on all my online activity and encouraged me to keep the momentum going.

"Every time a dead body turns up, a cash register rings," said Matthew during one of our weekly check-in phone sessions. "Now if we could just get one more right around your publication day. Another body would guarantee us a spot on the *New York Times* bestseller list."

FFS. My agent clearly had no shame. I didn't engage with him when he made comments like that. It was too ghoulish, even though deep down, part of me agreed. If another crime happened, I'd probably make enough money to cover the full investment in Teddy's restaurant. I wasn't exactly mainstream trending, but there was consistent chatter about me and my books on Twitter and the other social channels.

The police kept in touch fairly regularly keeping me apprised of any developments. Occasionally, they ran a new theory by me. The general consensus on the special task force was that whoever was responsible for the explosions and attacks had likely used my books as a guide. Duh. It was quiet for a few weeks but then things got really weird.

After Mercer's death was declared a homicide, the police believed they had a serial killer on their hands. They determined that all of the previous incidents including the fires were tangentially connected. For starters, Mercer was a distant relative of Walter S. Loomis, the man whose grave was marked with a knife and note. The dead Silver Man and Mercer were tied together by notes scrawled with the same color Crayola Midnight Blue crayon. That same crayon had also been used on all the notes from all the crimes including the drone fires and explosions. Crayola's Midnight Blue could only be found in large sized crayon boxes containing ninety-six colors. Turns out Midnight Blue was kind of a rare color.

When the cops did a deep dive into John Mercer, they discovered he wasn't what he appeared to be. Local residents had reported he was a nice person and a good neighbor, always lending a helping hand. Mercer would clean other people's snowy walks with his snow blower, or drop off a neighbor's mail if it were accidentally delivered to him. General consensus: Mercer was a good guy. But, the plot thickens, Mercer apparently had a hidden side.

After interviewing dozens of people, the police learned Mercer, a widower, had a grown son. That son had been incarcerated in a California prison for . . . wait for it . . . arson. Ding-ding-ding. Turns out Mercer Jr had been released three years prior to the beginning of the Connecticut crime spree. No one knew where the son was, not even his parole officer. Mercer Jr then became a major person of interest. With the son as the primary suspect, the crime puzzle fit neatly together — arson, murder and who knows what else. But was it too neat?

There's more. According to Brodsky and Marino, the dead father from the lake, John Mercer Sr, had a criminal record as a sexual offender. (What a lovely family.) Many people don't know this but, in the state of Connecticut, anyone can look through the state's database to find out if one of their neighbors has a record of sexual misconduct. It won't tell you exactly what their crime was. You wouldn't know if a person was an exhibitionist, Peeping Tom or a serial child molester, but you'd know they were up to no good.

The writer in me tried to get the detectives to give up what kind of sexual misconduct Mercer Sr had committed. I was dying to know but the only thing the cops divulged was that Mercer had committed a "serious crime". I tried to pry further but they said something about "privacy rules". IMO, privacy is so overrated.

As the cops dug deeper, they discovered old Man Mercer owned a small lake home under his dead wife's maiden name on fifteen acres in New Hampshire. On a gut hunch, Brodsky and Marino took a road trip up to New Hampshire to have a look around Mercer's property.

They found a ramshackle log cabin somewhat in disrepair. The grounds were littered with debris and the dead leaves so deep they practically had to wade through them. Discarded rusted yard tools lay in the front of the house next to a broken-down wheelbarrow and a bicycle frame with missing tires. The roof of the cabin was worn and covered with moss and empty chicken coops were spotted on the side of the house. An undisturbed blanket of leaves covered the wooden steps that led up to the front door. It was evident no one had been there in a while.

They tried the doors and windows but everything was locked tight. While the place was seriously rundown and falling apart, the locks appeared new and of high quality.

Unable to enter the cabin, they walked the property for a couple of hours. Wandering through the woods, the two men carefully combed the circumference of the house but found nothing. After their long drive and determined to make it a fruitful trip, the detectives split up to evaluate the grounds and buildings from their own unique perspective. Twenty minutes later they met up by the front door and walked together a second time down a narrow path hugging the north side of the house. That rocky path led down a slope to the far back of the building.

This time, as they passed the side door, Marino noticed a half dozen empty candy wrappers scattered under some leaves by a dead tree stump. They picked up the six empty Skittles bags, put them into a plastic evidence container and kept walking to the back. The path led down to the basement level of the house. From the matted earth on the path, it was clear it had been used on a regular basis. Fifteen feet from the back of the house, there was a cleared area with a fire pit overflowing with wet charred sludge. Next to it was a utility shed with a hole in its roof. Rusted tools, shovels, axes and rakes hung inside on corroded nails.

Using large sticks, the detectives sifted through the damp charred remains in the fire pit. When Brodsky hit something solid, he retrieved it with the stick. Using latex gloves he always kept in his pocket, he picked up the object and gently wiped it off. It was a burned, thick, grayish mass the size of a deck of cards. It appeared to be made of leather and whatever it was had originally been pink before it had been partially burned and melted. Brodsky carefully pried it open. It was the remains of a wallet.

The wallet contained half of a blackened melted Starbucks card and part of a white plastic card. Two thirds of the white card had also been melted and destroyed. All that was legible were a few remaining letters.

VER CO
nabe

Chapter 39

After finding the wallet, the detectives canvassed the property a third time but discovered nothing more. At 2 p.m., they got back in their car to begin their three-hour drive back to Medford. As they drove, the two law men reviewed the entirety of the John Mercer case including the things they had discovered that day: the Skittles wrappers and the charred wallet. Most of the drive, Marino stared at that piece of white plastic with the letters that spelled nothing.

Twenty minutes into their trip south, Marino got a phone call from his wife. His son's college tuition money was due the next day and she had called to remind him to make a deposit. After the call, the two men rode in silence each going over the particulars of the case in their own mind. As Brodsky turned off the turnpike, Marino continued staring at the charred white card inside the clear plastic container and something clicked. He called his son and asked him to send him something.

A minute later, he received a picture of his son's college student ID card and Marino told Brodsky to stop the car. Nearly having an accident, Brodsky pulled over to the side of the road, and faced his partner.

The two detectives looked at the image on Marino's phone and compared it to the burned white card they had found. There was no question. The partial white card was a Dover College student ID — a perfect match to the student ID Marino's son had just sent.

VER CO was part of the words DOVER COLLEGE. The size, font and location was an exact match to his son's card. Based on the position of the other letters, "nabe" had to be a part of the student's name. The wallet had originally been pink so they assumed it most likely belonged to a girl. Given the positioning of those letters, "nabe" was probably part of the girl's first name.

The Russian told me he put the car in drive to continue their trip back to Medford as both men tried to make sense out of what they had found. Within half a mile they both knew what they had. Brodsky did an illegal U-turn on the highway, cranked the car to ninety miles an hour and raced back to the cabin.

They had found missing college student Anabel Ford's ID. That charred plastic mess in the container was Anabel's wallet. The letters "nabe" were part of her first name, Anabel.

Eighteen minutes later, they pulled onto Mercer's property again, and ran up the path to the front of the cabin. They jiggled the doors hard but the locks held fast. Pounding on the doors and windows, they shouted Anabel's name over and over. Silence.

Brodsky pulled out his gun, fired several shots into the door lock damaging it enough to release it. It swung open and they entered, guns drawn. The rustic living room was musty but neat. Dishes had been washed and left to dry on the counter. At first glance, everything appeared orderly. They shouted Anabel Ford's name over and over. More silence.

The house was bigger than it appeared from the outside and had an alarm system. There were three bedrooms, one was being used as an office. That room contained a desk and two computer monitors. There was other assorted electronic equipment and a host of technology components the detectives could not identify.

Convinced they were close to something, they moved from room to room shouting Anabel's name. They moved furniture and pulled back rugs, they hunted for false backs or bottoms in closets and drawers and listened for hollow sounds in the walls. They opened cabinets and the doors to a Murphy bed hanging on the wall in the office. There was a queen-sized bed frame with a mattress hanging perpendicular to the floor inside of wooden louver doors. Nothing.

After half an hour, still coming up empty, they decided to return to Connecticut. As they were about to exit through the front door, Brodsky suddenly turned, walked out of the living room and back down the hall to the office. With Marino behind him, the Russian went straight to the Murphy bed and opened the louver doors again. This time, he pulled the frame and mattress down. A small pocket door was hidden behind the mattress.

Brodsky slid the door to one side revealing a ladder staircase going down. Feeling around the door for a light switch, the Russian flipped it on. A dim bulb illuminated the stairs and he descended with Marino following. At the bottom, was a small enclosed chamber with no windows, only a single, locked, reinforced metal door.

Marino and Brodsky pounded on the door and shouted Anabel's name identifying themselves as police officers. Every few seconds, they stopped to listen for a response but heard nothing, only dead silence. Pounding again, they waited. Then they heard it . . . a faint sound. It sounded like crying.

Brodsky shouted for the person inside to move away from the door as he used his gun to break the lock. He aimed and fired and seconds later the detectives pushed open the metal door.

The stench of urine and other unidentifiable foul odors were the first thing to hit the two men. Inside, lay a tiny emaciated teenaged girl chained to a metal cot. On one side of the space, a wall of shelving was stocked with non-perishable food like peanut butter and crackers, jams and pouches of tuna fish. An adjacent shelf was loaded with gallons of water.

Empty water containers, and dozens of Skittles wrappers littered the floor.

The imprisoned woman was painfully thin but didn't appear to have any significant injuries. The breaking news that night and the following morning's headlines across the country were all the same.

ANABEL FORD FOUND ALIVE IN NEW HAMPSHIRE.

Chapter 40

Right after the detectives found the missing college student alive, they called the New Hampshire police and summoned an ambulance. Anabel Ford was taken to a nearby hospital. Her parents were notified and within an hour the press went into a feeding frenzy. What had been a local southern Connecticut missing person case took on biblical proportions as tales of Anabel's captivity were splashed across the nightly news.

Brodsky and Marino became instant celebrities interviewed repeatedly by TV news, newspapers, websites . . . you name it. That week in November, every news outlet featured pictures and articles about the two detectives. How their persistent police work had ultimately cracked the case and saved Anabel's life. Never one to miss an opportunity, Tommy Devlin was at the front of the food line and milked the story for everything it was worth.

"The fact is," said Devlin's piece in the *Connecticut Advocate*, "if these two detectives hadn't gone the extra mile and followed up on a tiny detail, Anabel Ford would have died. She only had enough food and water for another couple of weeks. With her captor dead, it was only a matter of time before her supplies ran out. Boris Brodsky and Nick Marino are heroes."

The irony was that those detectives only went to the cabin in New Hampshire to solve John Mercer's murder. Never in a million years did they expect to learn their murder victim was also a victimizer himself. Mercer wasn't the genial, helpful tradesman that his neighbors in Connecticut had thought. As more information emerged, Mercer's demented proclivities shed new light onto the entire case.

"John Mercer was in my home a hundred times fixing this and that," said one local Connecticut mother. "He even watched my kids a few times when I ran to the market. I can't believe I left them with that sadistic psycho. What if something had happened to my children?"

After Anabel was thoroughly checked out in the hospital, the doctors wanted to keep her in for a few days for observation given what she had been through. Under their expert care, Anabel slowly disclosed the details of what had happened. But instead of bringing clarity, the new information about her kidnapping and horrific confinement only created more confusion and raised new questions.

When Anabel first went missing, the police had put together a timeline of that night based on anecdotal information from her college friends. Various eyewitness accounts confirmed that the young woman had been at a large party and had way too much to drink. Now, Anabel was able to tell them she got separated from her friends and decided to walk home alone to her apartment. Halfway home and very intoxicated, her right foot plunged into a narrow and deep hole in the road causing her to fall and severely twist her ankle. She managed to get her foot out but it immediately swelled to double its normal size. Despite the alcohol in her system, when she tried to get up and stand on it, the pain was excruciating and she was unable to walk.

They say timing is everything. At the exact moment Anabel lay on the ground unable to stand, John Mercer drove by and saw her sprawled out on the side of the road obviously in distress. Like any good Samaritan would, he stopped to help her.

Normally, Anabel would never have dreamed of getting into a car with a strange old man. But with the excruciating pain in her ankle and the alcohol coursing through her veins, caution went completely out the window. All she could think of was how lucky she was that Mercer had come by and she thanked him profusely. He gently helped her into his car saying he'd be happy to drive her home. He even offered her a bottle of water. Thirsty and grateful, she downed the water and woke up the next day chained by her neck to a metal cot in a basement bunker in New Hampshire. No one would ever know for sure because Mercer was dead but, based on Anabel's account of that night, the police suspected Mercer had drugged her, possibly spiking her water bottle.

The fully secure soundproof basement room in New Hampshire had been stocked with food, water and a drainage shoot where she was able to dispose of her own waste. The security of the room and the abundance of supplies led police to believe an abduction plan had been in the works for a long time. Mercer had been prepared.

From her hospital bed, Anabel confirmed it and told the police it seemed like Mercer had his house all set up in advance. She suspected he had been waiting for the right person at the right time which sadly turned out to be her. The subterranean room where she was held captive had been tricked out with video cameras and recording devices that watched her every move. The thick metal chain was attached to the metal collar that was fastened around her neck. The chain could be made shorter or longer. If she didn't do what Mercer said fast enough, or didn't act like she enjoyed his company, he'd shorten the chain so the food, water or sewage bucket was inches out of her reach. A few times after she didn't do what he asked, he shortened the chain and left for a week. That week she thought she was going to die. She hated him but at the same time wanted him to come back so she could live. Eventually, she realized it was easier to do what he wanted and do it with a smile. That's how she survived.

Her kidnapper had even provided old books and magazines for her entertainment which the police noted was oddly compassionate. Anabel told them that if she did everything Mercer asked, he'd bring her treats like candy and cookies.

Initially she was terrified of him. But over all those months, he never physically hurt her. Her biggest fear was spending the rest of her life in his dungeon. She had to follow his commands exactly, immediately and without argument. When he told her to stand, she stood. If he told her to dance, she did. If she complied, he'd bring her treats, extra food and speak nicely to her. Sometimes he even sounded kind. At one point during her captivity, he asked her to repeat a series of words in various foreign languages. When she did, he corrected her pronunciation. She was told to repeat them over and over, and did so until he decided she had said them right. He sometimes used hand signals as well as verbal ones to get her to do and say what he wanted.

He was training her like a poodle.

Anabel was asked about the dozens of candy wrappers found outside and inside the house, especially the empty Skittles bags. She explained that after one of her dancing sessions, Mercer had asked her to read passages in French to him from a book he gave her. She must have read the French well because he wanted to reward her with a special treat. He asked her what her favorite candy was and she blurted out the first thing that came to her mind — Skittles. On his next weekend visit, Mercer brought back a case of Skittles candy. He'd give her a packet whenever she followed his commands just right.

Gradually the cops pieced together the full timeline based on Anabel's recollections and statements from people in Connecticut who'd had regular contact with Mercer. During the year Anabel was imprisoned, Mercer went back and forth weekly between Connecticut and New Hampshire. While in Connecticut, Mercer was able to keep tabs on his "pet" through the video app on his phone. When he was in the cabin in New Hampshire, he'd watch her from the monitors in the office on the main floor. Rarely did he ever see her in person. Most of their interaction happened remotely. The only time he was in the same room with her was when he brought down food and water. When that happened, she would plead with him to let her go. He never spoke to her when they were in the same room. Their conversations only happened through the video monitor or his phone app.

While the FBI was in Anabel's hospital room taking a statement, Brodsky and Marino received a call from the New Hampshire police. The NH police had been at the cabin collecting evidence and had gone through the house three more times. On their last pass, a technician lifted up a brick in the basement and found twelve additional candy wrappers — but they weren't Skittles. They were from Kit Kat bars.

When asked about the Kit Kat wrappers and if she was ever given any of those, Anabel gave an emphatic no. Apparently, she was highly allergic to chocolate and absolutely certain she had never asked for nor eaten them. The case took a wild turn then, all because of candy. If Anabel hadn't had the chocolate, it meant someone else had.

Twenty-four hours later, after a canine squad combed the property, two female bodies were discovered buried in different locations on the site. The medical examiner ultimately determined that one body had been there for at least fifteen years and the other around five.

"It was strange. I was the one chained up. He was always in total control. But, when he came down to bring me food and water, he seemed nervous and uncomfortable. Maybe it was guilt," Anabel said in one of her first TV interviews.

"I've never seen anything like this," said an FBI agent at a news conference. "You've got your rapists, your torturers and even the guys who want their own concubine. But Mercer treated this young woman like a pet. Sit, stand, bark, play dead. Why didn't he just get a dog from a shelter?"

After Anabel was reunited with her family, and her captor dead, her case was essentially closed. Still, many questions remained. Who killed John Mercer and why? And, did the person who killed Mercer know about Anabel and the two other women? Or, if the killer was trying to avenge the abductions, why didn't they save Anabel?

According to California Corrections, Mercer's son, Jacob, who had been incarcerated for arson, had been paroled long before Anabel's abduction. Given the son's history with fires, the police investigation refocused onto him. If John Mercer was truly a demented lunatic who wanted a human pet, the cops thought it possible he might have abused his own son as well. If that was the case, it may have been what drove the kid to set the fires in the first place. It also may have driven the son to get revenge. They say the apple doesn't fall far from the tree.

As for me, I was so done with everything. All I wanted was to put my energy into my book launch that was less than three months away. Like everyone else, I was so happy Anabel had been rescued and proud of Brodsky and Marino. I hadn't heard from them in a while. With all the attention they got after finding Anabel, I guess there was no time for me which came as a welcome relief. Her rescue felt like the end of a chapter. Most people wrote Mercer off as a mental case who got what he deserved.

Chapter 41

Six weeks and counting until *The Soul Collector's* publication day. February twenty-second was circled in red on my wall calendar. It wasn't a circle exactly, it was more like a big flowery star with lots of tentacles. Advanced copy reviews had started coming in and they were, thankfully, pretty good. The buzz spillover from the Anabel Ford/Mercer/Loomis case had definitely helped drum up additional interest in my book, but even that wasn't enough to ensure a bestseller.

"How do you think it's going?" said Teddy as he and I shared a bottle of Chardonnay on a rare night he was home early. "Some of my regular customers at the Bistro heard about your book in the news and everyone is dying to read it."

"Are they?" I said smiling as we clinked glasses.

"Remember what Natalie said, 'keep plugging it on social media and don't let up'. This book will either make us or break us. It has to be a bestseller."

"I'm trying."

"If it tops the charts, the money we'll make will be a game changer. A couple hundred thousand, Jills, and we'll be set."

I wanted to come through for my husband. Over the past six months he had literally worked seven days a week, putting in twelve to fourteen hour days. I couldn't blame him for wanting a piece of the action on the new restaurant. Why wouldn't he? It had been his dream since before we met. I had my own literary aspirations but I really wanted to make the money for Teddy. The way things were going, it looked like I was going to achieve my dream. I wanted to help him have his, too.

With Mercer dead, the criminal investigation was centered in New Hampshire rather than Connecticut. Meanwhile, the Connecticut Police continued reviewing hundreds of missing person cases from the New York Metropolitan area hoping to find a match to the two female bodies found buried near the cabin. The FBI also remained involved. Further excavation of Mercer's New Hampshire property and his Connecticut house were underway.

Back home with her family in Connecticut, Anabel Ford tried to resume her life. After a few weeks, the local media frenzy quieted as more current headlines took their place. The police also had new crimes to investigate and Brodsky and Marino's caseload was reallocated with one exception. They were still charged with figuring out who murdered John Mercer. Old Man Mercer may have been a demented nut job but he was still murdered. The detectives intended to find out who did it and why. According to a variety of new sources, the smart money was on Mercer's missing arsonist son, Jacob.

Continuing with the Mercer murder investigation, the detectives reviewed everything they had and soon things came full circle. As they reconnected the dots, it led them back to me and my books — again. It was January, the busiest month in recruiting. It happens every year. Right after the holidays, every company wants to hire immediately. I was swamped and my boss was breathing down my neck.

At the same time, I had everything invested in my book launch — my literary career, my husband's happiness and our financial well-being. I didn't need any more distractions from the police. I'd already answered their questions ten times. I needed to stay focused on my business and wanted at that point simply to be left alone.

When my doorbell rang and I saw the detectives' car out front, I let out a groan and rolled my eyes.

"We have a few questions we'd like clarification on," said Marino, standing on my front steps next to Brodsky.

"I don't know what I could possibly add at this point," I said, "but come in. I've only got a few minutes before I have to jump on a conference call."

Once seated in my living room, they assured me they'd be brief and began firing questions. I'd already answered all of them many times before and got a little irritated. That's when it dawned on me that these two cops were relentless. They wouldn't stop until they found the answer. Note to self — if I ever go missing, I want those two looking for me.

"The crimes from all three of your books happened here in Connecticut," said Brodsky going full Putin, which by the way, no longer rattled me. "The man at the center of it all, John Mercer, ends up dead. His untimely death ultimately leads us to an abducted college student."

"Look, I've told you everything I know," I said losing my patience. "My answers aren't going to change. How many times are you going to ask me the same thing?"

"Until we're satisfied we've learned everything there is to know," said the Russian. I let out a breath of frustration and Marino took over the questioning.

"Have you ever written anything, maybe a short story or a magazine article, where someone kidnapped a woman or anyone for that matter?" said the Italian.

At last, a new question.

"No," I said. "I've never written any short stories or published articles of any kind about kidnappings or abductions. The three books you're already familiar with are my only public work."

"What about a novel that you didn't publish?" said Marino.

"There are none."

"How about classes or writing groups? Ever take a writing course and share your writing with other authors?" said Marino. "Could you have shown somebody something at one of those writing groups you attended?"

I hadn't thought about that before. I had taken a writing class at a local community college and another one in an adult education program. I'd also been a member of several different author groups. I nodded and gave them any details I could recall.

"Is it possible you worked on an abduction story in one of those classes or groups?" said Brodsky.

I thought for a minute and then shook my head. "The classes I took were at least four years ago. I don't recall writing any abduction story. Both classes were dedicated to thrillers and the writing groups were for mystery and suspense writers. So, I guess it's possible there could have been a kidnapping story discussed. It was so long ago, nothing comes to mind."

The detectives asked me for the names of all the people in my writing groups and classes.

"I really don't remember anyone in particular. I took the writing class through the Education Annex in New Haven. You could check with them. On the author groups, I only went to them for about six months. Most of the people changed from week to week. I didn't make any significant friendships there. I think the person who ran one of the groups was named Christopher. I don't remember his last name."

"Clearly, your writing is somehow connected to all the crimes. Once we figure out what, why and how, things will fall into place," said Brodsky. "I'm confident about that."

"Let me know when it does," I said. "No one is more anxious to put this sad saga to bed than me." As I showed them to the door, I had a feeling it wasn't the last time I'd see them.

An hour later, it was getting dark and I walked down our long driveway to get the mail. As I got closer to the street, I saw a car idling a few feet from my mailbox. A man was standing in front of it putting something inside. It was dusk and a little difficult to see who the person was. Lots of local people hand-delivered flyers or promotional materials in the neighborhood. I wasn't alarmed until I got closer. The man had his hand in my mailbox.

"What are you doing here?" I shouted.

Holding a package in his hand, he looked up and appeared flustered. "Hi, Jillian."

"Why are you at my house?"

"I guess I should come clean," said Ned LaGrange. "The truth is, I've wanted to get your autograph on my own copies of your books. I was too embarrassed to ask you at the post office, so I wrote you a note and put it in the package with the books. I hope that wasn't too presumptuous of me."

When did Ned start caring about being presumptuous? Seemed to me he presumed every woman on the planet had the hots for him. I stared at him.

"I never told you, Jillian, but I'm also a writer. I'm not as accomplished as you. I haven't actually finished my manuscript yet, but I will soon. You inspired me to keep going. I really love your books. They're so dark."

Holy shit, I had been completely wrong about Ned. He didn't have the hots for me, he had an author-fan crush. In a weird way, I was flattered. An infatuation for a married woman was one thing, but being cuckoo for Coco Puffs about my books, I kind of liked that.

I forced a very tiny smile. "Sure Ned, I'll sign your books. But before I do, I have a question."

"Lay it on me."

"Are *you* JollyRoger44?"

Ned looked down and started to squirm. I had my answer.

"I'm kind of a pirate geek," he said. "Jolly Roger44 is my social media handle. Cool name, right?"

I looked down at the license plate on his car. UR MYN. "What does your license plate mean, Ned?"

"It's the title of my thriller, the one I'm currently working on. It's called UR MYN. It's about a stalker. Catchy, right?"

And there it was. JollyRoger44 wasn't a stalker after all, he was a fan.

Chapter 42

February — Publication Month

With only twenty days to go, I was on permanent pins and needles. Despite all the distractions leading up to the magnificent day, it was finally happening. I could think of nothing else and tried to remain positive. Occasionally, however, flashes of self-doubt overpowered me. What if everyone hated it? What if the reviewers panned it? What if this was my one and only shot at success and I bombed? Would I drift into obscurity? No fifty-seven language translations, no movie deal, no money for Teddy's restaurant — nothing. When those negative thoughts popped up, I had to work hard to push them down.

That week, Teddy had a rare evening off. We were having dinner together at home.

I opened a bottle of Sancerre and poured us each a glass. He had cooked us a beautiful dinner of scallops in a lemon butter rosemary sauce served over jasmine rice. I can still taste it. Say what you will about my husband, the man can cook.

They say being married to a cop is hard because of the crazy hours, but being married to an ambitious chef is no walk in the park either. Teddy's day began at noon and ended at midnight. I was usually asleep when he got home and he was asleep when I got up. We grabbed an evening here and there whenever we could. With the upcoming opening of T. Samuels, our one evening together had become zero. It was only temporary and I kept reminding myself that after the restaurant opened, things would get back to normal.

Teddy was still trying to raise more money to invest in the new place. He'd been able to secure a fifty thousand dollar loan from one of his cousins but it had to be paid back within three years with interest. Fifty thousand wasn't even close to the half million Teddy needed, or I should say, wanted. He was knocking himself out trying to raise the cash, and it wasn't happening. If we borrowed money with bad terms and the restaurant failed, we'd be permanently screwed. But if my book was the mega hit I hoped, that would change the game.

I tried to focus on all the positives. Linton Books had set me up with multiple interviews on radio, local newspapers, magazines and even a few podcasts. I'll admit, I felt a little like a celebrity when I was interviewed. People wanted to know what I thought about all sorts of things; how I came up with my characters and my plots, and what was my inspiration. It was very exciting. I remember thinking I could get used to being a celebrity.

According to my editor, Eric, Linton had received some advance orders already from libraries and small booksellers. He said it was a good sign. Also, Linton's in-house marketing team had several promotions in the works for my launch week.

"Everything is going great and we even got Alex Kramer to give us an endorsement quote for your book," said Eric. "That's huge. You know who Alex Kramer is, right?"

Duh. Kramer was one of Linton's most popular thriller authors and a five time *New York Times* bestselling author.

"Of course I know who he is," I said. "Kramer's major, he may be the best. He's sold millions of books. What was his quote?"

"'Gripping, scary and fast. Buckle your seatbelt'," said Eric.

"Alex Kramer said that about my book?" I said thrilled that the famous author even knew I existed. "He actually read *The Soul Collector*?"

"Not exactly," said Eric. "We have a 'you scratch my back, I'll scratch yours' arrangement here at Linton. The big authors don't have time to read a whole book, they just give us a slug line. Kramer read the synopsis. He liked the synopsis."

"Oh," I said, somewhat disappointed.

"That's the way it works," said Eric. "The important thing is, we got his quote and he has a lot of sway with readers."

After the cops found Anabel Ford and her story was all over the news, interest in me and my books picked up again because of my tenuous connection to Mercer. Right after Anabel was rescued, my name surfaced in the news quite a bit. Natalie had come up for another weekend of debauchery then and declared after watching a news show that I would surely have a bestseller.

"You can't buy this kind of buzz. This is the stuff PR people salivate over. I'd kill for this kind of publicity for one of my clients. You had it fall in your lap. Be happy, Jills. The Anabel Ford story was a win-win for you."

"Don't say it like that," I said. "That poor girl was chained in a dungeon for over a year. It must have been horrible for her."

Natalie's big hazel eyes blinked twice indicating surprise at my naiveté. "Don't you get it, Jills? You write scary thrillers. Terrible stuff associated with you, even remotely, sells your books. Think about Stephen King. He's probably a pussycat. But, his fans think he's crazy crackers and an inherently frightening person in real life. His terrifying brand helps sell his books. Trust me, *The Soul Collector* will do great."

My BFF's absolute certainty I'd have a hit, helped calm me down.

The remainder of that girls' weekend went as it usually did. Teddy was working, while Natalie and I laughed, moaned and drank too much wine. Eventually, I passed out and woke up the next morning with a headache. Life was back to normal.

Later that same week, Matthew called to check in. "Your big day is almost here."

"After all this time, it's hard to believe. Everything still on track?"

"That's the reason for my call," said Matthew. "To be honest, pre-orders have been a little more sluggish than we'd hoped."

"But I talked to Eric a few days ago and he said things were going well."

"Eric's not good at delivering bad news," said Matthew. "He wants everyone to like him. Me, I don't give a shit if you like me, I'm all about being direct."

I wondered how it was possible. My book wasn't out yet. How could it not be doing well before it even came out?

"But, no one's read my book yet," I said, starting to freak out. "How could it not be going well?"

None of it made sense. I had a well-respected publisher and a well-connected agent. Why was I getting bad news *before* my publication day?

"When all those crazy crimes were going on, especially that whole Anabel Ford fiasco, we got some great pickup," said Matthew. "People were talking about the case in Sydney and Paris. Now everything's died down. All I can say is, it's a crowded marketplace."

"Can't you do something?"

"Linton is doing everything they can. Right now we need you to be out there promoting your book as much as possible," he said. "We're in the final countdown."

Disillusioned and depressed, as I hung up the phone I promised to bang on social media and anything else I could think of. Panicking, I posted a few pointless things on Twitter and Instagram about the life of a writer. But deep down, I knew it wouldn't help. I thought about the promise I had made to my husband. Teddy was counting on me and my book for his new restaurant. I couldn't let him down.

The following Tuesday evening was rainy, cold and miserable, typical February weather in Connecticut. A cranky

Teddy had called from the city to let me know the American Bistro had been overbooked that night and that I shouldn't wait up. Later, alone in bed reading, I was about to drift off when a big clap of thunder and a bolt of lightning roused me. I looked over at the clock, it was just after midnight. I figured Teddy would be home within the next hour and tried stay awake and wait for him. After yawning several times, I gave up, turned off my bedside lamp, and pulled the blanket up around my neck. I was about to fall asleep a second time when my phone rang. It was Teddy.

"Where are you, babe?" I said, still groggy, eyes half open.

"You're not going to believe this," said my husband. "I fell asleep on the train and overshot the Medford station by three stops. I'm in fucking Harwich."

"You're kidding."

"My car is still parked at the Medford station and it's pouring out."

I looked at the clock, it was 12.25 a.m. "Can you get a cab?"

"Everything's closed," said Teddy. "The taxi stand must shut down at midnight."

"What about an Uber?"

"I already checked. With this weather, there's nothing around here. Can you come get me?"

"I'll leave in five minutes but it will take me at least twenty or more to get to Harwich."

I threw on the clothes I'd worn earlier that day that were draped over the back of a chair, grabbed my bag and went downstairs to the kitchen to get my keys.

As I pulled out of the driveway, another loud clap of thunder accompanied by two giant bolts of lightning splattered across the sky. The weather was dreadful and I guessed it might take more than twenty minutes to get to my husband. The wind was strong and I had to hold extra tight to the steering wheel and drive very slowly. I squinted through the blinding rain on the windshield, the fast moving wipers doing little.

Humongous puddles had formed on the two lane road to Harwich. I worried water would get into my engine and my car would die. This part of Connecticut was semi-rural, which meant there were few traffic lights and hardly any other cars on the road. If my car died in the middle of nowhere, I'd be screwed.

Thirty minutes later, I pulled into the Harwich train depot. Teddy looked like a drowned rat standing alone in the dark. I honked the horn as I pulled in and my headlights washed over him. He smiled, waved and jumped into the passenger seat.

"You're soaked," I said feeling very sorry for him as I reached into the back for his dry sweatshirt.

"I'm so mad at myself for missing the stop. Did I wake you up?"

"No," I said, telling a little white lie. I didn't want him to feel any worse than he already did. "We'll be home soon and you can take a hot shower."

"First, we have to stop and get my car from the Medford station."

"Can't we get it tomorrow, it's so late?"

"I've got an early breakfast meeting in the city with the investors. I have to get the car tonight."

I let out a sigh as I headed toward the Medford station on the opposite end of town from where we lived. With the terrible weather and massive puddles, it would take us at least thirty-five minutes to get there. Then, another fifteen to twenty minutes to get back to our house. I calculated I wouldn't get into bed until three o'clock in the morning if I was lucky. But I didn't complain because Teddy was so wet and miserable.

Like the Harwich station, the one in Medford was also a ghost town. There were only three cars left in the lot. One of them was Teddy's blue SUV. I pulled up next to the driver's side so he could leap into the other car without getting too wet.

"See you at home," he said as he opened the door and climbed in. "The weather's really bad. Stay close behind me so I can see you in my rearview."

Chapter 43

I did as Teddy said and stayed right on his tail as he plowed through a deep icy puddle exiting the train station lot. His big SUV sat high above the water. My car was a two door Honda Civic and low to the ground. I pressed the hands free button on my steering wheel to call him.

"What's up?" he said when he picked up my call.

"Be careful of the deep water, my car sits much lower than yours. I don't want to flood my engine."

We ended the call and I continued closely following him on the dark empty roads. Suddenly, Natalie's phone number popped up on the screen in my car. The first thing I thought was, why the hell was she calling me at two o'clock in the morning? Something bad must have happened. Some guy probably dumped her. Before I had a chance to accept the call, her voice magically came through my car's speaker.

"Hey, everything alright? Been thinking about you."

I was about to say, "I'm fine. Why are you calling me so late," when I suddenly heard Teddy's voice.

"I just picked up my car and I'm driving home from the Medford station now," he said.

Wait? What was happening? Why did I hear Natalie and Teddy speaking? Was Natalie calling me? I didn't understand. Natalie never called me so late and why could I hear both of them talking in *my* car?

"Poor you. The weather is so miserable. You really did it tonight, didn't you? How could you miss your stop?" said Natalie.

I couldn't get my brain wrapped around how their conversation was happening in my car and more importantly — why?

"I guess you wore me out, babe," said my husband in a syrupy voice I had never heard before. "You were amazing, by the way. Did I tell you that before I left?"

I kept thinking, what's happening? How is this call coming into my car? Is this a joke?

"I hate it when you have to leave me," purred my best friend. "I want you in my bed the whole night. When is that going to happen, Teddy Bear?"

"I told you I'd take care of everything. I've got a lot of balls in the air right now," said Teddy. "You know I love you, right?"

"I love you, too, my little Mystery Man," said Natalie all breathy, "more than anything in the world."

Mystery Man? Teddy was her fucking Mystery Man? Teddy? I was so confused and nothing made any sense. I couldn't understand what I was listening to. I was almost more focused on *why* I could hear them, than what they were actually saying.

"You have to trust me," said Teddy. "Everything has to be done right. The timing has to be perfect or the whole thing will fall apart. You understand that, don't you?"

I stayed close behind my husband's car. As we got nearer to our home, I started putting some of the pieces together. The first thing I figured out was why and how I could hear their call. It had to be because Teddy's and my phones were synced to both of our cars. By traveling so close behind him, Natalie's call was picked up in both vehicles. Who knew?

I remembered one time I was out for a walk and listening to one of my favorite crime podcasts on my phone.

I was heading up our driveway when Teddy's car pulled up behind me. Somehow the podcast on my phone had over-ridden the Country music station he was listening to in his car. Suddenly, the voices on his radio were talking about a murder. He drove up next to me, opened his window and I heard my podcast blasting from the speakers inside his car.

That same technology glitch must have also happened with Natalie and Teddy's phone call. At first, I was so busy working out "how" that it took my mind away from "what" and "who". But, not for long. It didn't take a genius to comprehend that my perfect husband and dearest friend were having an affair. Apparently, they were in love and I was inconveniently in the way. But it was the *end* of their conversation that was the most horrifying part. As they said their loving goodbyes, I thought I was going to throw up on my steering wheel.

Talk about a double whammy, I had been betrayed by my husband *and* my best friend. They had been my "go-to people". Normally, I would have talked to either Natalie or Teddy about what had happened. Given the circumstances, however, that was out of the question. I continued driving behind Teddy feeling completely alone and frankly devastated.

The first half of the overheard phone call was difficult to process, but the second part and finale had me literally gasping for air. Honestly, I don't know how I was able to drive. It's a miracle I didn't kill myself after what I had heard combined with the horrendous road conditions.

We turned onto our street and I followed Teddy the last mile in silence. His car turned right onto our long driveway with me right behind. As I waited for him to pull into the garage, I realized my face was wet, tears dripping from my chin. I wiped my cheeks and chin with my sleeve and tried to put on a game face as I pulled my car into the garage next to his.

He waited for me by the basement door and let me walk first as we ascended the stairs to the first floor. Neither of us spoke, him because he was tired, wet and presumably exhausted from "the most amazing sex he ever had", and me because I was in shock. It was late and we bypassed the first floor entirely heading straight up another flight to our bedroom.

I washed my face while Teddy pulled off his clothes, tossed them on the floor and dove into our bed. It occurred to me that only hours before he had been in *her* bed. I looked at my reflection in the bathroom mirror wondering how things had gone so terribly wrong.

I had always thought Teddy and I were so happy. At that moment I started to question my entire marriage — every word, every late night, every moment. How could I have been so completely wrong? Until that night if anyone had asked, I would have said I had a wonderful marriage and was absolutely sure Teddy felt the same way. We were partners. But, if I had so poorly judged my husband and my marriage, how many other things in my life did I get wrong? Natalie, for starters — the duplicitous bitch. I questioned my judgment on everything I'd ever done, every decision I'd ever made, every person I'd ever trusted.

I knew Natalie was quirky and self-centered but I always thought she had my back. Turns out she *had* my back but it had a knife in it. I tried to figure out when their affair had started. How long had Teddy and Natalie been pretending? How many months or years had they been laughing at me? Natalie's Mystery Man went back quite a few years. Tears came again and I sniffled. It was late and I was exhausted on so many levels.

I didn't want to get into bed next to him but I had no energy to do a knock down drag out at that moment. On the flipside, it would have been strange if I went to sleep in another room. I needed to process things and come up with a plan. I couldn't let Teddy know I knew anything — not yet. Crawling into bed, I positioned myself as far from him as possible. I didn't want to accidentally touch him or even feel the heat coming off his body.

Typical man, by the time I got into bed, he was already snoring. I lay there wide awake consumed by a million sad and angry thoughts. Mourning the loss of my future, I knew then there would be no children or grandchildren, at least not with Teddy. My husband and my best friend didn't love me the way they pretended, the way I had loved them. They loved each other and more than anything wished I would disappear.

Chapter 44

While I tried to hold myself together and plan my next move, my publication date was fast approaching. It was ironic. My book suddenly seemed so unimportant after what I had learned about my husband and former best friend.

Regardless, the final countdown to publication day was well underway and I had to suck it up. I was teetering on the brink when my agent called and told me he and Eric had met for a pre-launch celebratory dinner at a steak place in Midtown. Apparently, when they clinked glasses Eric confessed he had worried they weren't going to pull it off. Then Matthew said something to me that I didn't understand, something about help from their "new friends". I was about to ask what he meant by "new friends" when he jumped off our call to pick up another. I didn't really care. After learning my husband loved it when Natalie dug her nails into his back while they're "doing it", not too much mattered to me. How do you recover after hearing a conversation like that? Teddy and Natalie's scorching words echoed in my head and I didn't know what to do.

Teddy on the other hand had no idea I was on to them. He carried on as he'd always done. The day after that fateful car ride and phone call, he gave me a kiss on the cheek before leaving to catch the train into the city. The touch of his lips on my skin burned and sent a chill through my body, every hair on end. It took everything in me to feign a loving look on my face and not push him away and burst into tears. That he could act so normally and even be slightly affectionate after what he said, told me everything I needed to know about the man I married.

I thought back to a thousand moments in our marriage including some recent ones. How Teddy had pretended to be jealous when my old boyfriend had contacted me on Facebook and when Ned LaGrange flirted with me at the post office. At the time, I thought Teddy's smoldering anger was a normal possessive spouse thing. His jealous outburst had made me feel wanted and I kind of enjoyed it a little. Obviously, it was a total act. He didn't care if I flirted with anyone. Teddy was too busy climbing Mount St Natalie to worry about me. My perfect husband had turned out to be a world-class liar.

As Teddy got ready to leave the house that morning, I maintained my composure and smiled sweetly. I hadn't figured out what my next move was going to be, but one thing I knew for sure: whatever happened would be on my terms not theirs. Since they were unaware I knew anything, it gave me the upper hand. From then on, everything I did had to be played just right.

Natalie actually called me the morning after I heard their "sexy love chat". I saw her name come up on caller ID and my stomach literally wrenched. I wanted to throw my phone against the wall as if somehow it would hurt her. I didn't do it. I had much to do and needed my phone.

"What's up?" I said trying to sound casual as I answered her call.

"You're not going to believe what just happened," she said in a totally normal voice.

Let me guess, Natalie? Did your best friend find out that you're sleeping with her husband? Like I cared what was going on in that lying bitch's life. She had known me long before she met Teddy. Despite that, she obviously had no allegiance to me at all. What happened to the girlfriend code? Even if she found my husband attractive, out of respect for our "best friend" status, she should have walked away. I would have. I'd been making excuses for Natalie Bloom for years and she finally showed her true colors.

I don't know why I was surprised. Natalie had always been out for herself with no regard for anything or anyone. She decided she wanted Teddy, and that was that. What bugged me was she was so physically beautiful, she could have had anyone she wanted. Why did she take *my* husband?

I'm not absolving Teddy for any of it. Still, he's not that smart. I don't think he orchestrated their affair or their horrific plan. Sure, he's a great cook but he's not that clever. My money was on the red-lipped walking time bomb. I was certain she had made the first, second and third moves and that Teddy was merely a fly caught up in her dark web. That doesn't excuse him, of course, he didn't have a gun to his head. However, I suspected Lady Macbeth was the one steering the ship. Natalie has to be in charge. Still, my husband went along with it and that made him her equal partner in crime — and punishment.

The big question remained: what the hell do I do? I couldn't play dumb forever. I had to take control of the situation, especially with my book about to launch. Teddy was "busy" in New York with the new restaurant and his demanding after-hours activities with Natalie, which gave me plenty of alone time to work things out. I approached the problem like one of my thrillers playing out several different scenarios in my head, each with different risks and rewards. But it wasn't until Brodsky and Marino showed up at my house again, that everything became crystal clear and I knew exactly what I had to do.

"We checked out the Education Annex in New Haven. That thriller writing class you took was taught by a Seth Glassman," said Marino reading off his phone.

"I remember him," I said nodding. "I got a lot out of his class."

Marino handed me a piece of paper with a list of a dozen names on it. "Glassman didn't save any materials or writing samples from that class. He said he gets rid of everything at the end of each semester. He did give us the class roster. Take a look. Any names jump out at you?"

I looked at the list. Given what was going on in my marriage, I had little interest in an old writing class. I didn't recognize a single name. "It was an eight-week course, one night a week for two and a half hours. We didn't socialize. The teacher gave us writing prompts, we wrote and then we went home."

"Maybe you read something out loud to the class," said the Russian eyeing me suspiciously as was his custom.

"A few times," I said. "But I don't remember writing anything about abductions or kidnappings. It's not really my brand."

"We're going to talk to everyone who took that class to see if anyone remembers anything," said Brodsky taking the list back. He also informed me they had been in contact with the Meet Up writing group run by Christopher, and taken statements from members who were in it when I was.

"One woman named Kathleen said she remembered you wrote pretty dark stuff," said Marino chomping on a piece of gum. "Maybe someone in your group latched on to you, read something you wrote and decided to reenact it to get your attention? Maybe someone had a romantic interest in you?"

"Look Detective, I write thrillers, they're dark. And, I don't remember getting any romantic vibe from anyone there."

"I'm sure this seems unnecessary but it's our job to track down every detail," said Marino. "It was a long time ago. Memories are fluid. You may not remember something but it's possible someone else will."

Those two detectives were going to be in my life for the foreseeable future unless I made a bold move. Obviously, something had to be done about Teddy and the slut. I decided Brodsky and Marino were going to be my partners and help me make things right.

Chapter 45

With all the insanity going on, I had missed several visits to see my mother and felt tremendously guilty. I was the only one she had left. The dementia unit had called a few times saying Mom had been asking for me. Despite recently learning my husband didn't love me, I put on my big girl pants and went to see my mother. When I arrived and spoke to the attendant, I learned that Mom hadn't been asking for *me*, she had been asking for Camille. After the whole Teddy-Natalie bombshell, being called Camille seemed so unimportant.

Armed with my usual sandwiches and the bag of candy for my mother, I walked through the lobby of the Fairview Gardens Senior Living Center that Friday at noon. I had learned the hard way that if I didn't show up with chocolate, things could get ugly. Mom was sitting in her wheelchair lined up along a wall next to a dozen other residents. Across the room, an old black and white movie played loudly. Based on the look or lack thereof in all their eyes, I was pretty sure none of them were following the plot. I wondered if they knew the TV was even on or if they knew they were in a dementia unit?

My mother was at the end of the row, a blank expression on her face. Carrying my bag of goodies, I walked over to her with a big, forced smile on my face.

"Hey, Mom," I said softly as I lightly touched her shoulder to get her attention. She turned her head and blinked several times as if to adjust her eyes to the new being standing in front of her — me. I expanded my smile as far as it would go making my cheeks hurt.

"How are you today, Mom?"

A few more seconds passed until a glimmer of recognition appeared in her eyes. She smiled. "Camille, you came. Where have you been?"

"Mom look at me, I'm Jillian." I don't know why I still corrected her. It was a habit and I did it almost every time. I so wanted her to remember me but she never did anymore. Somehow, I had been wiped completely out of her memory, replaced by my older sister. I told myself it didn't matter who she asked for. I knew my mother loved me. She was just confused. After all, she *was* in a dementia unit. Despite my inner dialogue, it still hurt every time she called me Camille. It seemed unfair given that I was the one who had taken care of her, not my sister.

After Camille died, my mother and I got closer without my sister's angry shadow looming over us. When I met Teddy, my mother was so happy. I remember her joyfully fussing over the details of my wedding and her excitement as she walked me down the aisle.

Since the beginning of her illness, all of her care had fallen on me. I did it with love but I'm not going to lie, it was a lot of work. Some weeks I could barely keep it together. That's why it was particularly galling after taking care of her all those years, that she didn't know who I was. She remembered the one daughter who had given her nothing but grief. I knew Mom didn't mean it, but it still cut like a knife.

Seated in her wheelchair, my mother rummaged furiously through the bag of candy on her lap. Ripping off the wrappers, she stuffed two at a time into her mouth.

"Slow down, Mom. You'll choke," I said gently as I took the bag from her hands and replaced it with a turkey sandwich. "Eat this first, then you can have the chocolate for dessert."

By some miracle, she didn't fight me that day and appeared content to do as I asked. I tried to entertain her by telling her about everything going on with the publication of my book and the surrounding publicity. I'm not sure my words made any sense to her. A few times she said "that's nice", but they weren't at the right times.

When I ran out of book stories, I told her what I had really come to tell her. After learning about Teddy, I really needed my mother. I told her about the call I'd overheard in the car between my husband and Natalie. I desperately wanted my mother's advice and prayed she might have a clear moment and offer me some wisdom. I don't know why I thought she would miraculously become lucid and provide me with answers. When I finished with all the torrid details of Teddy and Natalie's phone conversation, my mother looked directly at me. Her light blue eyes sparkled and she smiled just before she said, "That's nice."

I handed her the candy bag and her focus shifted to that. I had vanished once again.

"Mom," I said trying to get her attention as I stood to leave. "I've gotta go now."

She stopped chewing her chocolate and looked up at me. "Thank you for coming, Camille."

"I'm Jillian, Mom. Camille . . . is dead."

"Why would you say such a terrible thing? How do you know that?"

I stared at her for a moment as her attention shifted back to the candy bag.

"Because I killed her," I said softly as I turned and left the room.

Walking out of the Memory Unit, I took the elevator down to the main floor remembering so clearly the night Camille died.

I was eighteen, my sister was twenty. We had gone to a small house party in a neighboring town. I didn't want to go with Camille but we only had one family car. She had been relatively sober for a while but remained actively bitchy to me. I drove and we didn't say a word to each other on the way there. When we got to the house there were only a handful of people and Camille immediately proclaimed the party "dead". With a snarl on her face she wandered off to the backyard, presumably to look for some action. I saw a few friends and tried not to think about the black cloud who was my sister.

There was plenty of alcohol and weed at the party and around midnight Camille staggered up to me totally wasted. She couldn't stand upright without holding on to something.

"This party sucks," she slurred as she took a gulp of a beer. "There's a better party on the other side of town. I want to go there."

"I'm not leaving," I said. "I know what that other party is. Everyone there is doing drugs. Forget it."

"Fuck you," my sister said as she finished the last of her beer in a red solo cup.

I tried to move away from her but she followed me demanding to be taken to the other party.

"Come on, Jillian. This party is crap," she said. "Don't be such a selfish bitch."

When I tried to ignore her and turned to talk to one of my friends, my drunken sister grabbed my long hair from behind. Yanking it hard, she nearly knocked me over. Angry and embarrassed, I tried to get away from her by walking quickly to the side of the house. She followed me spewing a litany of nasty insults. Eventually, she cornered me and we were alone.

"I said, I want to go to that other party. Who put you in charge?" she said, spittle coming out of her mouth. "You're just a pathetic little bitch. I'll bet our father only left because of you. You make me sick every single day."

I stared at her full of fury.

"I want to go to that party, now," she demanded and poked me hard in the arm.

I felt myself shaking. I was so over her. Embarrassed and furious, I fumbled through my bag for the car keys and threw them at her.

"Take the fucking keys, Camille," I said as they fell on the ground in front of her. "Go to your stupid party. I don't give a shit what you do anymore."

She was so drunk, she nearly fell down trying to pick up the keys. "Fuck you," she said as she grabbed them from the grass and stumbled toward the front of the house. I was so mad and so sick of her ruining my mother's life and mine. Every waking minute of my life had been consumed with Camille. I hated her.

My sister never made it home that night or to that other party. The police said her car went over the divider and hit a tree. She was dead when the ambulance arrived. No one blamed me for Camille's death, but I knew I shouldn't have given her the car keys. I told my mother and the police I didn't know how drunk she was. I lied. I knew she was smashed, but I didn't care. I've never told anyone that except for my therapist. He said it wasn't my fault. The truth is, if I hadn't given her the keys, she'd still be alive.

She's dead and I killed her.

Chapter 46

Later that afternoon, the New Haven police contacted Brodsky and Marino about a large knife discovered sticking out of a grave in the St Regis cemetery. That came as a surprise to everyone involved. John Mercer's son, Jacob the arsonist, had been picked up but surprisingly had rock solid alibis for all the crazy crimes. After ruling Mercer Junior out, Mercer Senior the abductor, was the prime suspect. Convinced he had been behind all the crimes and was now dead, law enforcement hadn't expected another knife, fire, spray paint or any new loose end at this late stage in the investigation. The nagging question on everyone's mind: how were my books connected to the whole mystery and who killed John Mercer?

During one of our many police interactions, Marino explained his master theory about motives. Almost always he said, "People kill for four reasons. I call them the four Ls: love, lust, loathing and loot." He believed I had a fan who had read all of my books and recreated them as an homage, or more appropriately, "a sick tribute" to me. That put the perp in the "love and lust" buckets. It occurred to me that Ned LaGrange fit Marino's profile exactly. Ned had read all of my books, joined my exercise class and swam in the lane right next to me at the pool.

However, what the love and lust theory didn't explain was why John Mercer was killed. The detectives eventually concluded that Mercer's murder was only related to one of my books. They also determined the abduction of Anabel Ford and the murders of those two other women had no connection to me. Frustrated, their hunt grew cold with too many pieces that didn't fit together.

When I waltzed into the Medford police station that same afternoon the new knife was found asking for a private meeting with the two detectives, they were naturally surprised. I could see it in their eyes. As a writer who studies people, I spot little tells like that all the time, when I'm paying attention. Which of course begs the question, how the hell did I miss the whole Teddy and Natalie deception? I had asked myself that question a thousand times since that rainy night in the car. The only answer I could come up with was: I didn't want to know.

"Ms Samuels," said Marino as we all stood staring at each other in the Medford PD lobby. "We were on our way to your house. We just received a report that another knife was found at a grave in New Haven."

"Another one? Detectives, could we go somewhere to talk privately?" I said. They nodded and led me down an institutional green hallway and into an empty interview room containing a large metal table and four chairs. After we were seated, they waited for me to explain why I was there. After everything that had happened, I honestly wasn't sure where to start.

"What did you want to discuss with us?" said Brodsky peering at me over a pair of black reading glasses. I hadn't seen him wear those before. They made him look smarter.

I squirmed in my chair while attempting a serene composure. After learning my husband was in love with my best friend, creating the illusion of "serene" wasn't easy. How was one supposed to act under those circumstances? There's no playbook. Do I confront my husband? Do I tell him to pack his bags and get out of the house? "Take your things and leave, my divorce lawyer will be in touch?" That so wasn't me. I wasn't a yeller or a curser — okay sometimes. I typically approached conflict in a much more cerebral way.

It had only been a few days since I'd overheard that awful phone conversation. Since then, I'd had numerous interactions with both Natalie and Teddy. Each time, I had acted like everything was totally normal. Believe me, it was hard to keep that facade going when all I really wanted to do was cry and break things. I was at a critical juncture. There was a road in front of me with a fork in it and I still hadn't decided which path to take. I had to remain completely composed until I figured out what I really wanted. Only then could I design and implement my final plan.

What I really needed was time to think things through but I didn't have that luxury. Confused and in a heightened emotional state, there was a lot to consider. For two days after I learned the awful truth, I did a lot of meditation and yoga. Slowly, the fog lifted and I had to accept my new reality. My husband was in love with someone else and my best friend didn't give a shit about me.

For two anger filled days, I cobbled together my plan of action. To make it work, I would need help.

Sitting with the detectives in that putrid green room, I tried to act like it was just any other day. In retrospect, given the stressful circumstances, I don't think I maintained my usual poker face. Marino noticed I was agitated and brought me a cup of hot tea. While I slowly sipped, both men waited for me to reveal why I was there. Finally, I cleared my throat. I was ready to talk.

"I recently found out my husband is having an affair with my best friend," I said, waiting for astonished looks to cross their faces. None came. I guess cops have heard that one before. An affair clearly wasn't exactly big news in their line of work.

"Sorry to hear that," said Marino with a "hang in there" look on his face, which I appreciated. Not surprisingly, I got nothing from Brodsky. At least Marino offered me a little sympathy.

"It's always the best friend," said Brodsky with little emotion. "It's better for a marriage to not have best friends. They screw things up."

Call me crazy, but it sounded like the Russian was blaming Teddy's affair on me for having a best friend. Seriously?

"Is there a particular reason you're sharing your personal story with us? Is there some connection to the Mercer case?" said Marino gently.

I took a deep breath and let it out while searching my soul one final time. If I went ahead with my next statement, there would be no turning back. The wheels would be set in motion and the die cast. I took a moment to reflect. After what I had heard in the car that night, no amount of counseling could ever resurrect my marriage. There was no way I could ever trust Teddy again. I asked myself one last time if I was absolutely sure I wanted to go through with it. Before I had the answer straight in my own mind, I heard the words tumble out of my mouth.

"I believe my husband is responsible for everything that's happened."

Both pairs of eyes across from me opened wide. "Why do you think that?" said Brodsky leaning in so close I felt his warm breath on my face.

"I think he launched the exploding drones, painted the men silver and killed one of them. It was Teddy who left the knives and notes on the graves. And, I'm pretty sure Teddy was also the person who killed John Mercer."

"But, we found absolutely no connection between your husband and the victims." said Marino. "Why would he do all that?"

"Money," I said without emotion. "My husband needs money and a lot of it for his new restaurant venture. I believe he thought if he made the events in all my books come true, it would send my new book into the bestseller stratosphere and we'd make a bundle. Then, he'd invest that money into his new restaurant. What I didn't know was, he also intended to get rid of me and replace me with my former best friend."

"What about Anabel Ford? How does she play into this?" said Marino.

"I haven't worked that part out yet. I only learned about everything two days ago. I'm still trying to figure it all out, but I *know* he's behind it."

"How did you learn about your husband's affair?" said Brodsky.

I lowered my voice slightly. "It happened the other night. Teddy was on his way home from the city and missed his stop. It was stormy and raining. I picked him up and drove him back to the Medford station to get his car. As I closely followed him home, a phone call meant for him somehow also came through the speaker in my car. I knew the voice. It was my best friend, Natalie."

Chapter 47

Even now, I remember each word the two lovebirds said as if it had only just happened. Big mouthed Natalie encouraging Teddy the whole time. There were moments he seemed a bit reticent about the whole thing, but not her. She was all in, one hundred percent. Since Natalie never second-guessed herself, that wasn't surprising. She went after whatever she wanted with no consideration of repercussions — case in point, all those restraining orders. Up until then, I had always admired that about her — until she went for my husband . . . and my life.

It was bad enough hearing they were having an affair. But, it was the end of their conversation that nearly made me pass out in my car. That's when they went over the details of their plan to kill me exactly one week before my book's publication. They weren't even going to allow me to enjoy my publication day, the one I'd been waiting for my entire life. That was harsh, and oddly, the biggest slap in the face of all.

"It's got to be one week before the book comes out," said Natalie's voice as it boomed through my car's speaker. "The headlines about her murder will be huge when her book is released. We'll make a fortune, Teddy. You'll have all the money you need to launch your restaurant empire and I'll be right there by your side."

I thought about all those times I couldn't get either one of them on the phone. They were probably together at her place having a good laugh. An affair is one thing, but murdering me took their duplicity to another level entirely. Literally hearing Teddy and Natalie broadcast their deadly intentions gave me an idea. When I looked at the whole thing from a different perspective, I realized their selfish, treacherous scheme would solve all of my problems. They say God works in mysterious ways.

First order of business — I needed to protect myself. With that in mind, I came up with what I thought was a pretty solid idea. I do so appreciate a good strategy followed up with a well-executed plan.

When all the crimes related to my books started happening, Teddy had insisted we have security cameras installed all over our house for safety. It's funny now because I was the one who didn't want the cameras. In the end, those freakin' cameras played a pivotal role in my husband's ultimate take down.

Initially, I was so shocked my husband and best friend were having an affair that the secondary murder plot of me almost didn't register — until it finally did. On their call, the two star-crossed lovers had announced the date they planned to terminate me. Obviously, I had to stop them. I couldn't let them just kill me. I suppose I could have called the police and reported it, but what would I have told them? I had no concrete proof other than what I had heard on that random car call. The lack of concrete evidence put me in a bit of a bind. Surely, if either one of them were questioned by the police, they would deny everything. They'd chalk up my accusations to the stress I'd been under from the murders, the explosions and my book launch. I couldn't let them get away with that, not to mention, my life would still be in danger.

So, I came up with a far better more comprehensive solution. It took me a while to figure out exactly how to do it, but when it gelled, I was confident it would work. It also neatly solved several other nagging problems. I didn't have much time to prepare because "Ted-Nat" were planning to turn off my lights in only a few days. That following Tuesday night was to be my last. Given the time restraints, I got busy and worked out the scene the way I do in all of my thrillers. The devil is always in the details.

The following Tuesday afternoon, the day of my planned demise, I called Teddy at the restaurant. I told him I was exhausted and planning to go to bed early.

"Take a long hot bath," he said. "That always relaxes you. Put on some music. Pop a Xanax or two, light a few candles, and have a glass of wine."

What a dirty dog he was as he encouraged me to let my guard down with drugs and alcohol. "You deserve a good rest, Jills," he said. A good rest? If he had his way, I'd be "resting" for eternity. I wanted to scream but stopped myself. There was a much bigger agenda at stake so I kept my mouth shut.

"Good idea," I said, biting my tongue. "I got a new lavender bubble bath I've wanted to try."

I casually mentioned I planned to silence my phone so I could truly relax. I played Teddy like a world-class violinist at Carnegie Hall. Then, I got to work.

Why did I go to the police? My plan wouldn't work without them. The detectives were extremely supportive when I told them about my husband and his murder scheme. They got fully onboard and shortly thereafter, my Tuesday night takedown was hatched.

Brodsky and Marino along with a couple of uniformed officers came to my house that Tuesday morning. They made sure the feed for the house camera's went directly to a surveillance van parked in the woods on the outskirts of my property. I had purchased a stunningly lifelike female mannequin and outfitted her with a wig that was identical to my hair. She would be placed in the bubble bath, her back to the bathroom door. With the room only illuminated by a few flickering candles, it would look exactly like me in the tub.

"Do you think this will work?" I said to the detectives a few hours before the appointed time.

"If what you told us was accurate," said Marino, "we'll catch them. Everything will be recorded by the cameras. We'll have it all on video."

"Killing you so your new book would become a posthumous blockbuster breaks the entire case wide open," said Brodsky checking one of the cameras a second time.

"With the two of them behind everything — the drones, the paint, the murders and the marked graves, it all makes sense," said Marino.

"It also explains why John Mercer was killed," said Brodsky adjusting another camera. "Mercer's death had always been the outlier in this investigation. Your husband needed another body in the mix to keep the momentum going on your book. Teddy's been a busy boy."

Life can often be funny and unpredictable. Things don't always go the way you plan. I know that better than anyone. Despite all the steps taken to recreate the crimes from my books, it still wasn't quite enough to ensure a bestseller. In fact, the closer we got to publication day, the chatter on social media waned so much that my publisher and agent were genuinely concerned.

When Teddy and Natalie realized my book wasn't headed to the top of the charts, they concocted a plan to guarantee they'd get their pay day. Surely, they reasoned, if an author was murdered in the same way her main character is killed (strangled in her bathtub), on the eve of her book launch, it *had* to sell millions of copies. With me gone, my adoring husband would have all the money he wanted for his goddamn restaurant empire plus a little extra from my life insurance policy. I had never realized it before but it was always about the money for Teddy — "lust" may have been a part of it, but when all was said and done, it was about the "loot".

With the stage set in my bathroom and the cameras rolling, I waited with the detectives in the police van hidden in the woods behind my house. For nearly two hours, we sat there quietly with no activity. At one point Brodsky shared a split second look with his partner. I saw it. They were starting to doubt my credibility and story. Had I misunderstood Natalie and Teddy's phone call? Did I get the timing wrong? Where the hell were they? As the minutes dragged on I wondered if maybe they'd had a change of heart. Maybe they didn't want me dead after all?

I was just warming to that idea when I saw a flicker of headlights coming up the driveway. The half-moon in the clear sky provided enough light so that I could see it was Teddy's car. Oddly, he didn't pull into the garage. He drove to the outer perimeter of our two acre property and turned off the engine.

"That's Teddy," I whispered to the detectives, our eyes remaining fixed on the screens in front of us. There were no cameras out on the edge of the property so for a minute or two we were flying blind. The cameras were motion sensitive which meant we couldn't see anything until Teddy entered through the back door of the house. When he did, his image was picked up in the kitchen — clear as day. He was carrying a brown paper bag as he quietly walked across the room.

When I told him I was going to take a bath the same night they planned to strangle and drown me, he and Natalie must have done a happy dance. I had made everything easy-peasy. The only thing better would have been if I offered to choke myself to death while bathing. I presumed his original plan was to kill me first and then dump my body into a full tub. Now, he didn't have to go to all that trouble. I'd already be in the water. You're welcome.

Brodsky, Marino and I watched Teddy move around the kitchen. As he started to head up the stairs, he looked back. He remembered the cameras and walked directly to the master security panel in the dining room. We watched him erase the existing footage before he turned off the entire video surveillance system. That's when our screens went dark. Without cameras, Teddy could go upstairs, attempt to kill a dummy and there would be no recording of it, no witness of his perfidy.

"Shit," said Brodsky getting up when the cameras went off. "That fucking guy shut it all down."

"Don't worry. I've got an app to override that," I said already on my phone. "I can turn it right back on." Within three seconds the cameras were on and our monitors were receiving and recording the video feed again.

"That was close," said Marino letting out a held breath as we continued to watch the drama play out. Teddy's image was picked up again at the top of the stairs. He looked like a man without a care in the world. As he walked down the hall toward our room he stuck his head into the two other bedrooms, presumably to double check they were empty. They were.

Satisfied, he stood outside the doorway to our bedroom for a second before he entered. Once inside, he was picked up again by the camera in our dimly lit room. Without a sound, he went over to the bed, opened the paper bag he had been carrying and pulled out a rope.

"Looks like he's got all the toys," said Brodsky, his eyes never moving from the screen, "that's the kind of metal and fiber rope used by professionals. Your husband is deadly serious about this. This wasn't meant just to scare you."

"I never thought it was," I said.

Teddy took the rope and carefully wrapped it around both of his hands making a two foot taut line between them. He looked like he knew what he was doing and I wondered if he had practiced in advance. With the rope securely around his hands, he faced the bathroom door I had deliberately left ajar.

He pushed it gently and the door to the bathroom slowly swung open, the cameras inside capturing his movement. Why did we have cameras in our bathroom? That was all Teddy. When he was a kid he had watched an old black and white movie called *Psycho* where some blonde woman gets murdered in a shower. It had scared the hell out of him and started his lifelong shower murder phobia. I used to tease him about it, occasionally coming into the bathroom while he was showering holding a large butcher knife. He didn't find it amusing but it made me laugh every time.

When Teddy had the cameras installed in our house, he had insisted we put one in the master bathroom. At first, I vetoed the bath-cam but he was adamant that we had full security coverage. Aware of my husband's illogical bathroom death fear, I had reluctantly agreed. Little did I know then how important that decision would ultimately be. Technically speaking, Alfred Hitchcock may have saved my life.

Teddy waited just inside the bathroom door. From his vantage point, I appeared to be lounging or sleeping in a bubbly lavender bath. The soft rock music playing on the radio covered any noise Teddy might have made. I watched on the monitor as he walked up behind me, or what he thought was me, and lifted the taut rope high over my head.

"He's about to make his move," said Brodsky into his phone alerting the other officers stationed in the bedroom closet.

A second later, Teddy's hands swooped down as he swung the rope in an arc around what he thought was my neck. Wrapping it twice, he pulled — hard. From the angle of the camera, I couldn't see Teddy's face but imagined his look of horror when what he thought was my head, popped off and fell into the soapy water. When that happened, he jumped back and let out a blood curdling scream.

Brodsky shouted into his phone. "Move." Two uniformed police officers burst out of my bedroom closet into the bathroom. Still in shock from ostensibly seeing my head fall off into the tub, Teddy was easily wrestled to the floor and cuffed within seconds. At the same time, two other officers approached the parked car in our yard. Seconds later, my BFF Natalie, was read her rights.

That's the way it all went down. Within an hour, Natalie and Teddy were booked at the Medford police station for my attempted murder. They were also arrested for the drone explosions, the silver men killing and assault, and the murder of John Mercer.

It was clear to the police that my husband had been willing to do anything, including killing me, in his quest for money and power. I'm still not convinced he would have gone through with the whole scheme without Natalie's prodding. Regardless, he carried it out and because of that, would probably spend the better part of his life in a federal prison. Buh-bye.

Natalie too would likely be wearing an orange jumpsuit for a while, hardly one of the designer outfits she was accustomed to. Orange was so not her color. And that special "Sisters" mug she bought for me at that yard sale because she "loved me so much", I smashed it into a hundred pieces with a hammer in my driveway. Buh-bye.

Chapter 48

In an ironic twist, the news about Teddy and Natalie's arrest broke on my publication day. The story was carried nationally and internationally. It got media coverage in Europe, Asia and Australia. The next day it was picked up in South America and Africa. The world was talking about us, about me. I was everywhere.

A week later my agent and I did a Zoom session.

"You're not the only one with big news," said Matthew as he sipped his morning coffee wearing a satisfied smile. "When your book shot through the roof, I received several employment inquiries from a few big agencies. Alex Kramer wants me to represent him."

"Congratulations," I said.

"Not only that, your favorite Linton editor, Eric Shaw, has also been getting job inquiries from several major publishing houses. You didn't hear this from me, but Eric has an interview tomorrow with Bedminster Publishing for a senior editor position. Looks like your bestselling book paved the way for all of us to move on to bigger and better."

In only one week, my little book baby had done so well that it had impacted both Matthew and Eric's careers in a significant way. When the news of my dear husband's arrest hit the wires, *The Soul Collector* took off like a freakin' bullet train making publishing heads spin.

It was then Matthew finally shared how he and Eric hadn't been the passive agent and editor I had thought. According to Matthew, the two of them had cooked up a little plan of their own to move my book along the road to stardom. Their scheme was completely unethical but frankly, who am I to throw stones. Matthew said they manufactured personas of hundreds of fake people on every social media channel so they could create a groundswell of interest and chatter about me and my books. So those were their "new friends". Clever.

It kind of worked, too. Not to the extent of what was needed to become a mega hit but it did keep my books moving along in pre-sale. In the end, it was the carefully orchestrated murder attempt on my life that turned *The Soul Collector* into a global sensation. Even so, I was rather grateful that they had taken it upon themselves to go that extra mile. Professional commitment like that is so rare these days.

Ten days after publication, my book blew off the shelves and Linton Books had to order another print run. From all accounts, *The Soul Collector* was poised to become the number one Thriller of the Year. Everything had gone exactly to plan even with the detours I hadn't expected.

From the beginning, it had been clear I had to do something major to get my book noticed. That's when I implemented a twelve point tactical strategy. When I started, I never anticipated taking things as far as I did. Initially, I only wanted to get a little attention on social media. You know, send up a few tricked-out drones, light a few small fires and call it a day. I never expected to take it any further. But, when I saw how well the reenactments of my book crimes worked in terms of generating reader interest and sales, I couldn't stop. Who would?

Originally, I was only going to blow up a few sheds. Nobody would get hurt. I had absolutely zero experience working with explosives but like everything else in this crazy world, there's a video on YouTube. I watched a bunch of those along with a few on how to steer a drone. Turns out, sending drones loaded with explosives into buildings wasn't all that hard and kind of fun. Ka-Boom.

Then, there were all those messages from JollyRoger44 and that ominous note on the yellow religious pamphlet stuck on my front door. The whole Jolly Roger thing was totally legit. Ned LaGrange *did* send those messages and I later signed his copies of my books as he requested. But the yellow pamphlet left on my door, that was all me. When my friend stopped by my house with the Florida oranges I'd ordered, I deliberately asked her to come to the front so *she* would find the paper stuck in my door. That made her a witness. If the police ever talked to her, which they did, she'd say she found it. There would be no direct link to me.

I needed enough red herrings to keep everyone including the police and the press guessing. I fed ace reporter, Tommy Devlin, only the information I wanted him to have. Nothing more, nothing less. He was so consumed with getting his exclusive and ultimately seeing his smug chiseled face back on CNN that he lapped up every word I said, no questions asked.

I set off the first drone with the hope of creating a little excitement for my books and help me land an agent. After I signed with Matthew, he had trouble selling my book to a publisher. To help him out, I did a few more live drone reenactments and spray-painted that man at the dump and sure enough, Linton Books agreed to acquire my book. It worked like a charm. I guess Matthew had the same idea when he dragged Eric up to Connecticut and set off a few drones himself to try and keep my momentum going. I figured it out after my husband told me he'd seen Matthew and another man at our local train station the same day as a flying pig drone was spotted that wasn't from me. In a weird way, I have to applaud my agent for his ingenuity. Not many agents would commit felonies for their clients, at least I don't think so.

To be clear, when I painted that first homeless man, Argos, he was already unconscious. I didn't hurt him or do anything except turn him silver. He was alone, laying on the ground drugged out on who knows what. I happened to have a can of silver paint in my pocket (doesn't everyone?) and the next thing you know, Argos has gone full metallic. Same thing for the dead Silver Man or at least that's what I intended.

I had researched areas near me where drug addicts congregated. I wanted to find another zoned out person I could silver spritz to keep the mystery and social media interest going. It was a fairly bright almost full moon night when I entered a small park in the middle of nowhere that was known as a place to buy and sell drugs. The park was deserted and I was about to leave when I noticed a disheveled middle-aged man lying on the ground under some tall bushes. He appeared unconscious — the perfect person to spray-paint. It would have taken me all of two minutes if he had just remained still but he woke up in the middle and grabbed me. He pulled me to the ground, twisted my arms and attempted to climb on top of me. He was strong.

Somehow, I wriggled away from him and started to run but he was right behind me. For a guy who was presumably drug compromised, he was surprisingly agile. I sprinted and as I passed a large overflowing garbage can, I spotted an old metal golf club on the ground next to it. I grabbed the club just as the man growled and lunged for me. I swung at him but missed. To avoid being hit by the club, he turned, tripped, and fell flat on his face. Adrenaline coursed through my veins as I held the golf club over my head ready to strike if he moved even a pinky. Then, his arm moved. Terrified, I brought the club down on the back of his head a couple of times. Okay, twenty-six times. I was fighting for my life.

When he finally stopped moving, I nudged his shoulder with my foot. Even in the dark, I could see there was a lot of blood. I reached down and checked for his pulse. There was none.

Looking at him while trying to catch my breath and calm down, the wheels in my head started to turn. That's when it occurred to me that a dead Silver Man was far more newsworthy and headline grabbing than an unconscious one. When God gives you lemons, you make lemonade. What had happened was kind of a lucky break for me. After all, I didn't kill him on purpose, it was self-defense. So, I pulled the silver paint can out of my bag and finished the job.

After the dead Silver Man incident, things ratcheted up beautifully. Social media was loving the circus and me. With my helping hand, I got a nice little advance which validated me as a writer. It also gave me some money that I earmarked for my husband's new restaurant venture. It wasn't nearly enough, but at that point, I had no idea then what lengths Teddy would eventually go to in order to get the money he needed.

Which brings me to old demented John Mercer. My agent had been all over me on a daily basis to increase the visibility for *The Soul Collector*. I thought if I could simulate one more thing from one of my older books, it would be enough to satisfy everyone. But I knew, it had to be big. Dead drug dealers don't tug at the heartstrings the way a kindly old fisherman murder might. If I was going to get my book onto the bestseller lists, it had to be more sensational.

Here's the kicker. Walter S. Loomis' grave and his connection to John Mercer and how it all turned out, was simple dumb luck. I randomly picked Walter Loomis, the man in the grave, by closing my eyes and putting my finger on a list of people buried in a local graveyard. My finger landed on Loomis. I generated a list of his relatives, found three who lived reasonably near me and closed my eyes again. Without looking, I brought my finger down on the piece of paper with the three names and it pointed to a John Mercer.

With Mercer as my target, I googled the hell out of him and learned he was a handyman in his seventies who lived alone. After relentless searching, I found an article in a local paper quoting Mercer. It was one of those "Man on the Street" Q & A human interest stories on how people relax and de-stress in our over-scheduled world. Mercer was quoted saying he often fished at Fern Lake because it was so peaceful and hardly anyone went there. When I read that, the first thing I did was check out the park grounds myself. The next day, I started running at Fern Lake. I spotted Mercer fishing on my third visit.

After two weeks of running around the lake, I got a good sense of the older man's schedule. He was always there by himself. Sometimes fishing, sometimes sitting on a log drinking something out of a bottle in a brown paper bag. I waved to him once when I ran by. He seemed out of it and didn't wave back. As I passed, I felt his eyes examining me. I didn't know anything about him or his connection to Anabel Ford. In retrospect, I wonder now if he was sizing me up to be Anabel's replacement. All I know is, I got the creeps that day which helped me decide to make him my next perfect victim. No one would miss John Mercer.

Two days later, dressed in running clothes, I drove over to Fern Lake and parked under a huge pine tree. I was a little nervous because I'd never killed in a *premeditated* way before. That morning, before it was fully light, I did a reconnaissance run to the lake. While there, I found a large rock light enough for me to handle, but heavy enough to crack open a skull. I stashed the rock in the area where Mercer usually fished and waited in my car. A little later, I began my usual running routine. As I zipped along the lake path, I observed Mercer sitting on a log next to a small rowboat that had been pulled up on the shore. Three empty booze bottles in brown wrappers were strewn by his feet. I was relieved because I suspected killing him when he was drunk would probably be easier. As I ran by, I noticed the oars to his boat were on the ground behind him and changed my plans.

He never heard me come up from behind, probably because he was too intoxicated. I did one final look around the park and saw no one. Like a ninja, I picked up one of the oars and swung it high in the air slamming him squarely on the lower back of his head. Honestly, I hit him so hard, I was surprised I didn't take his head off. He went down like a brick, never moved a muscle.

For the second time in a matter of months, I leaned over and checked a man's pulse. Unbelievably, Mercer was still alive so I had to finish him off in the water. He was heavier than he looked. But, I was determined and dragged him in face down. From there, I let nature take its course. The whole thing turned out easier than I'd anticipated. When he was finally dead, I pushed his boat into the water and watched the back of his head bob for a few minutes. Up and down, up and down. It was oddly soothing. Wet and cold, I went back to my car and drove home. They found Mercer the next morning.

Looking at the big picture, if it wasn't for me, Anabel Ford would still be imprisoned in a dungeon in New Hampshire or possibly worse. It was only a matter of time before Mercer got bored with her and killed her like the others. In a weird way, I'm the hero of this whole story, although no one can ever know. The only reason Brodsky and Marino went to the cabin in New Hampshire was because they were investigating Mercer's murder in Connecticut. The murder I committed. When they found that missing girl, I was dying to tell people about the enormous role I had played in her recovery. But for obvious reasons, I had to keep all of my involvement to myself. That really killed me.

There was a little hiccup. I never anticipated the Anabel Ford connection. When Mercer's body was found and it led to the missing college student, the police investigation grew more intense and the press started swarming. It was great for my book sales but at that point, law enforcement was getting a little too close for comfort and asking me too many questions. I had hoped Brodsky and Marino would ease up in time, but not those two. They didn't know how to let things go. Like I've said, dogs with bones.

As I sat back and waited with anticipation for my publication day, everything went to shit when I learned my husband and best friend were "in love". I'm not going to lie

— it knocked me on my ass. That car call between Teddy and Natalie was devastating, but it also cleared up a lot of things that had been bugging me. That call was chock full of information. Apparently, on the weekends Natalie visited under the guise of "much needed girl time", she regularly slipped something into my wine glass so that I'd eventually pass out. I don't know exactly what she gave me, but based on my condition before and after her visits, I'm guessing it was something like a roofie. I listened to the two of them congratulating themselves for their cleverness on that call. They had it down to a science. Once I was unconscious, they'd put me in bed upstairs and then go screw each other's brains out in the first-floor guest room. That explained why I always woke up with a wicked hangover while Natalie was glowing and looked like she had been to a spa.

Their affair alone would have been enough to put me over the edge. But, there was so much more. At the end of their call, I learned they were also planning to kill me. Shocked, I had a mixture of emotions — betrayal, sadness, vulnerability, fear. Then finally those feelings were eclipsed by anger which soon turned into rage.

I'm not a vindictive person by nature but I had to protect myself. I did what anyone would do under the same circumstances and I had to act fast. That's when the big, and if I might add, scathingly brilliant, idea came to me.

Teddy wanted me gone for a couple of reasons mainly to do with money. Yes, Natalie made him "so hot", but more importantly, he was the beneficiary of a three-hundred-and-fifty-thousand dollar term life insurance policy we had each taken out with the other as beneficiary shortly after we were married. I never thought anything about it. On that call, PR expert Natalie Bloom had assured Teddy their plan was infallible. "Teddy," she had said, "Jillian dying the same way as her protagonist in *The Soul Collector* on the week her book comes out will start a media tsunami."

And there it was, they'd make a bundle from my demise. Teddy could start his food empire and at his side, Natalie would be Mrs Empire. Clearly, in order for their dreams to come true, I had to go.

It was actually my husband's affair and plan to kill me that led me to the really big idea. I would frame Teddy and Natalie for my attempted murder. This plan served a dual purpose. No question, John Mercer was a sadistic pervert and no one should have wasted a minute looking for his killer. But, Brodsky and Marino were determined to find out who did it. Their persistent hunting left me in an extremely vulnerable position. The detectives were also intent on still finding out who set the drone fires and did all the silver spray painting. As their investigation continued, they kept circling back to me. With the ongoing scrutiny, I worried that one day the jig would be up. I was clever, but those cops weren't stupid. After all I'd done to make my book a bestseller hoping my mother might see me, I simply couldn't go to jail, not with my book coming out.

So, I did what any normal person backed into a corner would do. I set up my lying husband and narcissistic best friend as the fall guys. The police concluded the two of them had been responsible for everything — Teddy and Natalie launched the drones, sprayed the silver paint and killed the homeless man. They were the ones who left the notes on graves and killed John Mercer for "loot and lust". Once the police nailed the two lovebirds for all the crimes, I'd be in the clear. IMO, it was a stroke of genius.

The devil is indeed in the details. I had a lot of work to do. I took one of Teddy's expensive Japanese Yaxell knives, the ones I had bought for him as a token of my love, and stuck it into the grave of a woman who had been buried at the St Regis Cemetery in New Haven in 2002. I knew the police would eventually find it, but, just to be sure, I left an anonymous tip on a hotline as time was critical. Since Yaxell was a fairly rare and very expensive knife often used by professional chefs, I knew they'd trace it back to Teddy. The introduction of the Japanese knife added another piece of solid evidence for the prosecutor's future murder trial. Imagine my surprise and delight when I learned Brodsky and Marino already had the knife in their possession when I marched into the police station asking for their help. Talk about perfect timing.

Throughout it all, I had gotten really good at hiding my tracks. I wore an old platinum blonde Halloween wig and put on a pair of big oversized sunglasses when I purchased a dozen boxes of ninety-six-count Crayola crayons from six different toy stores. I was very careful. You never know where a security camera lurks these days. I bought the ninety-six-count boxes because the smaller ones didn't have Midnight Blue. I wanted the color of my special crayon to be unique and uncommon. Naturally, I paid for everything with cash always wearing gloves.

My overarching mission had changed from promoting my book into a bestseller to making my husband and best friend the fall guys for my crimes. That's when I stashed a small bag of Midnight Blue crayons in Teddy's shave kit in his suitcase, right next to the box containing the three remaining Yaxell knives. When the cops searched our house, as I knew they eventually would, they found the sack of blue crayons and the knives with one missing. For a little added oomph, I put an instruction manual from one of the drone boxes and a half empty can of silver spray paint in a trunk in our basement. That trunk also contained all of Teddy's yearbooks and Samuels' family mementos. A few more nails in his coffin — bang, bang, bang.

When I finished laying it all out on a silver platter, Brodsky and Marino had an open-and-shut case. My handsome husband Teddy was charged with multiple counts of arson, two counts of murder, defacing a grave site and assault, among other things. The cherry on top? The attempted murder of me was fully documented on my home video security system and witnessed by two decorated police detectives. The case was airtight.

The prosecutor tried but he couldn't get Natalie for everything. Still, they did get her on conspiracy to commit *my* murder. She'll be spending some time at a medium security correctional facility somewhere in Connecticut. I suspect she'll have to trade one of her signature red lipsticks for a little in-house protection.

It will come as no surprise that *The Soul Collector* became a massive hit. I've now got over 206,000 reviews on Amazon alone and it's still climbing. My agent Matthew hooked my book up with a film agent and *The Soul Collector* movie is currently in production. As of right now, my novel is being translated into forty-seven languages, and I've been interviewed by every media outfit you can think of: *CNN, Vogue, CBS, Newsweek, BBC, GQ, The New York Times* and the *Hollywood Reporter* to name a few.

Here's the best part. When word got out about how my husband and best friend set me up, the public was almost more fascinated with my personal story than my novel. For weeks you couldn't turn on the news without seeing my picture, commentary about me, my husband, John Mercer and Anabel Ford. Not surprisingly, Tommy Devlin made the most of it and got his old job back at CNN. You're welcome.

The news avalanche was incredible and helped sell even more books including my older ones, which are all now massive bestsellers. Then, a Hollywood production company signed on to make a limited TV series about my life and tell my story. I still pinch myself every morning and think, this can't be happening. I have two film projects coming out surpassing all of my hopes and dreams.

After everything, I'm still the same ordinary person and trying not to let all the celebrity stuff go to my head. I recently completed a new thriller about a cannibal chef that makes Hannibal Lector look like a vegetarian. I've been kicking around a few ideas on how to make my new book even bigger than my last. It will take time and careful planning, but I'm confident I can do it.

What have I learned? You've got to be tough, focused and find ways to separate yourself from everyone else. Getting to the top might involve bending the rules a little — but it's so worth it. Take it from me, with a little creativity and a boatload of tenacity, anyone can have a bestselling novel.

Will you remember my name now, Mom? It's Jillian.

THE END

The Joffe Books Story

We began in 2014 when Jasper agreed to publish his mum's much-rejected romance novel and it became a bestseller.

Since then we've grown into the largest independent publisher in the UK. We're extremely proud to publish some of the very best writers in the world, including Joy Ellis, Faith Martin, Caro Ramsay, Helen Forrester, Simon Brett and Robert Goddard. Everyone at Joffe Books loves reading and we never forget that it all begins with the magic of an author telling a story.

We are proud to publish talented first-time authors, as well as established writers whose books we love introducing to a new generation of readers.

We have been shortlisted for Independent Publisher of the Year at the British Book Awards three times, in 2020, 2021 and 2022, and for the Diversity and Inclusivity Award at the Independent Publishing Awards in 2022.

We built this company with your help, and we love to hear from you, so please email us about absolutely anything bookish at:

feedback@joffebooks.com

If you want to receive free books every Friday and hear about all our new releases, join our mailing list: www.joffebooks.com/contact.

And when you tell your friends about us, just remember: it's pronounced Joffe as in coffee or toffee!